Carr

WANNABE IN WYOMING

ANTELOPE ROCK BOOK 1

J.B. HAVENS

SAMANTHA A. COLE

Happy Reading!

S Cole

AUTHORS' NOTE

Any information regarding persons or places has been used with creative literary license so there may be discrepancies between fiction and reality. The missions and personal qualities of members of the military and law enforcement within have been created to enhance the story and, again, may be exaggerated and not coincide with reality.

The authors have full respect for the members of the United States military and the varied members of law enforcement and thank them for their continuing service to making this country as safe and free as possible.

PROLOGUE

THE HARD PLASTIC edges of Willow's cell phone dug into her palm painfully, and the sharp sting brought her back to reality in a rush. She couldn't believe it. After thirty-three long years, she finally knew who her father was. The blank spot next to that title on her birth certificate was no longer a mystery.

Jason Hillcrest.

He'd been a little older than she'd imagined. For some reason, she'd always figured he'd been her mother's age, and that they'd been a pair of young lovers unable to handle the burden of an unplanned and unwanted pregnancy. Everything had been assumptions on Willow's part since her mother had never given her any information about her father, other than he couldn't be a part of their lives. No further explanation had ever been offered and Willow had long ago accepted it, albeit reluctantly.

In reality, Jason Hillcrest had been six years her mother's senior. He'd died alone of an aggressive pancreatic cancer at the age of fifty-six—unwed, and for all intents and purposes, childless.

Mr. Howard Smith, Esq. had called Willow a little over an hour ago to inform her that not only was her biological father deceased, but as his only living relative, she was his sole heir. Without warning, she was now the owner of a small cattle ranch in Antelope Rock, Wyoming—wherever the hell that was. Her heart pounded in a mixture of shock, fear, and pure excitement. There was also a heap of disappointment in there—her father had obviously known about her but had never reached out to her. She would've given anything to have been able to meet him and have a chance to get to know him.

Her own life was empty and hollow. Her mother had died three years ago from complications due to diabetes. And now, two years after her divorce, Willow had no boyfriend or close friends or relatives to spend time with. She worked, read, watched TV, and slept—not an exciting life at all.

Her tiny, one-bedroom, rented apartment had come fully furnished. All her worldly possessions would easily fit in her ten-year-old Chevy Colorado, with room to spare. As for employment, she stocked shelves at a local grocery store during the day and cleaned houses a few nights a week for extra money. She could quit both jobs at that very second and not be missed. Not to mention she'd be getting further away from her smarmy ex-husband, who couldn't seem to let her go even after being divorced for several years. Maybe putting half the country between them would finally beat it into his thick skull that she no longer wanted anything to do with him. It wasn't that he wanted to get back together with her. He only called or came by when he needed something—which, ninety-nine percent of the time, was money.

Could she do this? Drop everything, pack her stuff, drive to Wyoming, and start over with a clean slate? The lawyer had explained a lot in a short period of time, but one thing had stuck with her. She needed to go there to sign papers and make a decision on the property. Fix it up and sell it, or sell it as-is, had been his question. But another possibility had occurred to her. Up to that moment, her life had been boring, something she'd been regretting more and more as she got older. Maybe it was time to take a chance. Glancing around the apartment that'd never felt like a home, something sparked within her. If she had to put a name to it, the only two that came to mind were courage and...hope.

CHAPTER ONE

DRIVING from Pennsylvania to Wyoming was no joke. Thanks to scattered bouts of traffic, it'd taken a little over four days, more tanks of gas than Willow wanted to think about, and the last of her nerves. She'd left Nebraska and entered Wyoming late last night. After catching up on some sleep at a cheap but clean motel off the main highway, she was now on the final leg of the journey. Over 1,600 miles and countless hours in her beat-up truck, she was downright gleeful to see the GPS marking her destination as less than twenty minutes away. She'd remembered to get her Chevy a tune-up before leaving the City of Brotherly Love, and thankfully, it hadn't given her so much as a hiccup on the long trek.

She was in a bit of landscape shock. She'd been born and raised in Philadelphia, surrounded by the concrete, steel, and glass buildings and paved roadways that'd been erected in the city that still harbored some of the country's most historical sites. It'd always amazed her how quaint buildings from the 1700s sat peacefully among the monstrosities of the twentieth and twenty-first centuries. Between the traffic, construction, trains, and local residents coming and going at all hours of the day and night, her section of the city had never been quiet. The walls of her apartment had been ultra-thin, so she'd constantly known what her neighbors had been up to. The ones above her apartment often sounded like Bigfoot and his family dancing to loud music even when they weren't throwing wild parties. The ones below her would have loud arguments about the stupidest things just so they could have wild makeup sex that'd left little to the imagination. And the kid who'd lived in the apartment next to her smoked weed and bounced a ball off the other side of her bedroom wall whenever his parents weren't there. Philadelphia was definitely a huge difference from the open air of the upper Midwest with its flat landscape shadowed by buttes and snow-covered mountains in the distance.

When the GPS indicated she had to get off at the next exit, Willow changed lanes and slowed down to take the offramp. The rest stop looked like just about every other one she'd taken a break at along the way. Gas and air pumps, a few parked cars, and a store where you could buy cigarettes, lottery tickets, beer, condoms, coffee, soda, chips, and a hot dog in one two-minute shopping spree. According to the Google Maps directions she'd printed out at the start of her trip, she was in Butterfield, Wyoming—10 miles east of Antelope Rock, her new hometown, temporary as it might be. Maybe she was showing her age a bit, printing the directions out, but she'd been paranoid her GPS would break and she'd get lost.

After parking the truck, she climbed out and stretched her legs. Two vehicles were at the pumps, and she noticed the drivers gaping at her as they got their gas. One was a tall, lanky kid in his late teens who smirked at her with untamed lust in his eyes, while the other was a lady in her fifties whose eyes widened in horror as she took in the younger woman's appearance. Willow glanced down, wondering what might be wrong. She had on a loose pair of jeans, her favorite pair of pink Converse high-tops, and a black tank top that showed off the sleeve of tattoos on her right arm and the ones covering her shoulders. A peek at her reflection in the rear passenger window showed there was nothing on her face other than the tiny crystal stud on her nose. Her short, brown hair was perfectly spiked in its usual faux-hawk with hot pink tips a near exact match to the color of her shoes. Nope, nothing was out of place.

It wasn't the first time Willow had been on the receiving end of both of those looks, and as usual, she chose to ignore them. Hurrying inside, she located the restrooms and took care of business. Before leaving the store, she grabbed a Pepsi from one of the refrigerators and a bag of Cool Ranch Doritos. The stoned clerk at the register didn't give Willow a second look after he took her money. It was just after one p.m., and although she wasn't starving yet, she knew she would be if her meeting with Mr. Smith went longer than she anticipated. The last thing she'd eaten was a ham, egg, and cheese burrito and coffee at seven a.m., after checking out of the motel.

Thankfully, when she exited the store, the two vehicles and their drivers had disappeared. Before leaving the lot, Willow double checked the gas gauge on the dashboard—it showed two-thirds full. That was more than enough to bypass the pumps.

Climbing back into her truck, she followed the GPS, eventually turning down a long dirt road, dust kicking up behind her in a long trail. That was one way to announce her presence, she supposed. She passed under a wooden and metal arch that read "Skyview Ranch" in letters that had rivulets of rust running off them like blood. Way to be morbid Willow, she thought to herself. The lane cut through fields surrounded by leaning barbed wire fences. The disrepair was obvious to even her inexperienced eye. She didn't have a good feeling about this. Her sinking stomach dropped further as she pulled up to the ranch style house. Several barns and outbuildings were scattered around the property, but her eyes remained glued to the sagging front porch and peeling paint of the house she'd be calling home for the foreseeable future. She parked her truck between a white F-350 and a dark blue sedan. A man dressed in jeans, a navy-blue polo shirt, and a sport coat waited near the porch steps. She was unsurprised to see he wasn't on the porch itself, considering she was nervous about walking across it herself.

She climbed down from her truck, deciding to leave her bags for the moment. Who knew if it was even safe to stay there for the night?

"Mr. Smith, I presume?"

"Yes. Are you Ms. Crawford?" His furrowed brow, and his suspicious gaze sweeping her from head to toe and back up again told her she looked like a far cry from the woman he'd expected. When she nodded, he quickly recovered and smiled. "It's nice to finally meet you. Welcome to Antelope Rock."

"Thanks, and Willow is fine." Her gaze moved past Mr. Smith and strayed across the front of the house. The old-fashioned wooden screen door hung slightly askew, with its mesh ripped along the bottom.

"Then I'll have to insist you call me Howard." He put his hand out for her to shake, which she did firmly— just as her mother had taught her. You could tell a lot about a person by the way they shook your hand. "I'm sorry for your loss."

"While I appreciate that, it doesn't feel like a loss when you never had it to begin with. I never met my father or even knew his name until you contacted me. Curiosity, more than anything else, brought me here."

He didn't look the least bit surprised at her admission. "I can understand that. Would you like to go inside? I have a few papers for you to sign, transferring ownership of the property to you."

"Is it safe? Frankly, this place looks like it's about to fall down."

"Safe enough. I wouldn't worry about the roof caving in on your head, but it definitely needs some TLC, huh?"

She let out an unladylike snort. "More than that, I think. I'm assuming you have the keys?"

"Yes, but it's not locked. Most folks around here don't bother to lock their doors."

Shocked, she looked sideways at him as he carefully strode up the porch stairs. They creaked ominously like something straight out of a horror movie but held his weight. "I'm from Philly. We have multiple locks on our doors *and* windows. What if someone breaks in?"

"There are more guns than people in Wyoming. You break into a person's home, and you can be expected to be greeted by buck shot. I wouldn't be surprised to find a twelve-gauge leaning in the corner just inside this door." The words she thought were a joke had been delivered with such deadpanned straightforwardness that she couldn't help but realize he was absolutely serious. She came from a city where, for the most part, the only people with guns were cops, gang members, and criminals. This was going to be a bigger adjustment than she'd thought.

Howard opened the screen door and pushed open the, in fact, unlocked front door. Stale air wafted out into her face in an unpleasant rush, and she turned her head to get one last breath of fresh air before entering. "If there is, I wouldn't know the first thing about using it. I've never fired a gun in my life."

Stepping inside, Howard peeked behind the door, and sure enough, he lifted up and showed her a shotgun, painted a garish camo. "This is decent enough for home defense and has the bonus of being useful for the occasional critter."

Willow froze and gaped at him. "*Critter*? Um, could you, maybe, be more specific?"

"Raccoons, coyotes, and the like. If they wander too close to the house or barn, you can chase them off with this. You can also use it to kill a rattler if need be." He set the shotgun back where he'd gotten it from. "But until you learn how to properly and safely use a firearm, I'd strongly suggest banging loudly on a pot with a spoon for the 'coons and coyotes and using a shovel to take care of the rattlers. We wouldn't want any accidents, especially not all the way out here. The clinic in town isn't exactly equipped to handle gunshot wounds."

Horrified at the thought of doing battle with a rattlesnake, or any other animal for that matter, she blinked several times before simply saying, "Noted."

She followed the lawyer into the house, ignoring the stagnant smell of the place. Dust coated every surface in a thick grey blanket. Some of the furniture had been covered with sheets, but she wasn't about to lift them off until she got some windows opened. The living room was typical, about what she'd expected from a life-long bachelor. Her upper lip twitched when she spotted two deer heads hanging on one wall. A very old grandfather clock, that'd apparently stopped working at some point, and a creepy painting of some old dude, whose eyes seemed to follow Willow as she moved about the room, completed the simple and unappealing décor. The portrait hanging above the fireplace mantle couldn't be her father, since he'd only been fifty-six when he passed away, and the gray-haired person looked to be around seventy-five or eighty.

She'd keep the clock, if it could be repaired, but the rest of that stuff *had* to go. "I think I'll need to rent a dumpster or something, if I'm going to stay here for any length of time."

Howard nodded as if he agreed with her. "I can recommend someone for that, and if you need help hauling stuff, there are always a few guys around town looking to pick up some extra work on the side."

"Can you leave me a list of numbers or something?"

"Sure. Let's go into the kitchen and get those papers signed too, and then I can get out of your hair."

The kitchen was in a similar state of filth and disarray. Dated appliances and stained countertops greeted them. She'd never seen a fridge in that shade of puke green in real life before, having only seen ones like it in the movies. She shuddered at the thought of what it might contain. When Howard flipped a switch on the wall and an overhead light illuminated the room that was shaded from the mid-day sun, she was grateful to realize the electricity was on. Hopefully, that meant cleaning out the refrigerator wouldn't require a HazMat suit.

Howard pulled the sheet off the table, and a cloud of dust flew into the air around them. "Whoops. Sorry about that."

Coughing and waving a hand in front of her face, Willow crossed the kitchen, pulled open a sliding door that was also unlocked, and peeked out. There was a small deck that looked newer than its front counterpart and in decent shape at least. With a gentle breeze wafting in, the air in the kitchen soon began to clear, and they took a seat at the small rickety table. As Howard opened his briefcase and pulled out a folder, thick with papers, the mental list Willow had started of things she would need to replace was getting longer by the minute. A lot of it would need to be taken care of whether she sold the house or not, especially if she wanted to get a decent price for it. The only things she had going for her were that she lived alone and was used to not having much. The living room and kitchen of this house alone was bigger than her apartment in Philly.

Howard got right down to business. "The will is pretty straight forward. Your father left you this house, the surrounding land, twelve-hundred acres, and all his assets. You're his only living heir. The estate includes the remaining twenty head of cattle and two horses Jason owned at the time of his death, which are being temporarily cared for at the neighboring JP Ranch. I also have an offer for their purchase from Jeremiah Urban, who owns the JP. If you don't wish to sell them, he'll transport them back here for you when you're ready for them. Personally, I'd recommend selling them to him. This place isn't in good enough shape to house, care, and feed one cow let alone twenty steers and a couple of horses, if you don't know what you're doing."

"Is his price fair? I know the difference between a cow and a heifer, a steer and a bull, but that's the extent of my knowledge."

He nodded. "Yes, his price is more than fair. Especially considering he's been caring for them along with his own herd for some time now, even before your father's death. If you need me to, I can have my paralegal do some quick research and show you the current market value, so you can compare them to his offer."

She appreciated that he didn't seem to want her to get stiffed due to the fact she had no idea what the cattle and horses were worth. "Okay, yes, that's fine—thank you. Does he need to meet with me?" She lifted her elbows off the table where they'd been resting, grimacing as they stuck slightly to the surface. "And I'm going to need some directions to the nearest furniture store and grocery store." She waved a hand, gesturing around the room. "Do these appliances even work?"

"I think so, although the stove and washer/dryer in the mud room might be unplugged. I also have the number for a local, reputable contractor who can come out and give you an estimate on the repairs to the house."

"Thanks. Looks like I'm going to spend a good part of tomorrow on the phone."

He chuckled lightly. "Probably. Let's get these forms taken care of, and I'll leave you to it." Flipping open the folder, he handed her a pen and showed her where to start signing her name or initials.

Twenty minutes later, she stood alone in the filthy living room of her new house, a folder of documents clutched in her hand, including a long list of names and phone numbers for services she'd be needing. First things first though, she needed to check the place out and make a list of what she'd need at the store. The line of zeros in her new bank account gave her a sense of freedom she'd never had before. It wasn't to the point she'd never have to work again, but she was still in shock over the windfall. What a novelty, not worrying about paying rent or waiting for her next paycheck to roll around so she could buy food for the week. She glanced around, trying to decide if she should sell the place or keep it. She wasn't sure and wouldn't rush to make a decision either way.

"What the hell have I gotten myself into?" Jerking open curtains and windows, she got to work.

CHAPTER TWO

WITH A MASSIVE GROCERY list in hand, Willow headed into town in her father's late-model, Ford F-350. It was in much better condition than her Chevy and had a full tank of gas. She'd found the keys to it hanging on a hook by the front door and saw no reason why she shouldn't make use of the nicer vehicle. She slightly hated that it was a Ford, but she wasn't about to argue with a free truck, even if she cringed a little when she started it the first time. After driving Chevys all her life, it felt like a betrayal to drive anything else, especially something from their biggest competitor.

Her first stop was the cemetery behind the local Protestant church, where Howard had said her father's grave was. For some strange reason, Jason had demanded he be buried without a public funeral and before Willow had been notified of his death. Apparently, he'd paid the church and a funeral home for the grave and their services several years ago. On one hand, she was grateful she hadn't had to plan a funeral and a burial for a man she'd never met, but on the other hand, she was kind of peeved he hadn't wanted anything to do with her, even in death. It made her wonder why he'd left her his estate instead of donating it to a charity or something. If he had, she would've spent the rest of her life never knowing who he was.

It didn't take her long to find the fresh grave with a small marker bearing her father's name, the dates of his birth and death, and the name of the funeral home who'd taken care of the burial. No flowers or mementos had been left on his final resting place, like many of the others around it, and Willow was surprised to feel regret about not bringing anything. The grave was also one of only a few without a headstone, and she wondered if that was something else her father had pre-arranged. She remembered from when she'd interred her mother in a mausoleum at a cemetery that she'd been told it was common to wait a full year before erecting a stone or plaque in memory of a loved one.

Pulling out her phone, she made a note to contact the funeral home and find out if a headstone had been paid for yet. If not, she would arrange to have one made, since it was the least she could do after her father had left her everything he'd owned.

After paying her respects, her next stop was the bank Jason had used. Thankfully, Howard had been nice enough to inform the manager she'd be in today to fill out some forms, order new checks, and get a new debit card connected to the accounts she'd inherited. She'd found her father's wallet in what had obviously been his bedroom, but the two credit cards and one bank card in it were obviously in his name. Howard had given her copies of her father's death certificate and some paperwork saying she had power of attorney to deal with any accounts her father still had open at the time of his death. The ranch had only a moderate mortgage still left on it, which she could easily make payments on for the foreseeable future, and he hadn't left any other outstanding debts, for which she'd been grateful. One less thing to take care of.

Aside from the funny looks she'd gotten from the bank manager, clerks, and a few customers, the errand had been quick and relatively painless. It was evident she was going to stick out like a sore thumb in this tiny town, and she got the feeling that wasn't going to be a good thing.

She crossed the street to the grocery store where she'd parked her car earlier and grabbed a cart. She couldn't help but laugh out loud at the name of the place. The Pack & Sack was apparently Antelope Rock's only supermarket—if you could even call it that. There was nothing "super" about it, considering it was about one-third the size of the Wegmans Willow used to shop at in Philadelphia. However, Howard had assured her they would carry some of what she needed to get started on the housecleaning, and she could get a few more things at Ducky's Feed & Supply store up the street. Anything else would have to wait for a trip to the nearest Walmart which was about a forty-minute drive away in Ferndale.

As she strolled up and down the aisles, filling her cart with food, cleaners, and other stuff on her list, she garnered a few more weird looks. Was it the tattoos and her pink hair or the fact she was a stranger? The first person who didn't stare at her like she was an alien from another galaxy was a guy in aisle four, stocking the shelves with canned vegetables. In his late teens, he was tall and skinny, with dark hair sticking out in all directions. A red Pack & Sack vest covered a white T-shirt over a pair of baggy jeans and sneakers. He did a double take when he first saw her, then his eyes widened. "Wow, awesome ink—I love your sleeve." He took a step closer and gestured to her tattoos. "Do you mind?"

"Not at all," she said with a smile, as she extended her arm for him to get a better look, rotating it slowly, so he could see all the facets of the intricate designs.

"Wow, this is sick! I mean, it's awesome! Who did the work?"

"A guy back in Philadelphia. I just moved here from there."

His face fell for a moment before he went back to studying her tattoos in awe. "Damn. I was hoping the artist was local. My buddy got one last month, and between you and me, it was a shitty job."

"What are you thinking of getting?"

He shrugged. "Haven't decided yet. I have to wait at least seven more weeks until I turn eighteen. My mom won't let me get one until then. I think she's hoping I'll forget about it, but I've been saving up for one. I just need to find someone better than the guy who did Bubba's."

Willow held in a bark of laughter, but only barely. "Um, is that a nickname or do people really name their kids Bubba around here?"

The young man chuckled. "Some people might, but in his case, his real name's Bobby, but everyone's called him Bubba since he was little. I'm Cody Moore by the way."

He extended his hand which she shook. "Willow Crawford—it's nice to meet you, Cody."

"Same here. So, what made you move from a big city to this hick town?"

Before she had a chance to respond, an obnoxious male voice boomed from behind her. "Cody, quit yer yappin' and get back to work. Those shelves ain't gonna stock themselves."

Willow turned to see a heavyset, balding man striding towards them. The blue tie he wore, over a white button-down shirt, barely extended past the start of his swollen beer belly. He was red-faced and sweating, even though it was a comfortable sixty-five degrees or so in the store. The name tag above his left chest pocket read "Al Sanders, Manager".

"Sorry, Mr. Sanders, I—"

Not wanting Cody to get into trouble, Willow cut him off. "He was just telling me what aisle the aspirin was in for this headache I suddenly have." She smiled at the teen. "What aisle was it again?"

The look he shot her said he was grateful for her attempt to appease his boss. "Uh, aisle seven, Ms. Crawford. Let me know if you have trouble finding anything else."

"Thank you, Cody. You've been very helpful." She bit her tongue against saying anything rude to the manager and gave him a forced smile as he eyed her hair and tattoos. As she began to push her cart away, she added, "Have a nice day, gentlemen."

Twenty minutes later, her cart was overflowing with bags as she steered it toward the exit. In between the interior and exterior sliding doors, there was a large community cork board where it seemed anyone could post announcements, business cards, lost and found flyers, and more. She paused and let her gaze scan them. Someone's cat named Muffin was missing, and another person's dog had puppies and they were free to good homes. A teenage girl was looking for a babysitting job. There was an announcement for that week's Women's Club meeting, and another for an upcoming book fair at the town's library. A notice from the local American Legion Hall caught her eye.

Pen Pals Wanted:
Any Soldier, Inc.

The members of our armed forces would love to hear from
you. The mission of Any Soldier, Inc. is to connect our
deployed soldiers with people back home willing to write to

them and send care packages when appropriate. Receiving mail greatly affects the morale of any soldier. Go to our website to be connected to a soldier in need today . . .

She finished reading the flyer and smiled. Back when she'd been in fourth grade, her class had adopted a soldier who'd been serving overseas. The students had sent him written letters and a care package twice a month during the school year, and their teacher would read his replies to them. Even though he would write one long letter to the entire class as often as he could, he'd taken the time to mention each of the students and comment about something from the individual messages they'd written to him. Two weeks before school ended, he'd come home from his deployment and surprised the class with a visit and a pizza party. Staff Sergeant Greg Sweeney—that'd been his name. Wow, she hadn't thought about him in years. She remembered he'd said their letters had meant the world to him while he'd been away from his friends and family. Every time his name had been announced during mail call, it'd felt like he'd won the lottery when he received one of the class's care packages filled with things to make his week a little brighter.

Willow didn't have a pen and pad handy, so she pulled out her phone and snapped a photo of the flyer. Maybe after she was done with the massive cleanup job she was facing, she could send a soldier a "thank you for your service" letter.

CHAPTER THREE

THE NEXT MORNING, Willow groaned as she sat up in bed. Between cleaning all afternoon and a restless night spent on an old worn-out mattress, her back was aching. Her first errand after coffee today would be a visit to both the furniture and appliance stores in Ferndale. A new bed was a priority, but she also needed to re-outfit the entire house, including a new fridge, stove, and microwave to start with. After uncovering a couch and a recliner yesterday, she'd been greeted by burnt orange fabric from the seventies that smelled like it hadn't been cleaned once in its entire existence.

A trip to Walmart was also going to be in order for the day. She needed new linens, rugs, shower curtains, etc. for the bathrooms and bedroom, not to mention a bunch of things for the kitchen. She wasn't a skilled cook, but even she saw the need for a decent set of pots, pans, plates, utensils, and glasses. The ones she'd found during her inventory check yesterday were unusable, in her opinion, and since she'd donated her old ones to a halfway house in Philly before she'd left, she had a list of everything she needed to buy.

Last night, she'd ended up having a pre-made salad for dinner that she'd gotten at the Pack & Sack, using the included plastic utensils, but tonight, she wanted to cook an actual meal. Snorting softly, she couldn't help but giggle every time she thought of the store's name. Who was the genius that named a store the Pack & Sack? The dick jokes she could come up with for that were endless.

Willow didn't know much of anything about her father, but the more she saw of his house, the more she doubted they would've had anything in common. The man had not only been a slob, but he'd also been a bit of a pack rat. The closet in the bedroom was crammed full of boxes that appeared to be stuffed with old papers and receipts. Who needed a receipt for a gallon of milk they'd bought fifteen years ago? Her father had apparently.

That thought reminded her to call one of the numbers Howard had given her and have a roll-away dumpster sent over. She also needed to hire a crew of guys to come help toss the old broken-down furniture and appliances before new stuff could be delivered.

Sighing heavily, she rose and shuffled to the kitchen to start the coffee. Thankfully, it was the one appliance in the entire house that seemed new and in good shape. She guessed a single, male rancher could live with a craptastic bed and only two threadbare towels, but he couldn't live without coffee. Who knows, maybe she did have something in common with the old man after all.

Two cups of coffee and a shower later—she'd cleaned and disinfected one of the two baths in the house before going to bed last night—she was on her way to Ferndale. At least in the bigger town and stores, she wouldn't stand out so much. The pink hair and tattoos didn't seem to be well received in

Antelope Rock, but the people there would just have to get used to it.

Spotting the Walmart sign first, Willow pulled into the parking lot, grabbed a cart, and followed a few shoppers into the store. She hadn't fully decided if she was keeping the ranch or fixing it up and selling it. Based on the property value Howard had showed her, if she did some improvements to the house and land, she'd clear a very nice profit in the sale after the last of the mortgage was paid off. She'd have enough to live comfortably just about anywhere she wanted. She'd even be able to travel for a bit, if she had the mind to, without worrying about a job. It wouldn't last forever, but taking a few years off did sound appealing. With images of white-sand beaches and blue waves dancing in her mind, she tossed beach-themed bathroom accessories into her cart, along with blue and white towels.

She continued with the color scheme in the bedroom department, selecting a light-blue and grey comforter and matching sheets with a higher thread count than she'd ever purchased before. A painting caught her eye. It was a picture of the ocean at night, a full moon shining down on the rolling waves, stars sparkling and reflecting off the water. The dark water seemed to hide untold secrets. There were footprints along the sand, right above the water line, left behind by a woman in the distance. Long dark hair touched the small of her back, just above a sarong tied around her hips. She was as mysterious as the ocean itself. The painting was a mass-produced print, no doubt millions of them were in existence, but it spoke to Willow. She saw herself in that lonely woman. Without a second thought, the painting went into her cart to replace the creepy portrait she'd taken down in the living room.

Two overflowing cartfuls later, she checked out, trying not to cringe at the total before she remembered she could afford it. Her trip to the furniture store was, surprisingly, just as quick, easy, and relatively painless. She splurged on the new bed a little, but the living room set she picked out was simple, functional, and on clearance. She wasn't convinced she'd be staying at Skyview Ranch forever and wanted to get things she could leave behind if necessary. Of course, she hadn't applied that logic to her bed, but by the way her back felt this morning, she figured the expensive queen-size mattress would be worth its weight in gold. In the appliance store next door, there'd been a black refrigerator and matching range on sale, so she'd picked those, not really caring what they looked like beyond function. She also added a stacked washer and dryer set, to replace the ancient ones in the laundry room. The salesman had been nearly giddy as she'd placed her large order. It was probably the biggest sale he would have all week and possibly all month.

After arranging to have the furniture and appliances delivered and installed as soon as possible, she made the long drive back to the ranch. She switched radio stations often, searching for something that wasn't new-age country music and didn't have much luck. She only liked old-school country singers like Cash, Haggard, and Hank Williams Jr. Finally giving up, she connected her music app to the radio via Bluetooth and set the vehicle's cruise control. Rolling down the windows, she sang along with her favorite mix playlist, not caring at all that it switched from Etta James to Eminem to Frank Sinatra and onto DMX.

Forty minutes later, she turned down the dirt lane to the property she now owned, passing under the ranch sign and continuing to the house. There was a red pickup parked in front next to her Chevy, and she slowed, approaching cautiously.

"What the hell?" she muttered since she wasn't expecting anyone. Her confusion eased when she noted the lettering on the strange vehicle's tailgate that read "JP Ranch." It must belong to Jeremiah Urban, her new neighbor.

Willow parked, turned off the truck, and climbed out, deciding to leave her bags for now. She glanced around but didn't see anyone. "Hello!" she called out walking around to the back of the house. "Can I help you?"

A figure emerged from around the side of the larger of the two barns. All she could make out from the distance between them was that he was average in height and sported a tan cowboy hat and dark jeans. He waved and hurried over to her. If he was taken aback by her pink hair and tattoos, he didn't show it.

As he drew closer, she noted he was about forty years old, and as he took off his hat, she was able to see that he had dark red hair and sharp features. A thick reddish-brown scruff covered his jaw. While he had white streaks near his temples and a little in his beard, it only made him more attractive. He was lean but roped with muscle, and she doubted there was an ounce of fat on him.

"Howdy, ma'am. I'm Jeremiah Urban. I talked to Howard, and he told me you'd like to sell your father's cattle and horses to me. I just wanted to introduce myself and take a gander around here. Jason wasn't too keen on visitors. I can see why you'd want to sell, if that's what you're planning on doing. This place needs too much work right now to be suitable for any animals."

He'd stuck one hand out and taken off his hat with the other, all while keeping up a running dialogue. He was friendly enough, but she got the impression he was of the type to talk your ear off if he got the chance.

She shook his hand. "Pleased to meet you––I'm Willow Crawford. Considering I don't know the first thing about taking care of cattle or horses, I'd be selling to you even if this place was in perfect shape. I haven't decided what I want to do with it yet, but for now, I just want to focus on bringing it into the twenty-first century. Then I'll go from there."

The man grinned. "Fair enough. Howard said you agreed with the price I quoted, so I'll have a check for you by the end of the week, if that suits you. Is there anything I can do for you in the meantime? Being out here in a new place all alone must be a shock for ya. We were all surprised to find out you existed. No one at the Rock had any clue the old bastard had any kin." He slapped his hat against his thigh and settled it back onto his head, talking non-stop all the while. "Pardon my French, ma'am, I don't mean to speak ill of the dead, but your father was a mean cuss when he had a mind to be, which was often."

"I never knew him, so I'll take your word for it." She shrugged and quickly changed the subject before he could start up again. "I was wondering, do you happen to know a few men who wouldn't mind making some extra cash? I need to clear out a lot of junk and old furniture from inside the house. I'll be renting a roll-away dumpster and could use a hand. I also need someone who could tell me about the equipment in the two barns. I don't know what's useable or what's just scrap."

"Oh, sure thing! I got myself a couple ranch hands who would be glad to help out, you just let me know when. Most folks around here are willing to help out for free. Neighbors gotta take care of each other, ya know? But if you're willing to pay cash, you'll have a crew here in no time. Especially for easy work like hauling broken couches, or what not."

Hauling furniture was easy work? Though she supposed compared to ranch work, it must seem that way. "Great. I'll be in touch soon. I'm going to call and make the arrangements for the dumpster today. I have new furniture and appliances being delivered in three days, so I'd need the help pretty soon, if that works."

"Did Howard give you my number?"

"Yes, he did. Yours is at the top of a very long list."

He chuckled. "I'm sure. Howard takes good care of his clients. Well, you just call me anytime, as soon as you have a day and time. I can get five or six guys here and have this place cleaned out in an afternoon, after they're done working at the ranch. While they haul the junk out, you and I can take a look at the barns, and I'll help you decide what to keep and what to get rid of. Does that work for you?"

His offer to help took a load off her mind. The smaller of the two barns on the property was full of equipment she didn't know the names of or what they were used for and one of the things she hadn't been looking forward to confronting on her own. "Yes, thank you so much." He looked as if he was about to open his mouth and continue the conversation, but she was anxious to get her bags inside and set up the house more. "I'll be in touch later today. I have a whole list of calls I need to make and a lot more cleaning to tackle." She hoped her dismissal was polite enough because he was a nice man, and if they were going to be neighbors for however long she would be there, she didn't want to start off on the wrong foot with him.

Jeremiah smiled and tipped his cowboy hat to her. "Yes, ma'am. We'll talk soon."

CHAPTER FOUR

June 1

Dear Any Soldier,

Hi, my name is Willow, and I wanted to take a moment to thank you for your service. It's very much appreciated. It must be hard on you being away from your family and friends for long periods of time, and I hope this letter brightens your day.

I'm probably not supposed to ask where you're stationed or deployed, so I won't. I'll just assume you're somewhere on the other side of the world and pray you're safe.

I guess I should tell you a little about myself. I'm thirty-three years old and originally from Philadelphia, where I'd lived my entire life until three weeks ago. That's when I found out I'd inherited a ranch in Wyoming, of all places. Talk about a culture shock. This little podunk town has a population of just under 1000 people, and everyone seems to know everyone else. I probably had that many people living within a two-block radius of me back in Philly, and no one knew who any of their neighbors were beyond nodding hello as they passed each other on the street.

I've spent the last few weeks doing an overhaul of the house here—it really needed it. I'd been hoping all it would need was a fresh coat of paint, but that turned out to be the least of my worries. The front porch needed major work—all new steps and most of the boards needed to be replaced. Thankfully, the supports were in good shape, so the whole thing didn't need to be torn down. I even managed to save the old porch swing, sanding and refinishing it. I think I'll rehang on the side porch though—it faces west—and get another one for the back porch. The painters come in a few days to re-paint the outside of the house. I picked a light green color—I think it'll look nice against the blue sky.

I also tackled the kitchen and two bathrooms and had a plumber and an electrician come in and update what needed to be. While there is still a lot to do in the three rooms, at least I can now say every surface has been bleached and disinfected, the water is clean, and the plugs are updated for the new appliances I ordered. Now I'm moving onto the rest of the house. Every room needs, at the very least, to be painted and new furniture and rugs.

With the help of some local guys, I got rid of the old, very outdated furniture (think of the 1970s if you need a visual), junk that was lying around, and anything else I didn't want to keep. There are a bunch of boxes and trunks left, mostly filled with papers and stuff, but I put them in the attic until I have more time to devote to going through them. Thank goodness I also now have satellite internet and TV access—

*it was really quiet here without them for the first two days.
I'm learning a lot about living in the country, thanks to
Google.*

*Tomorrow, I'm going to do the craziest thing—well, at least
the craziest thing I've ever done besides leaving
Pennsylvania to move to Wyoming where I know absolutely
no one. I'm going to buy some chickens! Me, the tattooed,
pink-haired chick from Philly is going to get, well, some
chicks (lol). Two of the guys who helped me clear out the
house came by yesterday and fixed up the coop in the
backyard for me and put up some new fencing around it.
The other night, I spent three hours researching chickens,
from which ones to get and what to feed them, to how to
collect their eggs and know when there's something wrong
with them (just in case). There's a local vet who deals with
farm animals, so at least there's someone nearby who I can
consult with. I was surprised to learn you don't need a
rooster for the hens to lay eggs. You only need one if you
want baby chicks. I'll do without the rooster for now.*

*I must be crazy (well, the last paragraph probably
confirmed that), but I'm actually thinking about keeping the
ranch. At first, I was seriously thinking of fixing it up to
sell, but the longer I stay here, the more I like living out in
the middle of nowhere. Weird, huh? There's really no reason
for me to go back to Philly other than it's familiar. People
move all the time and start over in new places, so why can't
I? The only thing is I'll need to figure out what to do with
all this land I now have (1200 freaking acres!). It used to be
a cattle ranch, but I sold the last few cows, steers, and horses
to my new neighbor, since I have no idea how to take care of
them or what to do with them. He'd already been taking
care of them, so it just made sense to let him buy them.*

I want to raise some animals or plant something I can sell, but this is all so new to me, and I have no clue how to be a rancher. If you have any ideas on what I could use the land for, I'm all ears.

Oh, I forgot to mention. I have a new friend. He's a white-tailed prairie dog that comes and hangs out on my back porch. After the third day of him showing up, I named him Fred. I had to take a picture of him with my phone to find out what in the world he was because, needless to say, we didn't have prairie dogs back East. The guy who owns the feed store, whose name is Ducky—if you can believe that— gave me a quick education on them. Thankfully, they're herbivores. I bought some seeds that Ducky said I could leave out for Fred. I can also give him some vegetables. From what I'm told, he probably has a family somewhere nearby, so I'm sure he's sharing the meals with them. Maybe one of these days I'll follow him and see where he lives.

Anyway, I'm obviously rambling on about nothing, and I'm sure you have lots to do. If you want to write back, that's great, but I'll understand if you don't. In the meantime, thank you, again, for your service, and I hope you're back with your loved ones soon.

Sincerely,
Willow
Wannabe Rancher

P.S. - I know it would be easier to exchange email addresses to write back and forth, but if you don't mind, I kind of like writing letters and mailing them the old-fashioned way. We did that when we adopted a soldier in my fourth-grade class, and it was so exciting when the teacher announced we had a letter from him each month.

June 15

Dear Wannabe (I love your name but got a kick out of Wannabe lol),

Getting your letter did what you'd hoped it would—it brightened my day. And I don't mind writing snail mail. You're right—it is more exciting to receive a handwritten letter as opposed to an email. Getting letters here is like Christmas morning for us. A lot of the guys I know carry them around while on missions, so they always have that connection to their families. The Army is known for its 'hurry up and wait' attitude, so having letters to re-read during downtime is a treat.

My name is Nathan, I'm thirty-three years old, and I grew up in a small town in Colorado that sounds a lot like where you're living now. There are good and bad things about small towns. One of the good things is neighbors help out neighbors without batting an eye. One of the bad things though is the gossip. The minute you let anyone know a secret there, it'll be running through the rumor mill faster than you can say, "Don't tell anyone."

You didn't say who you inherited the ranch from, but I assume that means someone close to you passed away and left it to you in their will. I'm sorry for your loss.

It sounds like you've done a lot of work on the place already

*and have plenty more to do. With 1200 acres there are a few
animals you can raise other than cattle. Hogs
and sheep come to mind. The hogs and lambs (baby sheep)
would need to be slaughtered for their meat, and I'm not
sure if you're up to doing that (I know I wouldn't be), but
sheep and llama farms are known for their wool or fiber,
and you don't have to kill the animals to get it. Either way,
you'd have to research what you would need in order to
raise any of those animals. You'll also need to hire people to
work for you to maintain the herd, since it's not as simple as
just giving them food and water. As for crops, there are a
few options for you there too. I looked it up (thank you,
Google), and it seems like hay, barley, wheat, beans, and
corn are the main crops grown in Wyoming. Again, you'll
have to research them and will likely need to hire at least a
few people to help you throughout the different seasons.*

*Speaking of Wyoming, isn't it beautiful there? I was only
there once, the summer between my junior and senior years
in high school. My friend's parents took us and another
friend camping in Glendo State Park. I'm not sure how close
that is to you, but it's gorgeous. If you get a chance, you
should visit it. That was a great trip. Even though his
parents were with us, they were cool, and we had an
amazing time.*

*How are the chickens doing? Glad to hear you didn't get a
rooster since you don't need one yet. Those damn things
wake you up at the ass-crack of dawn. Not to mention they
can be mean little bastards sometimes—actually, most of the
time.*

What tattoos do you have? I have two—a Celtic cross above

my left shoulder blade and Celtic knot over my heart. I'm Irish by the way.

Tell me about the town you live in now. Does it have a hamburger joint on the edge of town that has the greasiest yet most delicious burgers and fries? Oh, and don't forget a chocolate shake! How about a town square with a gazebo? A movie theater that only shows one movie at a time or is there a drive-in nearby? If it's like the small town I grew up in, you'll probably be having a parade and/or carnival coming up for the 4th of July weekend. I'd love to see pictures of it if you take any. When I was growing up, I couldn't wait to be old enough to move to a city, or at least a much bigger town, but now there's so much I miss about living in a small town. I guess your perception of things changes as you get older.

Well, I'm heading over to the mess hall to grab some dinner. Hope to hear from you again soon. Tell Fred I said hello.

Sincerely,
Nathan
Pen Pal Extraordinaire

CHAPTER FIVE

June 29

*Dear PP Extraordinaire (I like your name too, but the
nickname gave me the giggles.)*

*Thank you for writing back. I was so excited to see a
handwritten envelope in my mailbox. Yours has the honor
of being the first one I've ever received at this address!
Congratulations! You win two-thumbs up and a huge smile!
Sorry it couldn't be more. LOL.*

*I wanted to respond the other day, right after I got your
letter, but I've been so exhausted every night after working
all day. I didn't have the energy to do more than fall asleep
right after dinner. I'm proud to say I've become an expert
(sort of) on hammers, nails, screwdrivers, and drills. I also
have a new personal library of how-to books for plumbing,
electrical, woodworking, tile, general home improvements,
and more. A lot of it is gibberish to me, but at least there are*

a bunch of things I can do now instead of paying someone to do them for me.

My chickens have settled in, and last Saturday morning I got to eat my very first fresh-from-the-chicken-coop egg. I don't know if I'm imagining things, but damn those things are better than any other egg I've ever had. Not to mention, the yolk is such a dark yellow! I always figured an egg was an egg, but apparently not. I also learned that I don't have to refrigerate them as long as I don't wash them after I collect them. That's taking a lot longer to get used to. I keep thinking I'm going to get salmonella if I don't put them in the fridge. How's the food where you are? I've heard about those MREs, and I hope you're not living on those. They sound pretty nasty.

On the Any Soldier site, it said that care packages are always welcome. I was thinking of putting something together for you. Any requests? I know chocolate is a no-go because it melts all over everything, but is there anything special you need, or are craving, that I can send you?

It is beautiful here, and once I get a printer for my computer on my next trip to Walmart, I'll send you some pictures. In the meantime, I'll do my best to describe it, and you'll just have to use your imagination. I'm sitting on the side porch swing I hung yesterday. The chains creak a little as I rock. I'll have to remember to put some WD-40 on them tomorrow. Right now, the sun is setting, and the colors are like something out of a dream. Pinks and reds, mixed with oranges and just a hint of purple above the hills. There's a breeze blowing through the fields, rustling the tall grasses against each other. The air smells fresh and sweet, like flowers, grass, and dirt.

It was creepy when I first moved here, but I've gotten used to the different noises. The frogs and crickets are loud tonight, and lightning bugs are blinking all around through the fields by the barn. It's beautiful and serene. I can't see another house or building other than my own. I've never known peace like I feel here. The chickens were clucking and carrying on earlier, but they're in bed now that it's dark outside. I need to make sure the coop is locked up once I finish writing this, so no predators can get at them.

Nights like this make me feel maudlin and restless. I've been alone a long time, and it normally doesn't bother me—I enjoy my own company. Tonight though, I wish there was someone I could sit with on this swing and just enjoy each other's companionship.

I know I didn't mention who I inherited the ranch from in my first letter, because I'm still trying to come to terms with it. I never knew my father, but he still left me everything he had. My mother rarely talked about him and only if I asked. Even when she did, there never were any details, not even his name. All she would tell me was they weren't meant to be, and he left before I was born. She was sixteen when she had me, and I now know he was twenty-two at the time. Despite their age difference, I did get the impression she'd been in love with him and having me was something she never would've changed. Mom always made sure I knew I was loved and wanted. She's been gone a few years now, so I can't even go to her for more information, although I'm not sure she would've given it to me, even with what I know now.

Growing up, I tried to imagine what he looked like and what his personality was like. I wondered if he knew about me or if he didn't know my mom was pregnant when he left. Again, she was never forthcoming with details and always changed the subject when I asked about him. Hell, I only found out his name a few weeks ago, when his lawyer called me to say my biological father had passed away and left me his ranch. Now, I know his name, Jason Hillcrest, and what he looked like from his driver's license—it was in his wallet that I found in his bedroom. I think I have his eyes. I'm hoping there are other pictures of him in the trunks and boxes I still have to go through and some information on his family. Maybe I'll find something about his parents and if he had any siblings, although his lawyer said I was the only living heir.

The only other thing I've discovered about him, so far, is that he wasn't the nicest guy in the world. The words I've heard a few times to describe him since I've gotten here are "cranky," "eccentric," and "curmudgeon". (I actually had to look that last one up, since I'd never heard anyone called that before.) Thankfully, a few people I've met have determined I fell far enough away from the paternal family tree to not have the same personality as him. Some other people in town still look at me funny—probably because of the tattoos and my nose stud—but others have started to warm up to me.

So, what about your family? Are your parents alive? Do you have any siblings, cousins, aunts, uncles, etc.?

I know I told you I had pink hair—it's actually just the tips of my spiked hair—but I'm letting it grow out. It wasn't intentional at first, but there's only one hairdressing shop in town, and it's owned by one of the people who hasn't taken a liking to me yet. When I met her at the feed supply store, *she turned her nose up at me. I'm afraid if I ask her to color or cut my hair, it'll be a disaster. Maybe on my next trip to Walmart (forty minutes away), I'll stop at their hair salon and get a trim.*

You asked about my tattoos. I have a full sleeve on my right arm that has a bunch of things in it. I'd describe them for you, but honestly seeing them would be easier. I have ink from my right wrist, up my arm and shoulder, and across onto my upper chest and collar bone area. A lot of it is stuff that has special meaning to me or random things from Philly that I love. I even have a small cheesesteak tattooed on the inside of my forearm. LOL. I know, weird, right? But if you're a Philly native, cheesesteaks are like a staple in your diet. I can't imagine you were able ever to get a REAL cheesesteak in Colorado.

Your questions about this town were dead on. There's a hamburger joint a block in from the edge of the main drag (which doesn't have a single traffic light on it), a gazebo in the middle of the town square, and a theater that only shows one movie at a time. Apparently, Wednesdays is when they show classic films—this week's oldie is Casablanca. The closest drive-in is about twenty-five minutes away, so still doable. I've never gone to a drive-in, but I don't think I want to go by myself—that would be just too pathetic. I've made a few acquaintances here, but I'm not close enough to anyone yet to say we're friends. My neighbor, Jeremiah, who bought the cattle and horses from me, has been really nice and helpful. He's about forty years old and single, not that I'm interested in dating him or anyone else I've met so far, but I can see us becoming good friends.

There will be a parade AND a barbecue in the town square

(no big carnival, but there will be some games and stuff) this coming weekend for July 4th. I'm sure I'll be meeting more of the townspeople then.

Well, I'm going to wrap things up for now. I hope you're safe and that this letter brings you a measure of joy.

Sincerely,
Willow
Wannabe Rancher

P.S. Fred says hello and that his new favorite snack is carrot tops.

CHAPTER SIX

STAFF SERGEANT NATHAN CASEY tucked Willow's letter into his shirt pocket, keeping it safe against his chest, before slipping on his body armor and helmet. She may never know, but her letters were saving his sanity. Days of training, hauling gear, unbearable heat, and the constant grit of dust were wearing him down—and he wasn't the only one ready to get out of this hellhole. His buddies were itching to get back home too.

When their unit's mail clerk had come around two months ago, he hadn't even looked up, knowing there wouldn't be anything for him. Much to his surprise though, he'd been handed an envelope addressed to "Any Soldier." He knew about the program, of course, but he'd never been picked to receive a letter. He hadn't realized until then how much mail from anyone, even a stranger, would make him feel. As he'd read the words Willow had written, he'd felt an instant connection to her that'd caught him off guard. He'd then counted the days until he might hear from her again. It took seven-to-ten days for her to get his letters via snail mail, and then another seven-to-ten for him to get one back from her. Two to three weeks between her letters, and that was if she wrote him back right away. Since he didn't get any personal mail from anyone else in the States anymore, he savored every word she'd written, reading the letters over and over again.

Checking the time, he temporarily pushed Willow out of his mind and finished getting dressed before heading out for breakfast. Slinging his weapon over his shoulder, he locked his door behind himself and prepared for yet another day in this God-forsaken country. He'd had enough of the sand, the dust, and the high temperatures, not to mention the blood. He didn't even jump anymore when he heard a distant explosion. They had to be a lot closer to get a reaction out of anyone who'd been there over a month or two.

Hueys flew overhead, the vibration from their rotors shaking the ground beneath his worn boots as he headed to the mess hall to grab some breakfast. The stink of smoke from the burn pits and the thick acrid stench of diesel exhaust hung in the air around him, the heat baking the smell into everything. His mind briefly flashed to a sunset-lit porch and a swing.

Entering the mess hall, he got in line, quickly loaded up a tray, then located an empty seat at a table with a few of his buddies. Running late, he wolfed down the food as fast as he could force himself, washing it all down with a cup of coffee strong enough to burn a hole in his gut. The faster you ate the less you tasted it. That was his theory anyway.

Willow had asked for care package ideas, and he was already compiling a mental list—beef jerky and chew being right at the top. He wasn't a smoker, but chew helped keep everyone awake on long shifts. As disgusting as it was, it was another tool they all used. Nathan would probably never touch the stuff again after his discharge.

After he reported for duty at his station, he struggled to

pay attention, which was a problem he'd never had before. Being distracted while on duty was dangerous for him and, more importantly, everyone around him.

Thankfully, his buddies didn't notice, or he'd never hear the end of it. He thought ahead to what life would be like once he was no longer in the Army. The only thing he was truly going to miss was the tight-knit brotherhood he had with the men of his unit, even though they busted each other's balls at every available opportunity. The humor got them through the long days and nights.

Why was he so messed up over her letters? He kept replaying her words in his head, thinking of what he was going to write back. A broken record of "I should tell Willow . . ." or "I wonder what Willow would think about . . ." was on a near constant loop in his head. It'd only been two letters, which shouldn't be a big deal at all, even considering the fact he never got personal mail anymore while deployed. But for some strange reason, it *was* a big deal to him.

After work, which included a rocket attack and a small engagement with the enemy, followed by a debriefing and reports, he'd decided to spend some extra time in the gym, hoping to sort through his feelings. There wasn't much else to do over there anyway. Work, exercise, sleep, rinse, and repeat.

Was that why he was so hung up on Willow? The novelty of something different in his routine?

There was no room in his brain for thoughts of her when he was on duty. He needed to focus on his job—fucking up could cost lives. If there was something between him and Willow, then he'd figure out his feelings for her when he got back to the States.

He finished his workout, left the gym, and headed to the showers. After spending a few minutes under a tepid spray of water with some soap, he only felt a bit cleaner than before because, let's face it, no one was ever really *clean* when they lived in a sandy desert.

It was another long day in the books, and one less he had to spend there. Returning to his quarters, he unlocked the door to the room he shared with Zach Ramsey and set his weapon down with a heavy sigh. His boots immediately followed.

He stretched out on his narrow bed and grabbed his note pad and pen. Writing back to Willow would take his mind off this place for a while. When he'd first joined the Army fourteen years ago, he'd been full of hope, wanting to make a difference in the world. He knew that'd been a pipe dream now. Sure, his presence in Iraq made a difference to a degree, but he was tired. He was counting the days until this final deployment was over and he could start over again as a civilian in the States.

July 12

Dear Wannabe,

Today was a long day, but now I'm sitting in my rack, trying to ignore the usual sounds of the base and, instead, pretending I can hear those crickets and frogs you mentioned. Over here it's engines, shouting, and explosions. You speak of the peace you feel in Wyoming, and I'm not ashamed to say, I crave it for myself.

This is my last deployment. Once it's over (in sixty-eight more days, but who's counting?), I'll be done. I didn't re-up. Then it'll be a few more months before I process-out. After that, I'll be a free man. Like you, I want to start over somewhere new, but I'm not sure where or what I want to do. I can operate weapons that I'm sure you've only ever seen on TV, but my skills as a civilian are limited. I guess I'll just have to find my way, same as you are. If you can, I can, right? That's what I'm going to go with anyway.

I really appreciate the offer of a care package. While the Army provides the basics, there are a lot of things we need that we can't get here. Beef jerky would be amazing. Not only is it a perfect snack, but I can trade it if I need to. Same with chew and smokes. Coffee is another commodity in high demand—that, however, I wouldn't be trading. LOL. Sunflower seeds and similar snacks are good. I can carry them with me, and they don't spoil or take up too much space.

Anything you can send would be appreciated. Keep a tally, and I'll pay you back when I'm back in the States.

You asked about the food here—no, it's not MREs, but honestly, it's not much better than them. For dinner tonight, I'll probably have a choice of meatloaf with cheese sauce and corn, or spaghetti and chicken gravy. The foreign cooks the army hires have no damn clue what sides go with which dishes. I'm still trying to decide which is the lesser of two evils.

I'm happy to hear your chickens have settled in and you're getting your first eggs. How's the house coming along? Did you get a garden planted? I'd give anything to have some cherry tomatoes fresh off the vine right about now.

That story about your father was surprising. I can't imagine what it felt like to get a call that you'd inherited a ranch from someone you never knew, especially your biological father. I'm glad some of the people there aren't holding his surly disposition against you. Just from your letters, I can tell you're nothing like him. I hope you find answers to some of the questions I know you have about him in the boxes you still have to go through. If you want to talk about your findings, I can be your sounding board.

Sorry this letter is a little shorter than the last one. I won't go into detail, but today was a hard one. I keep re-reading your letters, and they remind me of what's waiting for me when I get home. Not to imply that it's you, but the freedom and simple day-to-day life you're enjoying. It's keeping me focused on staying safe and getting home in one piece.

I hope you don't think this too forward of me, but I'm including a picture of myself. Just thought you might want to put a face to your Pen Pal Extraordinaire.

Sincerely,
Nathan
Pen Pal Extraordinaire

P.S. - Tell Fred hello and give him some celery tops from me. I bet he'd like those too.

P.S.S. - I know you asked some questions that I didn't answer this time. I will when I write again. Didn't want you to think I didn't want to answer them.

P.S.S.S. - Hope you had a blast at the parade and bbq and took lots of pictures!

CHAPTER SEVEN

July 27

Dear PP Extraordinaire,

I hope this care package gets to you okay. I included everything you wrote about in your last letter, plus I added a few things that Cody Moore suggested. He's a nice, seventeen-year-old kid who works in the grocery store here and loves my sleeve. His cousin is in the Marines and is deployed right now too. Cody gave me a list of things his mother and aunt send over every month.

Sorry to hear you were having a bad day the last time you wrote. I guess you tend to have a lot of them where you are. I hope you've had some better days since then, and I don't blame you for wanting this to be your last deployment.

I picked up a 35mm camera I've always wanted and a printer on my latest trip to Walmart and printed out some photos of the parade and bbq to enclose in the package. I also added some pictures of my property, the house, the chickens, Fred, and the amazing sunset we had the other night. I might have gotten a little snapshot crazy. I even put in a photo of me, since you sent me one of you. I shouldn't tell you this, but I took about two dozen selfies before I found one that I liked enough to send. As you can see, I still have some pink hair, but it's growing out. I can't remember the last time it was down to my shoulders. There's also closeup pictures of my sleeve and the tattoos that cover my right shoulder.

Speaking of the parade/bbq, I had a great time. It definitely had that small-town feel to it that I've seen in the movies. (I hate to admit I'm a sucker for the Hallmark channel.) The marchers included the bands from two high schools in the county, the volunteer fire department and ambulance corps, a search & rescue unit, a bunch of horses, some bagpipers, Little League baseball players, 4H Club and the Boy and Girl Scouts. I sent you pictures of a lot of the different groups. I thought of you when the veterans from the local American Legion marched by.

At the bbq, there was a band playing in the gazebo in the town square. There were food contests for the best chili, pulled pork, homemade pies, hot wings, jams, and more. I was almost completely stuffed before the pigs cooked on spits were ready to be served. That was a little gross to see for the first time, but it was the best damn ham I've ever had in my life, after I got up the nerve to try it.

I also got a kick out of the 4H club's competitions for best cow, chicken, and pig (not the ones on the spits). Too bad I'm too old to enter one of my chickens to win a blue ribbon— you had to be under sixteen.

47

My neighbor, Jeremiah, introduced me to some people, most of whom are all from their late-twenties to their mid-forties. One of them, Maddie, who's my age, invited me to a wine & Jenga girl's night at her house this weekend. That should be an interesting combo! The others were all really nice too, even though some other people in town still gave me the evil eye. I can't figure out if it's because of who my father was or if it's because I'm an outsider with pink hair, tattoos, and a tiny nose stud. Either way, I'm not going to let them bother me.

I have a new addition to the ranch since I last wrote to you —a kitten I've named Ethel (I figured that was a good name since my "dog" is named Fred). Someone was giving away their cat's kittens when I went to the store the other day, and this little gray one wormed her way into my heart. (Her picture is included too—did I mention I got a little crazy with the new camera?) I've never had a cat before, or a dog for that matter, but always wanted one. Jeremiah said it's good to have one here because she'll keep the field mice and other rodents away. Surprisingly, or maybe not, Fred doesn't seem to be afraid of her. There was a little hesitancy when they first met on the back porch, but now they seem to be fine with each other. Ethel wants to play, but Fred is more interested in getting his daily seeds into his cheeks to carry them back to his family. Oh, and I finally followed him to his home, and I counted ten others in his little group or coterie as it's called (thank you again, Google). They didn't seem as trusting as Fred, so I stayed far enough away so I wouldn't scare them.

You'll be happy to hear I started a garden (thanks to your question). I'm growing green beans, zucchini, cherry tomatoes, carrots, and green peppers. I didn't go crazy planting a huge amount of each one, since it's only me here and it was a little late in the season to start them. Next year, I'll start earlier.

I've done a LOT of research on animals for the ranch, and I think I'm going to raise alpacas. There's an alpaca ranch about an hour from me, and I emailed them through their website and asked if I could go visit and talk to them about it. They were really nice, and I have an appointment with them set up for next week. I'll tell you all about it in my next letter.

Oh, one more update and then I'll let you go. I start horseback riding lessons next week too! One of the women I met at the bbq has a horse ranch and gives lessons. I figure if I'm going to be a rancher, I need to learn to ride a horse, right? Do you know how to ride one?

Well, I guess that catches you up on everything happening in Wyoming. Looking forward to your next letter. I'm counting the days until you're back on US soil. Stay safe.

Yours truly,
Wannabe

P.S. I am NOT keeping any sort of tally, Nathan. The things I sent are a gift—accept it with good grace. I don't want to hear another word about you "paying me back." As far as I'm concerned, we're square. You're fighting for our country, for our freedoms, and the safety of the men beside you. A box of goodies is the least I can do. Understand?

WILLOW TUCKED the letter to Nathan into its envelope before sealing it inside the care package she had all set to go out with the mail in the morning. Sitting at her desk by the window in her bedroom, she looked out over the fields. The blinking glow of lightning bugs appeared as dusk settled, in even greater numbers than there'd been a month ago. Fall would be approaching before she knew it though, and she'd been warned that winter came early there, and seemingly all at once. The picture Nathan had sent her was propped against the growing stack of letters from him. Picking it up, she studied it closer, as she'd already done hundreds of times. If she wasn't careful the edges were going to start to wear.

He was handsome, incredibly so. It was a photo of him from the knees up but still close enough she could make out his facial features—those not hidden by his helmet anyway. He wore camo and cradled some kind of rifle in his arms. A thigh holster held another gun. She didn't know much about guns, including how to tell one caliber weapon from another, but Jeremiah was taking her shooting soon, deeming it a basic skill she needed to have, which she agreed with. While she was nervous, he was obviously very comfortable with them, considering he often openly carried a handgun on his right hip, which was legal in Wyoming.

In the photo, Nathan was standing between a pair of Humvees, which gave her an idea of how tall he was. Even under his layers of clothing and armor, his strong build was apparent. A sharp jaw was lightly dusted with dark stubble. She was guessing his hair was equally dark, but none showed from under his helmet. Did he keep it buzzed short or shaved completely? She wanted to ask him to send her a more casual picture, one where he wore civilian clothes and looked relaxed, not so tense and gruff.

His eyes were what grabbed her attention the most. His gaze was piercing, boring into hers even through the inanimate photograph. She couldn't make out their color. It was hard to admit it to herself, but she kept dreaming about him, his big, calloused hands cradling her face as he devoured her mouth. He wasn't smiling in the photo, but even in its indifferent state, his mouth looked sexy as hell. Would he kiss her roughly and hard or softly and sweet? A bit of both? Light bites and slow drags of his tongue along her lips?

Her face heated at the thought. She patted her cheeks, grateful there was no one around to see her blushing like a schoolgirl fantasizing about a cute boy in her class. Though there was nothing boyish about Nathan, not in his posture, his profession, or his attitude. He was all man. She shivered. They didn't have men like him in Philly, that was for damn sure—at least not that she'd ever run into. These corn-fed mid-west boys were something special.

She could kick herself for sending so many pictures. The box was already sealed, and she wasn't going to waste the tape by reopening it now. Would he like them? Was she being too forward, sending shots of her tattoos the way she did? What if he thought she was weird and stopped writing her? Why did that thought sink a stone of disappointment into her belly? She knew she'd be spending the next couple weeks, tied in knots of nerves, waiting for his reaction.

"Don't be an idiot. He's writing you because no one else does. He writes back for something to do, not because he has any sort of feelings for you. No doubt a man like him has women throwing themselves at him every chance they can get. Sure, he's a nice guy and sweet, and seems to care, but people are very different on paper than they are in person. And now you're talking to yourself like a lunatic."

Shaking her head, she tried to force her thoughts to her upcoming riding lesson and the renovations she was still dealing with. Nothing good could come from pining after

Nathan. He was half a world away and even when he was back on US soil, she'd probably never hear from him again. She highly doubted he'd want anything to do with her in a romantic way. Her ex-husband certainly had preferred the company of other women to her. Logically, she knew that wasn't her fault, but doubts and insecurities still lingered.

Speaking of her ex-husband, her phone vibrated, showing yet another incoming call from a Philadelphia area code. She let it go to voicemail, knowing it was probably him again. He'd been trying to get in touch with her for the past week, calling from different numbers which she blocked without remorse. When the phone signaled the person had left a voicemail, she raised it to her ear, and listened to the message, just in case it wasn't him.

"Willow, baby, it's Andrew. Is it really true? Did you inherit a ranch in Wyoming? I've been trying to get ahold of you. When you wouldn't answer your phone or call me back, I went to your apartment and your landlady said you'd moved out. She had this address for some hick town called Antelope Rock to forward your mail and security deposit to. Where the fuck is that? Call me back, please, baby. I miss you."

Rolling her eyes, she deleted the message, blocked the number, and made a mental note to call her former landlady tomorrow and remind her not to give her personal information out to anyone. Shuddering, she wished she could block Andrew from her life as easily as she did his number, but like a swarm of mosquitoes, he kept bugging the hell out of her. Marrying that man had been such a huge goddamn mistake. Granted, he hadn't turned into an asshole until after they'd been married a few months, so it wasn't like she had any warning things would go downhill so fast. Andrew had done a good job of hiding his gambling and recreational drug use until after Willow had said, "I do." She'd felt like such a fool when she'd finally found out.

She hadn't dated since her divorce, beyond meeting someone for drinks a few times, being too gun-shy to commit to anything more since the fiasco that'd been Hurricane Andrew. None of those men had ever made it past her front door, and now that she thought about it, she realized she hadn't even been kissed in years. How long did one have to go without sex to be an honorary virgin?

Even as she prepared for bed and turned off the light, her mind kept unwillingly shifting back to Nathan. He was already beginning to haunt her dreams, and now it seemed he was going to star in her waking thoughts as well. She was determined to keep her romantic notions to herself though, chalking them up to going too long without sex and nothing more. Of course, the first guy in years that treated her with respect and care was going to lead to a crush. It was only normal.

Right?

CHAPTER EIGHT

August 13

Dear Wannabe,

Thanks so much for the care package! Everything you included is greatly appreciated. I'm sitting here with the best cup of coffee I've had in ages. I love that you got a brand that's veteran owned. It was a tough decision which flavor to have, but I went with the dark roast since it's an eye-opener. I didn't get much sleep last night. There was stuff going down a few klicks (which is short for kilometers) away from the base, and we saw some action. No casualties on our side, which is always a good thing. Can't tell you much about it, just that I'm glad it's over and we're all in one piece.

As for your P.S. in the last letter, yes, ma'am, whatever you say, ma'am! I'll accept your care package in good grace as ordered. On one condition—you accept this bracelet I got for you. The local kids make them. I try to give them candy when I have it, but buying from them is better sometimes. I know the little boy I bought it from will eat today. I hope you like it.

I LOVED all the photos—they definitely made me homesick for the good ol' USA. The guys in my platoon made me pass them around. I might have growled a bit when a few of them asked me if you were single (sorry, not sorry). Your tattoos are awesome—I absolutely love them—although now I feel a bit like a slacker in that department. I'll have to add some more ink when I get home. Maybe you could give me some ideas on what I should get.

It looks like you had a great time at the parade and bbq, and I got a better idea of what the town and your property look like from the photos. As I suspected, Antelope Rock (I assume that's the name, since it was on the big banner hanging across the street above the parade) is a lot like the one I grew up in—Foxborough, Colorado. I haven't been back there in years, so I loved seeing something similar to it.

I got a kick out of the pictures of Fred and Ethel—I know some people have prairie dogs as pets, but I've never heard of a wild one being that friendly before, especially with a cat around. I hope they stay friends as Ethel gets bigger.

As for horses, yeah, I know how to ride them. My friend's family (the one I went camping with) had a bunch of them. They bred them, gave horseback riding lessons, and boarded them for people who needed it. It's been ages since I've been on one, and I really miss it. If you're sore from the lessons, get some arnica gel. It'll help with the aching muscles.

I owe you the answers to a few questions that I skipped over last time. It's kind of hard to write about—or even talk about. My folks and my younger sister were killed in a car accident nine years ago while I was deployed. Shannon was seventeen, a senior in high school, and my only sibling. They'd taken a day trip to check out Colorado State University—it was one of the schools she was interested in going to. On their way back home, a tractor-trailer jack-knifed on the interstate during a freak hailstorm, setting off a chain reaction. Twenty-two cars and trucks ended in a massive pileup that killed eight people. From what I was told, my parents and Shannon died instantly when their car was sandwiched between two semis. The three-pointed Celtic knot I have over my heart, along with the date of their deaths, is in memory of them.

I'd never planned to be in the Army as long as I have been, but after losing my family, I had no one to go home to, so I re-upped the next few times I was asked to. My mom's best friend, Melinda Jackson, and her family were a godsend during the aftermath. They helped arrange the wakes, funeral, and repast while I was flying home. A week after it was all over, I couldn't stand being in the house I'd lived in for most of my life all by myself, so I got back on a plane to rejoin my platoon. The Jacksons packed up the house for me, sold what I told them to, and put the rest in storage for me, then put the house on the market. My dad's lawyer and accountant helped out too, and I was able to handle a lot of the paperwork over the internet. It took a heavy load off my mind when I was back over on this side of the world. I honestly wouldn't have been up to doing all that, even with their help. I threw myself into work because I didn't know what else to do without my family. Nine years later, all that stuff is still in storage waiting for me. I have a few pictures of them at my place off-base in the States, and one of all of us that I carry over here. I know there are so many memories in that storage unit—maybe after I'm discharged, I'll find the courage to finally go through everything.

You would've liked my sister. Shannon was one of those people who made friends with everyone she met. She'd walk into a room and bring joy and laughter with her. She wanted to be an elementary school teacher because she'd loved her summer job as a camp counselor. She was great with kids. I always thought she'd grow up and give me a dozen nieces and nephews someday, but it wasn't meant to be.

My folks were great people too. They gave us a loving, happy, and stable home. I miss them so much, and there are mornings, when I'm in that foggy state between sleep and consciousness, that I think they're still alive. But then it hits me full force that they're gone, and I grieve all over again. Anyone who ever says the pain of losing a loved one goes away is lying or they truly don't get it. The pain is always there—we just have to learn to live with it.

All right, that's enough sadness for one letter. Tell me, how did the drunken Jenga night go? How's the garden doing? And fill me in on how things went with the visit to the alpaca farm. Are you still interested in raising them?

Looking forward to your next letter. I was never one to get excited about mail call, since I rarely get anything, but you've changed that. Thank you, Willow. You've given me something to smile about, and some things to think about other than how much time I have left in this crappy sandbox. You'll never know how much you've brightened my world with your letters. Maybe when I'm stateside again, I can come to Wyoming and we could meet, that is, if you're okay with that.

Until next time . . .

Yours affectionately,
Nathan

CHAPTER NINE

WILLOW FOLDED the letter carefully and added it to the stack with the others. She would write back a little later tonight after she got her thoughts and feelings back under control. Her heart broke for him as she'd read about his family. Her mother's death had been difficult, but she couldn't imagine what Nathan had gone through, losing both parents and his sister all in the same instant.

Her mind shifted to other parts of his letter. He wanted to meet her? She couldn't believe it. And he was growling at his buddies who were asking about her? Was she reading too much into it? She didn't know, but maybe she'd be finding out someday.

For now, she needed to get ready for her shooting lesson with Jeremiah. He'd told her to wear comfortable clothes and a hat. Well, comfortable described all her clothes, because who wanted to wear things that weren't?

Going downstairs, she opened the hall closet and grabbed the ball cap she'd noticed one day on the top shelf. She shook it out and looked at the patch above the brim. She was surprised to see it was the Philadelphia Flyers logo. Her father had been a hockey fan? Being from Philly, it was hard to escape the constant bombardment of sports teams from the city, and while she didn't follow the sport, she'd recognized the team's logo immediately. The cap's bill was perfectly curved to protect her eyes, and the sweatband was worn from years of use. It was ragged, but well-loved. Settling it on her head, she stepped out onto the porch to wait on the swing for Jeremiah.

Not even five minutes passed before her neighbor's massive red pickup truck came rolling down her drive, kicking up dust in its wake. Walking down the steps to greet him, she tried to disguise her nerves. Knowing she needed to learn to shoot was one thing, actually doing it was another. The main thing pushing her to follow through with the lessons was the fact she'd spotted a rattlesnake near her mailbox the other day, and it'd scared the crap out of her. Actually, she'd heard it first before seeing it. In a panic, she'd run back into the house and called Jeremiah. Of course, by the time he'd gotten there, the reptile had been long gone. Thankfully, she hadn't seen it since, but she now carried a spade shovel whenever she went to get her mail. She didn't want to be some damsel in distress that had to run to her best friend every time something slithered by around here.

"Hey, Jeremiah," she greeted him as he climbed from the truck. Smiling, he gave her a big hug. As they'd gotten to know each other better, she'd discovered he was a hugger in a genial way. There was nothing sexual about his embraces, just warmth and comfort.

He squeezed her tightly and lifted her clear off her feet. "There's my Willow-girl! How are ya this fine day? Ready to sling some lead?"

"People actually say that?" she questioned, laughing at his antics. She was so glad she'd met him because he was turning into a close friend—something she hadn't had in a long time.

"No, not really, but it sounds good, don't it?" Keeping an arm across her shoulders, he led her to his truck. "Now, seeing as you're a gun virgin, I brought a couple different choices for you, plus we'll take that nice Mossberg you got by your door." Releasing her, he opened the crew cab door of his big rig and waved her forward. "I brought my two-twenty-three hunting rifle, two pistols, and both a pump action and double barrel shotguns. A well-rounded education is ideal, yeah?"

"That's an awful lot of firepower, Jeremiah." She didn't want to admit to him that guns intimidated her. She was a strong and independent woman, right? She was living in the wilds of Wyoming, where guns were commonplace. Shit, most trucks in Antelope Rock had gun racks mounted on the back windows.

"It's good to be familiar with different types, so even if you're around one that you've never fired before, you'll know the basics and your way around them. I can tell you're a bit intimidated, but don't be. Ain't nothing to it."

She wasn't sure that was true, but she was willing to give it a try. "If you say so. Let me go get the shotgun from inside, and we'll get going. I don't have shells or bullets or whatever it uses though."

"Don't worry about that—I brought plenty."

Willow jogged back to the house and returned with the heavy shotgun, holding it awkwardly. She had enough common sense to keep the barrel pointed at the ground, but she didn't have a clue if it was loaded or how to check.

"Here, take this. I don't know if it's loaded or where the safety is."

A guffaw erupted from him as he took the weapon from her and checked to see if it was loaded, which it was. She should have known, since it made sense if her father had kept the shotgun in the house for protection. "Willow, my girl, shotguns don't have a safety. You've watched too many movies."

She blushed and looked down at her feet, kicking stones with the toe of one of her new boots she'd picked up the last time she'd stopped at Ducky's Feed & Supply. If she was going to be a rancher, she figured she might as well look the part. "No need to make fun of me."

"Oh, honey. I was just teasing you. I didn't mean any harm." Keeping the shotgun off to the side, he hugged her with his other arm. "Come on, by time I'm done with you, you'll be a regular Annie Oakley."

Nodding but not believing him for a minute, she climbed into the passenger seat when he held the door open for her. After securing the shotgun in the bed of the truck, he got in and didn't hesitate to drive straight across her field as if it were any other road that could be found on a GPS. As they bounced along, Willow held onto the "oh shit" handle to keep from flying out the window. By the time Jeremiah pulled up to a small incline and stopped the truck, she'd been laughing harder than she had in ages.

When they got out of the truck, she noticed there was a small hill and depression ahead of them. Behind her, Jeremiah lowered the tailgate and began to line the guns up on it. He nodded toward the hill. "This is perfect for target shooting. First rule, always be aware of your surroundings. Bullets travel a long distance, much farther than you probably figure, and it's important to know where they might end up. In this case, the only place they'll go is into the dirt."

"What are the other rules?" she asked as she watched him check each weapon.

"Rule two, always, always assume the gun is loaded, even if you just checked it. Over-caution is the rule of thumb here. Three, never point a gun at someone unless you intend to shoot them. When you're handling a gun, always have it pointed at the ground or downrange away from anyone near you. Four, never, under any circumstances walk into the line of fire of someone else. Even if they have finished, wait for the other person to unload and secure their weapon before you approach. Accidents can happen in a split-second of carelessness. Five, never shoot up into the air. You hear about this all the time, especially around the holidays. What goes up, must come down. People have been hurt and even killed because some jackass was shooting into the air to celebrate something a half mile away. Gravity always wins."

"Okay." Her nerves had ratcheted up another few notches as he'd rattled off the rules. It was a lot to remember, but it all seemed like common sense. "Anything else?"

"Treat your weapon with care—clean it, secure it, respect that it's a dangerous tool, and it will serve you well. Today, we'll shoot for a while and later I'll show you how to clean them. It's important to clean a gun after each use. Firing them releases gunpowder residue that can gum up the action. The last thing you want is to need to fire your weapon for some reason and have it jam on you. Just like you change the oil in your truck and fill it with gas, you have to keep proper maintenance of your guns. Understand?"

"Makes sense." She jutted her chin to the cache of weapons. "Now tell me more about each one of these."

Pointing at each gun, he told her the make, model, and caliber of each. "This is yours—it's a Mossberg pump-action twelve-gauge, takes a three-inch shell, and yes, they come in different sizes. Here's my pump, same as yours. Next is my double-barrel ten-gauge. This one here is my two-twenty-three, bolt action. I use it for deer hunting. Next are my pistols. I brought both a semi-automatic and a revolver. I've got a Smith & Wesson three-fifty-seven and a Glock nine mil."

"Wow." Words beyond that failed her. "If I didn't recognize most of the words that just came out of your mouth, I would've sworn you were talking in a different language."

"You'll be talking like that soon enough," he responded with a chuckle. "So, where would you like to start?" He rested his hands on his hips and looked at the guns all lined up in a pretty row of death on his tailgate.

"I've never fired a gun, of any caliber, in my life. In fact, today was the first time I ever had one in my hand. So, I'll let you pick."

"Okay, fair enough. Let's start with your shotgun. It's the one that'll be in your house, and the one you should be the most familiar with anyway."

"Makes sense. Show me what to do."

He pointed at the end of her shotgun that rests against the shooter's shoulder and then at the same spot on his. "This is the stock, see how it's shorter on yours than it is on mine? Your daddy was only a few inches taller than you, maybe five-ten, which means his arms were shorter than mine. Same as yours. The shorter stock makes it easier to hold the weapon properly against your shoulder. If the stock is too long for the person shooting it, there's a good chance it'll shift out of position after the first shot. That happened to one of my nephews—he fired two shots, one right after the other, and on the second one, the kickback had the base of the stock nail him good in the bicep. Nothing broken, of course, but he was badly bruised for a good two weeks.

An hour later, Willow's shoulder was sore, her right palm was stinging, and the smell of gunpowder was thick in the air around them. She'd shot all the shotgun shells Jeremiah had brought and most of the rounds for the pistols. The three paper targets he'd stapled to pieces of plywood attached to long stakes stuck into the ground a few feet in front of the hill, were in tatters, and over time, her confidence with the weapons had grown.

"You're a natural. I just can't believe it," Jeremiah said as they removed the eye and ear protection he'd brought for both of them. "You're sure you're not pulling one over on me? You're a secret marksman—excuse me—markswoman, aren't you?"

Laughing with delight and pride in herself, she shook her head. "Nope, I swear. This is my first time. Did you not see my first dozen shots? I missed the targets by a mile."

"Well, remind me never to piss you off and be on the wrong end of your shotgun, woman. You're deadly with that damn thing now. Ready to call it a day?"

"Sure, on one condition. You let me make you supper. We've spent all afternoon out here, and I'm sure you're starving."

"You won't see me saying no to a home-cooked meal. Bachelorhood does have its downsides, that's for damn sure."

His comment gave her pause, and she wanted to ask why he was still single. He was handsome and funny, not to mention sweet and kind. She couldn't believe he hadn't been snatched up yet. He wasn't her type, but surely, there was someone in town for him.

She helped him pack up and secure the guns into his truck, and then he drove them back to her house.

Leading the way into the kitchen, she said, "Let me wash up, and I'll see what I have that I can throw together quick. There's beer in the fridge if you'd like one. Help yourself."

"Thanks, don't mind if I do." He grabbed a bottle for himself, holding another out to her in question.

"Please." After he opened the twist top, he handed her the bottle, and she took a long drink of the cold brew, the flavor hitting her just right. "Damn, that's good."

"Nothing like a cold beer after a day outside in the fresh air, am I right?"

She switched the radio on and the rumbling voice of Johnny Cash singing about Folsom Prison filled the air as she found some chicken and veggies from the fridge. "Stir-fry okay? It's quick and easy."

"You could serve me peanut butter and jelly, and I'd just be happy not to be making it myself." He sat on the barstool at the island before removing his Stetson and setting it beside him. His dark-red hair gleamed under the light. Not for the first time, she thought how lucky he was to have such gorgeous hair without a salon's aid.

"Why is that? You don't like cooking?"

"Nah, I cook just fine. Just gets lonely eating by myself sometimes is all." He worked on peeling the label from his beer, not looking up as she diced the chicken and put a skillet on the stove.

"I apologize in advance if this is none of my business, but why are you single, Jeremiah? You're handsome as all get out and a great guy. Any woman would be lucky to have you. No one around that strikes your fancy?"

He froze, before slowly rising his head and meeting her gaze. He studied her carefully, seeming to be debating something with himself.

"Can I trust you?"

Hearing the seriousness in his tone, she gave him her full attention. "Of course, you can. You're the closet thing I have to a best friend around here. Anything you tell me stops with me."

He paused, as if weighing his words. "I don't like any of the women around here. Actually, I don't like women at all. I'm—I'm gay."

The implications of his confession hit her like a ton of bricks. The small town of Antelope Rock wasn't progressive in any way. There was not a single rainbow flag anywhere in town. It was an archaic boys-club type of place where homophobia was alive and well. To be gay and a rancher in a small community had to be . . . hard. She was honored he trusted her with his secret, and she would take it to her grave if he wanted her to.

His eyes were downcast, as if he didn't want to see her reaction, so she did her best to lighten his load. "So, does this mean we can check out hot cowboy asses together? There's just something about a tight pair of Wranglers . . ."

Jeremiah threw his head back and laughed so hard, tears welled up in his eyes. "Oh, woman, you never cease to amaze me. Thank you for that. Coming out is never easy for anyone, and you're the only person in my family or this backwater town that I've ever told. I'm sure my parents suspect at this point, but we don't talk about it. They're retired and live in Arizona, and we don't see much of each other anymore. And to answer your questions, yes, ma'am, a nice tight ass in Wranglers is a sight to behold."

As she finished cooking, they laughed, joked around, and teased each other. Their conversation flowed easily, as if they'd known each other their entire lives. She hadn't had a close friend since before her marriage. Having one now meant everything to her. Being here, in Antelope Rock, was beginning to be the best thing that had ever happened to her.

"So, what about you, Willow? Have any of the single guys in town caught your attention yet?" When she blushed, his eyes widened, and he leaned forward. "Oh, c'mon, girl. I just bared my soul and came out to you, so you can damn well give me one of your secrets in return. Which one is he?"

Smiling, she shook her head. "It's no one in town. No one in Wyoming even." As they ate, she proceeded to tell him about Nathan, doing her best to stick to the facts and keep the adolescent gushing to a minimum. She held out her left wrist where she'd been wearing the bracelet Nathan had sent her ever since she'd received it. It was colorful but would've gotten lost against her tattoos on her other arm. "He got this for me. The locals make them where he's deployed."

"It's pretty. He's got good taste."

"Do you think I'm crazy, fantasizing about a guy I've never met in person, Jeremiah? Hell, we haven't even spoken on the phone or video chatted—just old-fashioned, hand-written letters."

He shrugged. "People find their soulmates in all different sorts of ways. Over a hundred years ago, mail-order brides were a thing, and I've heard of romantic relationships that started out as pen pals before. Nowadays, people are marrying the love of their lives that they met over the internet. When that boy gets back to the States, invite him up here. Just wondering about it will get you nowhere. Maybe he'll get here, and you'll find you're not attracted to him romantically, but you could still be good friends. Lord knows you can never have enough of those. But maybe you'll discover he's your soul mate. You won't find out until you take that first step. And if you really want to win him over, cook him this dish." He used his fork to point to his almost empty plate. "It's the best damn thing I've eaten all year."

Her smile grew. "I'll keep that in mind."

As they finished their meal, Willow realized it'd been forever since she'd had a friend over for dinner. Even back in Philly, there had been very few times she'd had people over to her apartment. Since she was starting a new life here in Wyoming, she mentally added having company over more often to her list of things to do.

Jeremiah was helping do the dishes when her cell phone rang from where it sat on the kitchen island. The sound startled her, making her drop a plate into the soapy water with a splash. "Damn, no one ever calls me. Who the hell could that be?" Although she suspected she already knew.

When she picked it up, however, she didn't recognize the number or area code. It wasn't from Philadelphia or any of its surrounding counties, so she swiped the green button and said, "Hello?"

"Willow? Oh hey, babe, it's so good to finally hear your voice."

Her blood ran cold, and she felt the blood drain from her face.

"Andrew, what the hell do you want?" Jeremiah looked sharply at her upon hearing her icy tone. He mouthed, *you okay?* She frowned in response, plopping down on a barstool at the kitchen's island in disbelief and agitation, but held up a hand to stop him when he reached for her phone. The last thing she wanted was for her new friend to get caught up in whatever mess her ex had found himself in. And she was sure that was the reason Andrew was calling. "Did you not figure out I didn't want to talk to you after I sent your calls to voice mail, blocked the numbers, and didn't call you back?"

"Ah, come on now, baby. Don't be that way. I can't call you up?"

"No. You fucking can't. You gave up that right when I found you balls deep inside Mindy." She ignored Jeremiah's eyes bugging out of his head.

"Now you know that was a mistake, and I regret it. She didn't mean anything to me."

She gritted her teeth as fury assaulted her. The nerve of her bastard of an ex-husband never ceased to amaze her. If only she'd realized it before she'd married him. "You have two seconds to tell me what the fuck you want, after that I'm blocking your number. Again."

"Well, honey, I heard about your father, and I just wanted to call and give my condolences. I didn't know you'd found him." She wasn't going to explain it all to him, but before she could tell him to never call her again, he asked, "Why did you move out there? Your home is here, baby."

God, she hated the syrupy endearments he threw out at the drop of a hat. At one time, she'd thought the words proved he cared about her and loved her, but now she knew they meant nothing to him—just like she meant nothing to him. "It's none of your business. You've given your regards, now fuck right off." She ended the call, cutting off whatever he'd started to say and sorely missing old phones that you could slam onto the cradle. Swiping a button just wasn't as satisfying.

"Willow?" Jeremiah sat on the stool next to her and placed a comforting hand on her shaking arm. "Are you okay? Who was that?"

She sighed heavily, dropped the phone on the counter, and ran her free hand through her hair. "Andrew Phelps is the slime ball I had the misfortune to marry a few years ago. I came home from work one day, happy to be out early for once, to find him doing his level best to fuck Mindy, my best friend, through our mattress. Yes. He was fucking my best friend. In our bed. With no condom, I might add. Not to mention, anytime I ever managed to save some money he pissed it away gambling."

"You're fucking kiddin' me." He looked equal parts shocked and appalled.

"Wish I was. I kicked his ass out right then and filed for divorce the next day. That was two years ago. And this isn't the first time he's called me. I block the numbers he calls from, but he keeps getting new ones. I should just get a new phone number and be done with it." Picking up the phone again, she hit the appropriate buttons on the screen to select the latest number he'd called her from and blocked it like all the others. "I wish he'd just leave me alone. I came here to start over, to have a life as far away from him and Philly as possible, and here he comes, fucking with me all over again."

Jeremiah squeezed her arm gently. "Listen, I'm here. If he bothers you again, you let me know, and I'll track him down and bury his body where it'll never be found—Marty Olsen's pig farm. Those things eat everything you toss in their sty and don't leave a trace of body parts." She snorted a laugh as he continued, "What? I saw it on the Discovery channel! A couple pigs can eat an entire human body, bones and all, in a matter of minutes, if they're hungry enough. He's a bastard and never deserved you anyway."

That she agreed with. "I know. To be honest, our marriage was already falling apart by the time I caught him cheating, but it doesn't excuse that he did it. My mother had just died, and I was really struggling, both emotionally and financially. He didn't get the attention from me he thought he deserved." She shrugged. "I've moved on, honestly." Her thoughts immediately zinged to Nathan. Oh boy, had she ever moved on. "One of these days he'll get bored and stop. I mean, it's not like he's going to come to the middle of nowhere Wyoming to see me, right?"

"But if he does, I've got Marty on my phone's speed dial." Putting his arm around her shoulders, he tucked her into his side. "You're a strong woman, Willow-girl. Don't let a bastard like that get you down."

"No worries about that. He doesn't have power over me anymore."

CHAPTER TEN

August 30

Dear PP Extraordinaire,

I hope you have a good day today. My day was half good, half shitty, but before I go down that road, let me tell you about where I am. I've taken to sitting outside on one of my porch swings when I write to you. If the weather is nice anyway—if not, I sit at the desk in my bedroom. Tonight is a gorgeous night. Warm but not too hot, and there's a nice breeze coming through. I think it might rain later, because I can hear thunder pretty far away and see flashes of lighting in the distance. Do you like thunderstorms? I adore them in the summertime. The chickens are quiet this evening too, no doubt sensing the bad weather coming. Do you get thunderstorms where you are? I know it's hot during the day and gets cold at night in the Middle East, but I admit I don't know much else beyond that.

My friend Jeremiah just left—he took me target shooting today! Not only was it fun as hell, but I made that target my bitch! I don't know if I'll ever be totally comfortable with guns, but now I feel a measure of confidence handling them. My shoulder is a little sore from my father's shotgun, and my right palm is pink and sore from the kick on the pistols I was firing, but Jeremiah said I did an awesome job. Who knew that a city girl from Philly would be wearing shit kickers and blasting a target with a 12-gauge shotgun? I sure as hell never imagined I would be that person.

After we finished up with my lesson, I cooked him dinner, and we had a great time laughing and getting to know each other better. Did I tell you he owns the neighboring ranch? He's really nice. If I hadn't met him, I don't know what I would be doing right now. Probably running back to Philly with my tail between my legs.

Now, here I am, thinking about getting alpacas and raising chickens. Not to mention Fred and Ethel. If you miss horseback riding, maybe one day you can come see me, and we'll go riding. The land here is so beautiful. I can see why the Lakota hold it so sacred. It IS sacred land. There's something holy about sitting here on my porch and looking out across my property. Seeing the sage brush and grasses, smelling the wind and soil. I'm not a very religious person, but this place makes me feel like I'm on holy ground when I step outside. There's a magic here that's hard to put into words. I guess what I'm saying is that even though I didn't know my father, I'm grateful to him. For giving me this place and making it possible for me to find myself here.

I was so sorry to read about the loss of your parents and

sister. My heart breaks for you. After losing my mom, I know that kind of pain and wouldn't wish it on anyone. I'm sure your family is very proud of the man you have become. I know I'm happy to call you my friend.

I'm glad you loved the photos and care package. I'll have to send you another one soon. Any new requests? That coffee really is the best. It's the only kind I drink. I was supporting veteran causes before I wrote to you, but now I have even more incentive to do so.

I will admit I blushed like a teenager when you said the other guys asked if I was single when you showed them my picture. The answer is yes and for good reason. I'll explain, but I'm warning you, it's not a great story. Speaking of pictures, before I forget to ask again, is that the only photo you have of yourself? Do you have any others where you're not in uniform? Okay, that sounded like I was asking for naked pictures of you and now I'm blushing again. Since I don't want to toss this letter in the trash and start from scratch to save myself from embarrassment, let me clarify— what I meant to ask is if you have a photo of you in civilian clothes.

Anyway, back to me being single. This isn't something I talk about often, but there's a safety in writing to you that I don't feel when speaking otherwise. I was married before. I met Andrew six years ago. He was kind and handsome, seemed successful (seemed being the operative word here), and was interested in me. I realize now that I was more flattered by his attention than really in love with him, but sometimes emotions get the better of us, and like most people, I just wanted to be loved.

We dated for a year and when he proposed I said yes. For a while, things were good. Then when my mother got sick, and I devoted more and more time to caring for her, he started coming home later and later. Often, I was so tired from working and being a caretaker for Mom that I didn't notice. Truthfully, after a while, I didn't really care either. I was pulling double shifts to try and help Mom with her bills, so I didn't have a lot of time left over for him or even myself at the end of the day.

I'm sure you've figured out where this is going. It reads like a cheesy Lifetime movie. I got out of work early one afternoon and I came home, thinking I would surprise him. Turns out I was the one in for a surprise. I was greeted by the sight of my husband and my (now former) best friend, Mindy, going at it like animals in our own damn bed.

I kicked them both out, filed for divorce, and bought a new bed the next day. Fast forward to today. During dinner this evening, I got a call from none other than Andrew. He was asking if I really did move to Wyoming and tried to give me his condolences about my father. The slimeball. Let's just say, that conversation was brief, and I've blocked his number, yet again.

I was blindsided. Let me be clear. I do not in any way harbor feelings for that bastard. If I never saw or spoke to him again in my life it would be fine with me. He just keeps creeping back in, calling me up, and I don't understand why. I wasn't enough for him then, so what the fuck does he want with me now? No offense, but men can be such bastards sometimes.

So, if you're curious why I'm cursing more, this is why. But I had a great afternoon with Jeremiah, (who offered to feed Andrew to Marty Olsen's pigs if he ever shows up here—I haven't met Marty yet, but I might have to some day), and now I'm sitting here, talking to you. Well, sort of. Even though I know you won't get this letter for a week or two, it still feels like I'm having a full conversation with you. I can pretend that you're here beside me on this swing. Sorry if that sounds a bit sappy, but I'm feeling a bit sappy today.

All right, I want to end this letter on a few high notes. Drunken Jenga night was a friggin' BLAST! My head was pounding a bit the next day, but it was so worth it. Maddie is a sweetheart, and she really made me feel welcome in the group. I had them add my name to the list of rotating hosts, but everyone's schedules are always so crazy, it might be a few months before I get a turn.

My garden is coming along really well. The tomatoes are in flower, and I hope that I'll have some fresh ones soon. Or green ones. Fried green tomatoes are delicious—one of my favorite summertime treats. What are some of your favorite foods? Beside beef jerky of course. I've been thinking of trying my hand at making some. This is beef country, right? I found a few recipes online that look good, and if it comes out right, I'll send you some to try.

The trip to the alpaca farm was AMAZING! They are so damn cute! The Brodericks, who own the place, were so nice and gave me the grand tour. They gave me all sorts of reading material and websites to look into and told me how I could start off slow with only a few head, a couple females and one male. Their operation is huge now, but they started small way back when. I even got to see the ranch hands shearing the fleece off a few alpacas. The fleece is then sold to companies and individuals to make yarn. Gail Broderick also spins some of it to make her own yarn. I learned how to take care of them, what to feed them, etc. Gail said if I had any more questions (even though I'd asked around a hundred of them already) to call her or shoot her an email. She's going to check around and see if anyone has any secondhand equipment that might be for sale for me. Thankfully, I don't need a whole lot beyond a barn, hay storage, corrals, and feeding equipment. They aren't as much work as cattle can be. Again, she and her husband Mark were awesome. So, it looks like I really might do this! I'm so excited!

It's getting late, and this letter is so long that I'm probably boring you. As always, I hope this finds you healthy and safe. Stay that way, okay? For me? The thought of something happening to you . . . I don't even want to think about it.

Yours,
Willow

P.S. Fred and Ethel say hello, and he loves the celery tops just as much as the carrot tops.

NATHAN CLUTCHED the letter tightly in his fist, his heart slamming against his ribs. Who is this Jeremiah fucker? He was proud of Willow for learning to shoot, but dammit, Jeremiah better keep his hands off his girl.

Wait, what?

His girl?

When had he started thinking of Willow as his? She was a person, not a piece of property. They'd never met or even spoken on the phone. All he had of her was a stack of letters and an envelope full of pictures, but he felt possessive all the same. Maybe it made him more than a little crazy, but he couldn't help but hope he wasn't the only one who thought there was something between them. Was writing letters back and forth all that different from online dating? He didn't think so. He knew he wasn't imagining it. She'd said, right here in black and white, that she wished he was on that porch swing with her, watching the sunset together. It might make him a pathetic sap, but he wanted that more than anything. That she was there, alone and hurting, broke his heart more than a little. He hated that she had to deal with her ex by herself.

But she wasn't alone, was she? *Jeremiah* was there. *Jeremiah* was nice and kind and her neighbor. *Fucking Jeremiah.*

As for her ex, Nathan wanted to track that Andrew fucker down and beat him to a pulp. He wasn't normally a violent guy outside of work, but cheating bastards like that got his back up. Gritting his teeth, he swallowed his anger and put her letter safely away in his footlocker with the others. He needed to get to work, focus on getting through the day, and the next day, and then the one after that—on and on until he could get out of this shit hole.

He'd stay safe, he'd do his job, and he'd go home because now he had something to go home to.

Willow.

His girl. She was his, even if she didn't know it yet, he would make damn sure she understood that too. That bastard Jeremiah didn't stand a chance. Already mentally writing the next letter, he vowed to step things up a bit and put aside any sort of subtlety. He refused to let her have any doubts that he was interested in her.

It was a risk but one he knew he had to take. Losing Willow to her neighbor, or anyone else for that matter, wasn't an option.

CHAPTER ELEVEN

A LITTLE OVER two weeks after her first shooting lesson and dinner with Jeremiah, Willow pushed her cart through the Pack & Sack, stocking up on groceries for herself and goodies to send to Nathan. As always, he was never too far from her thoughts. Jeremiah had opted to come with her after she'd called and asked if he'd needed anything.

"Here, Willow-girl, you need these." Jeremiah tossed a box of condoms into the cart with a wink and a grin.

"I do not! Jesus, put them back." She grabbed the box and threw it back at him with a glare and a frown. She was on the shot and free of any STDs, not that she was about to discuss her sexual health in the middle of the Pack & Sack. And the last thing she needed was for someone to see her buying condoms with her single male neighbor, who everyone thought was straight.

"When Nathan comes to see you, it would be a good idea to have them on hand. Better safe than knocked up." He poked her in the belly with the box, smirking like an asshole.

Her eyes widened as her jaw dropped and slammed shut a few times before she found her voice again. "You did not just say that to me." After smacking his arm, she snatched the box from him and shoved it onto the shelf, not caring that she'd put it with the wrong brand. "I don't even know that he's interested in me that way. He's probably just lonely and grateful for the distraction of my letters. Like watching late night TV—it's just something to do to kill time."

They pushed their carts around to the next aisle. Willow had been hoping to run into Cody while they were there, but he apparently it was his day off. Tomorrow was his eighteenth birthday, and she'd stuffed a twenty-dollar bill into a funny card for him, figuring he could add it to the money he'd saved up for his tattoo. They'd discussed different design options, whenever they'd run into each other, and he'd narrowed it down to three really nice ones but was still undecided which would be his final choice.

"See, I'm calling bullshit right there. Maybe it started out that way, but it's changed, and you know it." Jeremiah reached over her head, adding chips and dip to his cart. "I think you're afraid to let yourself like him."

"There's nothing to be afraid of, because there's nothing going on. Grab me those crunchy Cheetos on the top shelf, will you? Two bags, please." She was trying to send some different things to Nathan this time. Spotting the rack of beef jerky, she ignored the high price and threw several packages in a variety of flavors into her cart.

"Girl, stop doubting yourself so much." Leaning closer, he lowered his voice. "I may not like women, but I have eyes. You're sexy as hell. Trust me. That man is on the hook, and you just need to reel him in a little. He'll be putty in those hands of yours. Oh, and if you need any blow job tips, just let me know." Straightening, he whistled as he strode further down the aisle to the beer, leaving her gaping after him.

"Blow job tips?" she said to herself softly, stunned at the direction their conversation had gone in a heartbeat. Had she fallen down a damn rabbit hole? What world did she live in now, where she owned a ranch and had a gay best friend offering tips on giving hummers?

Chuckling and deciding to go with it, she followed Mr. Blowie Expert, snagging a twelve pack of beer for herself.

Arriving back at the ranch after dropping Jeremiah at his place, she was hauling the last of the bags inside when she heard a vehicle coming down the driveway. Thinking Jeremiah must have forgotten something in her truck, she waited just inside the screen door for him to pull up. Only the silver, mid-sized sedan coming toward her in a cloud of dust wasn't what she'd expected to see.

Warning bells clanged in her head, and she stepped back deeper into the shadows of the door. The car stopped next to her truck and shut off. The windshield was dusty and shadowed, making it impossible for her to see who was inside. The car's engine ticked as it cooled, and Willow waited patiently, glancing down at her shotgun in its normal place by the door. Patting her pockets, she realized her cell phone was in the kitchen, and she didn't want to take her eyes off the car long enough to retrieve it.

The driver's door swung open, and the man that emerged set her teeth on edge.

Andrew.

As a litany of curses ran through her head, she didn't move, not wanting to give her presence away. Ethel came slinking out from the shade of the porch and approached the unwanted visitor. She'd almost doubled in size since Willow had adopted her. Andrew scowled down at the cat, making a move as if he was going to kick her.

"You kick my cat, and you're not going to like the consequences," she barked.

His head jerked up, and his foot returned to the gravel, leaving Ethel unharmed. "Willow? Where are you?"

She took a step toward the still closed screen door, keeping the barrier between them. Ethel had clamored up the steps at the sound of Willow's voice. "Get off my land."

"Now, Willow, that's no way to talk to your husband." He strode closer, clearly intending to come up onto the porch.

Before his foot hit the first step, she picked up the shotgun, not giving herself a chance to think about it. She kicked at the screen door's frame, sending it flying, and shouldered the weapon. Her hands shook a little, but it was definitely from anger and not from the fact she was pointing a gun at someone for the first time in her life. The *chh chh* of the pump action had Andrew freezing where he stood. "You're not my husband, Andrew—you haven't been in a very long time. Now, you're nothing to me other than a trespasser. And around here, we shoot trespassers."

His hands were raised, and actual fear appeared on his face. "What the fuck, woman? Put that thing down before you hurt someone!"

Taking two steps closer, she aimed the barrel to the left of him and fired into the dirt. Andrew paled and jumped about a foot straight up in the air, yelping in alarm. Quickly pumping the action again, she ejected the spent shell as a live round loaded into the chamber. "I have four more where that came from."

"What the fuck! You shot at me!"

"If I'd shot at you, you'd be dead. I'm going to say it one more time, really slow, since you're such a dumb ass. Get the fuck off my property before I decide you're too stupid to live."

"I'll have you arrested! You tried to kill me!" he shouted as he quickly retreated to his car. "I'm calling the police!"

"Go ahead! I'll be waiting right here." She kept the shotgun trained on him until he was in his car and backing away in a cloud of dust.

Sure enough, twenty minutes later, the sheriff arrived at her house. She'd taken the time to put her groceries away before deciding to wait on the porch swing for him. There'd been no doubt in her mind Andrew would file a complaint against her. Sheriff Grady Minor was in his fifties and had been with the county's sheriff department his entire adult life, having been elected to the top position after fifteen years as a deputy. Maddie Fisher had told her everyone loved him so much, he'd run uncontested during every election. He had the reputation of being firm but fair. Willow had been introduced to him briefly at the fourth of July parade but hadn't had a chance to say more than hello to him because he'd had to run off for someone having a medical emergency. He'd seemed like the good guy everyone proclaimed him to be though, and as she waited to find out how much trouble she was in, she hoped that was true.

The lawman climbed out of his SUV and slowly ambled up to her side porch. He was dressed in his official brown uniform, complete with a badge over his heart, a duty belt around his hips, and a cowboy hat on his head. He had a strong physique that probably had most criminals thinking twice about going toe to toe with him.

"Where's the shotgun, Ms. Crawford?"

"Inside by the door, where it's always been. You here to arrest me, Sheriff?"

"Should I?" He took a step closer before crossing his arms and leaning his shoulder against one of the porch's columns. "You shot at a man, trespassing or not, that's against the law, unless he was threatening you, which he says he didn't do."

She tamped down her reemerging anger, remembering this man had the ability to toss her into a jail cell and throw away the key. "To be clear, I shot *near* him, not *at* him—a good eight-feet away from him. I'm sure I skirted the law a bit, but he got a fair warning."

She should be afraid about being arrested, but for some reason she wasn't. If she was still back East, she would already be face down in the dirt with her hands cuffed behind her back. But as she was learning, things were far different in Antelope Rock than Philly, and she was hoping this was one of those times where the cultural differences would lean in her favor. "Look, he's my ex-husband, and he's been harassing me since the divorce. I keep blocking his number, but he keeps getting new numbers to call me from. Shit, I moved across the country, Sheriff, and the bastard still tracked me down. The way I see it, if doing all that doesn't get him to leave me alone, maybe buck shot will convince him."

The corners of the sheriff's mouth ticked upward, but he quickly ran a hand over his face to hide what she was sure had been the start of a smile. "Fair enough." He pushed his hat higher up on his head and eyed her closely. "Mind if I sit?"

"Knock yourself out, Sheriff." She scooted over on the large swing, making room for him as he climbed the steps.

"I ran your name before coming over here. You've never been in trouble, not so much as a damn parking ticket and now you're shooting at a man." He held up his hand when she opened her mouth to clarify she'd shot near him. "Jeremiah took you for some target practice, huh?"

"Yeah. He's a good guy." Sighing, she turned to look directly at him. "Look, if you're going to take me in, fine, but I need to call Jeremiah, so he can come check on my chickens and cat."

He shrugged. "As far as I'm concerned, everyone has the God given right to protect themselves and their property. Maybe more so since you're out here all alone. No one was hurt. If you'd clipped him or his car, we might be having a different conversation. Your ex has been advised to be on his way to the airport, by the way. If you hear anything more from him, let me know. Keep that gun close. You never know what folks like him'll do. I've seen situations like this go south real fast. I'd hate for something to happen to you." He patted her leg and stood. "Remember, Ms. Crawford, I'm here to help. Call me if he shows back up before you go blowing holes in him."

"If you're not going to arrest me, please call me Willow. And I can't make any promises about not blowing holes in my ex if he harasses me again, though I do promise, if he does, I'll call you before it escalates."

"I guess that's going to have to be good enough, huh? Just make sure it's justified. In fact, next time, yell that you see a rattler before you pull the trigger." The smile he'd hid earlier appeared on his face, accompanied by a twinkle in his eyes. "Stay safe, Willow, and tell that cousin of mine not to be a stranger—I know the two of you are getting on pretty well." At her look of confusion, he continued, "Jeremiah's my cousin. His mom and mine are sisters, although they had a falling out years ago. He's still kin though." He descended the steps and strolled to his cruiser. He opened the driver's door before pausing and looking back at her. "Oh, and Willow, welcome to Antelope Rock. Since you've officially discharged a weapon at someone, you get an honorary shot at Spurs & Bulls. See you later."

Once again, she felt as if she'd fallen into an alternate reality. One where shooting *near* someone got her a visit from the sheriff, but instead of being hauled off in cuffs, she'd been invited to go out drinking like it was a rite of passage to get a visit from the local fuzz. Apparently, times had changed in the past decade or so. From what she'd heard, it used to take years, a blood pact, and the sacrifice of a firstborn before newcomers in a small town were accepted into the fold. There were still people who talked in hushed tones or avoided her when they saw her, but they were far less than she'd expected. Antelope Rock was feeling like a home, where she could put down roots, more and more each day. Nice.

She couldn't wait to tell Nathan.

With that in mind, she hopped off the swing and wandered down her long drive to the mailbox, hoping another letter was waiting for her.

CHAPTER TWELVE

Dear Wannabe,

NATHAN CRUMPLED UP THE PAGE, tossed it into a nearby
wastebasket, and started over.

Dear Willow,

Tell that jackass neighbor of yours that you already have a
boyfriend and to keep his dirty hands off you.

"Arrgh." That piece of paper ended up in a ball in the
bottom of the trash too.

Dear Willow,

You're so damn sexy, I can't stop thinking of you. Hell, I
jacked off in the port-a-john to images in my head of
having you naked underneath me.

"Get a freaking grip, Casey. That's not something you tell

her in a letter when you've never even been in the same damn room with the woman." He threw the crushed-up page toward the basket to add to the others, but it bounced off the rim and onto the floor.

"You talking to yourself over there, man?" Hector Garcia asked from across the multipurpose room a few members of Nathan's squad were hanging out in during their downtime. "Or just playing a crappy game of trashball?"

"Neither. Mind your own business."

His roommate, Zach Ramsey, made kissing noises before announcing, "He's writing to *Willow* and trying to not tell her how badly he wants to bang her the first minute they meet."

With that, everyone in the room started up with the kissing noises and moaning and yelling like they were getting some tail.

"Fuck you, all," he responded without any heat. They always gave each other shit about one thing or another. Today was just his day to get razzed apparently. He ran his hands through his hair as his captain strode into the room.

Before anyone could stand, Capt. Matt Santana waved both hands in a downward gesture. "At ease. I come bearing gifts . . . well, actually good news. A week from Thursday, we're outta here—a little earlier than expected. So, give your significant others, and anyone else you want, a heads-up. We're going home, boys and girls!"

The room erupted into a cacophony of whoops, hollers, and whistles. That was the best news they'd gotten since they'd arrived in this hellhole. If all went well, Nathan would leave Iraq next week and never return.

September 10

Dear Willow,

We just got the greatest news! My platoon is heading back to the States next week! I think I might kiss the ground as soon as I get off the plane. It'll take about another week or so to settle back in, but after that, I should be able to take a few days leave. I was thinking of taking you up on your invite to visit Wyoming, so I can sit on that porch swing with you and watch the sunset. Is that okay with you?

Don't bother mailing another letter or care package to me here, because I'll be on my way home, if not already there, by the time you do. I'll put my email address and cell phone number at the bottom of this letter, so you can send me yours. That way, when I get home, it'll be easier to contact you.

I want you to know, I'm saving all your letters. They've meant the world to me, and so have you. When I get a chance, I'd like to take you out on a date, like a proper date. Please say yes. Pretty please! Okay, enough begging. I'm probably coming off as a desperate schmuck, but I feel like I've known you for a lot longer than these past few months. Oddly, it doesn't seem strange to me that we haven't met in person, yet I feel like we already have. I hope that doesn't sound creepy. Anyway, let me know if you're up for me visiting you, and I'll make the arrangements. Maybe you can scout out some tattoo shops within driving distance and help me choose some new ink. We could also go horseback riding, shooting, and if we're lucky, watch a thunderstorm roll in. (As I wrote that, I was struck by how cool it is that we have so much in common. It must've been fate when our mail clerk chose me to give your first letter to.)

To answer your questions about thunderstorms—yes, I love them, and no, we really don't get them here. In fact, there is very little rain, if any, from May to September. Instead, we get sandstorms, and those things are a bitch. You feel like you're coughing up sand for days after getting caught in one of them.

I'm sorry to hear about your douchebag ex-husband. No one deserves to be treated like that. I'm glad you're half a dozen states or so away from him now. Maybe he'll get the picture. And if he doesn't, I'll be more than happy to make sure he does.

The Brodericks sound like nice people. It's great of them to take you under their wing, sort of, and show you the business. I think you should go for it, if that's what you really want to do. I have a feeling you'd excel at anything you put your mind to. I mean, you packed up and moved halfway across the country and transitioned from a big city woman to a small town one with more ease than most people could. I'm proud of you. Just do me a favor and don't name any of the alpacas after me, okay?

Well, I gotta go—my buddies want to celebrate the good news, and they're making such a racket, I can barely hear myself think. The next time I write, I'll be in the States! I can't wait. Talk to you soon.

Yours,
Nathan

(719) 555-9420
NCasey@zmail.net

WILLOW'S HAND shook as she finished reading. "Oh my God!" She wanted to scream out loud for the world to hear, "He likes me! He really likes me!"

She refrained, but just barely. As it was, she'd let out a squeal that probably sounded like a mating call to any nearby pigs. As she'd walked to her mailbox, she'd been hoping for, but not really expecting a letter from him so soon. She'd been so surprised and excited, she'd ripped it open and read it right there, standing on the side of the road, oblivious to any rattlesnakes that may have slithered by.

She traced her finger over the carefully written numbers at the bottom of the page. His phone number. Flipping the envelope over she noticed the post mark was almost two weeks old. That meant . . . he was home! She could call him, like *right now*—just dial the number and talk to him for real. She'd be able to hear his voice. His breathing. His laughter.

Did she have the guts?

Tucking the letter safely into her back pocket, she sprinted up the dirt driveway to the front door. If she could pull a shotgun on her ex-husband, she could pick up the phone and take a chance. The first thing she was going to tell him was, yes. Yes, to the date. Yes, to the visit. Yes, to everything!

Dammit, maybe she should've bought those condoms after all.

Barreling into the house, she skidded to a stop by the island where she'd left her cell phone. She snatched the letter from her back pocket and smoothed it out on the countertop. Her hands trembled, hitting the numbers wrong three times before she got it right. Taking a moment, she tried to calm her racing heart before she pushed the green button. Raising the phone to her ear, she held her breath and waited as it rang.

"Staff Sergeant Casey."

His voice was deep and thick, sounding more than a little annoyed.

"Hello? If someone is there, you've got two seconds before I'm hanging up and blocking this number."

She shivered at his commanding tone, never thinking he'd sound like that.

"N-Nathan? It's Willow," she replied, unsure and hesitant. Nerves jumbled around in her stomach until she was sure she was going to puke. Had it been a mistake to call him?

"Willow?" he replied, the air of command now absent in his tone, having been replaced clearly with disbelief. "Is that really you?"

"Yeah. Yes. It's me. I, ugh . . . I just got your last letter. Is this . . . um . . . is this a bad time? I should have waited until later this evening, but I was just so excited to call you."

"No! No, this is a perfect time. I was just leaving work for the day. It's so good to finally hear your voice. Hang on, let me get in my truck." She could hear people talking in the background, their words and laughter rising and falling in volume, as if he'd walked by a large group. The sound of a vehicle's door opening was followed by it shutting again before he spoke again. "Willow . . . I just . . . wow. I don't even know what to say. I'm smiling so hard my face hurts."

Relief was coursing through her over the fact he was happy to hear from her, Willow began pacing back and forth . "Same here. I'm . . ." she trailed off, struggling to get her thoughts into words. "I'm just so glad you're home safe. Where are you?"

"Fort Riley, in Kansas."

"Really? That's not that far away here. You could . . ." She smacked herself on the forehead. "Oh my God, that was really presumptuous of me."

"No. Stop. It's not. I told you I wanted to come see you, and I meant it." He paused. "Did you think about what I asked?"

"The date?"

"Yeah." His voice was quieter than it'd been a moment ago and sounded a little insecure. Maybe he was as nervous as she was.

"Yes."

"Yes, you thought about it?"

Laughter bubbled from her lips before she put him out of his misery. "Yes, I thought about it, and yes, you can take me on a date."

His sigh of relief was audible, making her giggle even more. God, when had she become a woman who actually *giggled* at a cute guy? She didn't know or even care. All she knew was that Nathan made her feel lighter and happier than she could ever remember being.

"You laughing at me, Wannabe? You know how damn nervous I was? I thought for sure Jeremiah would've beaten me to it."

That sent her into another fit of hysterics that soon had her stomach hurting. She had to brace herself against the counter otherwise she would've ended up on the floor in a pile of mirth. "Oh shit, Nathan!"

"Why you laughin' at me, woman?" he growled into the phone, but she could tell there was a smile behind his indignation. "That's not very nice."

"Oh, Nathan, trust me. Of the two of us, Jeremiah would much rather be taking *you* on a date, not me."

There was a long pause, and she almost thought the call had dropped before she heard him say, "Wait, you mean . . ."

"Yup. He's just a friend."

"Thank fuck. I was ready to fight him for you."

She gasped. "Seriously? Wow. That's a first." More relaxed now, she took a seat at the island.

"Are you kidding me? Of course, I'm serious. There's nothing I want more than to get to know you better. To be, well, your man, your boyfriend, whatever term you're comfortable with. I know it's sudden, and we haven't actually met yet, but I just . . . you're special, Willow. I don't know how I know that, I just do, and I'm not willing to let you go without finding out what this thing between us can be."

Her breath caught in her lungs. Was he for real? Gone was his hesitation—now he seemed sure of himself and of her . . . of them. "Your confidence is a huge turn on." She slapped her free hand over her mouth, shocked she'd said the words she'd been thinking out loud.

He groaned, long and deep. "Wannabe, you can't say things like that to me when I'm so far away. You trying to torture me? Do you know how long I've been thinking about being with you, in every way?"

Grinning, even as she felt her face heat, she traced an invisible figure eight with her finger on the countertop several times, wishing it was his bare chest. "Probably as long as I have been wondering the same thing. So, when can you get those few days off?"

"Next Saturday, I start a week of leave. Does this mean you want me to come see you? For real?"

"For reals."

"Awesome! You've just made me the happiest man on base."

Laughing, she got comfortable at the island, propping her feet up and settling in. "You're kind of a dork, aren't you?"

NATHAN COULDN'T GET ENOUGH of the sound of Willow's voice. His boring day, full of meetings necessary for him to process out of the Army, had taken a turn for the better.

"Maybe I'm a bit of a dork, but you agreed to go out with me, so what does that say about you?"

"That I have good taste in men."

Barking out a laugh, he ignored his growling stomach. He could switch the call over to his truck's Bluetooth and drive home, but he didn't want to stop talking to her even for the few seconds that would take. He'd spent his deployment counting down the days until he could come home to actually talk to Willow, and now he was counting down the days until he got to see her.

Their conversation continued, neither of them wanting to stop talking now that they'd begun. He loved the sound of her voice and laughter. She told him about her day, including the run-in with her ex. As angry as he was about that, he was delighted she'd pulled her shotgun on the fucker. He almost hoped that rat bastard would show up while he was there. He'd take great pleasure in explaining, in no uncertain terms, that Willow was taken and protected by a man capable of killing him with his bare hands. A man who would, in fact, take joy in the act. He didn't tell Willow that, of course. He didn't want her to think he was a bloodthirsty animal. His feelings for her seemed to bring a protective streak to the forefront.

After their call ended, Nathan was still reeling. Putting his car in gear, he headed right for a drive-thru for dinner, not wanting to take more time than necessary to feed himself. He needed to get home and look at flights. He was going to see his woman and hopefully claim her in every way.

CHAPTER THIRTEEN

WILLOW THOUGHT nothing could pierce the ecstatic mood she'd been in since her phone call with Nathan yesterday, but someone decided to prove her wrong. She still couldn't believe he was coming to visit in just six days. They'd ended up talking on the phone for over an hour before he finally confessed he was starving and had to eat something to quiet his growling stomach. It'd been obvious he'd been as reluctant to end the call as she'd been.

She'd stayed up late last night, making a list of everything she needed to do to prepare for his visit. There were still things she had to do around the house, like paint the walls in one of the spare bedrooms and buy a full-size bed, a nightstand, and a lamp to set up for him, at the very least. She hoped Nathan wouldn't mind her putting him in there— even though she felt like she'd known him forever, the truth was they still had so much to learn about each other. Yes, she'd fantasized about sleeping with him often, but she wasn't sure if she was ready to actually do it. And what if the chemistry they seemed to have was all in their heads, and once he got there, they found out they weren't really attracted to each other?

When she'd woken up that morning, she decided to go into town, get some paint from the hardware store, and stop into Shear Genius hair salon to see if she could get a trim. Ginger Moore, Cody's sister, who Willow had met at the drunken Jenga night, had told her she worked there and to come in anytime and she would take care of her. Hopefully, she was working today, because she didn't want to deal with Martha Watkins who'd already made her disdain of the Rock's newest resident known.

The last time Willow had gotten a haircut was about five months ago in Philly, and she really needed to get rid of the dead ends at the very least. The last of her pink tips would be cut off, but that was okay. It was time for something new anyway, and she wanted to look nice when Nathan got there.

When she pulled the door to the little shop open, a little clapper bell tinkled, announcing her presence. It was apparent she'd interrupted a hen-house gossip session because the two stylists, Ginger and Martha, and three customers immediately shut their traps and turned their attention to the newcomer. Willow felt like a side-show freak as one much older woman sitting in Ginger's chair regarded her, her lip curling in distaste as her eyes tracked along Willow's tattoos. No doubt also noting her pierced nose.

"Hey, Willow! Did you have an appointment I forgot about?" Ginger asked after turning off the hair dryer she was using on the woman.

"Hi, Ginger, I didn't make an appointment—sorry. I just need a quick trim and was hoping you could squeeze me in." Willow really liked Ginger, who was about five years younger than her. They'd hit it off immediately at Jenga night, bonding over a love for rock bands, body art, and bright hair dye. Ginger kept her ink hidden from most people—it was on her hip—and had a beautiful electric-blue tint in her dark-brown hair. Surprisingly, none of the other women in the place seemed to have had a problem with her choice of color, so it must be Willow's hot pink they had an aversion to. Or maybe it had nothing to do with her hair at all and what they had an aversion to was her. "If it's not too much trouble. I can always come back another day."

"It's no problem at all. I'll get you fixed up just as soon as I'm done with Mrs. Jenkins here." Ginger patted the shoulder of the gray-haired, seventy-something-year-old woman in front of her. "Have a seat for a few minutes, and I'll be right with you."

"Thanks, I appreciate it." She took a seat near the window where a few chairs were lined up. There was a stack of magazines on a small table beside her. Picking one up, she flipped through it absentmindedly while trying to ignore the conversation around her.

"Kids these days have no respect. Did you hear about what a group of those football players did?" Mrs. Jenkins nasally voice cut through the light chatter that'd started again like a knife through butter. "They took a steer onto the football field, painted it red, and took turns trying to ride it. That animal tore up the turf and ruined the field! In my day, that sort of thing was punished severely. Not this suspension nonsense. Kids don't *want* to be at school. So how is giving them what they want a punishment?"

"It is a shame," Ginger agreed. Her pacifying tone and expression told Willow she'd clearly had this conversation, or ones similar to it, with the older woman before and was simply humoring her.

"Jesus is what they need. Just like folks who choose to mark up their bodies with filth and fill it full of holes the good Lord didn't put there." Mrs. Jenkins cut her eyes to Willow, not hiding her contempt.

Ginger met Willow's gaze over the older woman's head, wincing in sympathy. "Now, Mrs. Jenkins, everyone has the right to make choices with their own bodies. It's not for us to judge." Willow understood the stylist's diplomatic response to a paying customer, and she barely bit back a scathing retort herself.

Mrs. Jenkins wasn't done with her preaching yet, however. "More church is what this world needs. Not rock music and those disgusting, shameful displays young folk call dancing. The world would be a better place if there were more bibles in hands and knees on the floor in prayer."

Willow gritted her teeth, fury bubbling inside her. *Keep your mouth shut. Putting this old biddy in her place isn't worth it, even if it would be so satisfying.* She cleared her throat and turned another page in her magazine. Her mother had taught her to respect her elders, even when they were being small-minded judgmental assholes.

"Just like divorce. Marriage is a sacrament not to be broken by anything less than death. That's why the vows are 'until death do us part.' Not until we get sick of each other."

That's it! Willow's mouth opened and words poured out before she even realized it. "Marriage is a sacrament, but when one party decides he'd rather stick his prick in another woman, the sacrament is broken. Maybe God should be a little more understanding in that regard."

It was as if a silent bomb had gone off in the room. All eyes were back on her, this time in shock. Mouths gaped. Ginger's and Martha's hands were frozen in the air above their clients' heads. It was surprising when Martha seemed to recover first and quickly did some damage control. "Now, ladies, you're here to enjoy an afternoon getting pampered. No need for us to be sniping at each other. Ginger, I think Mrs. Jenkins's hair looks lovely. Why don't you get her checked out, so she can enjoy the rest of her day and show off that lovely hairdo?"

Willow remained quiet, actually astonished that Martha hadn't kicked her out of her shop after she'd snubbed Willow the previous time they'd crossed paths. Dropping her gaze to the magazine in front of her with an air of nonchalance, Willow did her level best to calm down and ignore the nasty older woman. Her week was going to be wonderful—Nathan was coming to stay with her—and she refused to let the poison the woman spewed to ruin it for her.

"You know," Willow looked up to see Mrs. Jenkins standing in front of her with a pious look on her face, "like father, like daughter. I'm sure that awful man that sired you is burning in Hell. No doubt you'll be right beside him."

Stunned, Willow's mouth fell open, but her temper rose faster than her shock. Somehow, she managed to keep her tone as sweet as molasses. "Since we're all born sinners, I'll be seeing you in Hell too, no doubt. Have a good day, Mrs. Jenkins, I'll be praying for you." She smiled as broadly as she could force herself, thinking that two could play at this game. If the old bitch was so shocked by her tattoos and nose ring, wouldn't it just chap her ass to find out Willow had her nipples pierced too? Willow was almost tempted to whip those puppies out, just to see the other woman faint.

Mrs. Jenkins huffed and stormed out of the salon in a cloud of perfume and indignation.

Ginger coughed and ducked her head to hide her grin. "Willow? Ready, sweetie?"

"Sure am." Setting her magazine aside, she followed Ginger to the back of the salon where the sink stations were as the other three women stared at her in shock. "I need to look good for my trip to Hell, right?"

CHAPTER FOURTEEN

NATHAN SAT NERVOUSLY at the small desk in his bedroom in the apartment he shared with Sergeant Zach Ramsey near the base, with his laptop open in front of him. Willow had agreed to Skype him at 7:00 p.m. that night, and he'd sat down with fifteen minutes to spare, just in case she called a little early. He hoped he didn't babble like an idiot when he was finally face-to-face with her. It was bad enough he'd sounded like a teenage dork when she'd surprised him with the phone call yesterday.

Taking a quick glance behind him for the third or tenth time since he'd sat down, he made sure everything was uncluttered and there were no stray dirty clothes in view. Being in the military for so long had instilled the need to be clean, orderly, and prompt, three traits that would probably follow him until the day he died.

His knee jiggled under the desk, and he double-checked the Skype app on the computer, making sure it was open and working. Damn, he was going to go nuts if she didn't call soon. The clock in the upper right corner of the screen read 6:55.

He was just about to get up and quickly run to the kitchen to grab a soda from the fridge when the quirky Skype music for an incoming call erupted from the computer's speakers. His nerves ratcheted up several notches as he wiped his sweaty palms on his jeans and then clicked his mouse to accept the call. Suddenly, there she was, looking more beautiful than she'd been in her pictures. Her hair was perfectly styled, but the pink tips were gone, and she was wearing subtle makeup which only enhanced her facial features. The emerald-colored t-shirt she had on made her hazel eyes appear more green than brown. Squinting closer, he noticed the script on her shirt read "Stop Chicken Me Out" with a white outline of a chicken wearing sunglasses below the words.

Staring at her, he almost swallowed his tongue. He'd tried searching for her on social media sites, to see if there were any other pictures of her on them but hadn't been able to find her accounts. When they'd spoken on the phone last night, he'd learned she wasn't on Facebook, Instagram, Twitter, or any other sites anymore. There wasn't anyone from her past she really wanted to stay connected to, so there'd been no reason to keep the accounts she'd made years ago, since she never used them. Nathan didn't blame her. He only had a Facebook account that had all the security measures in place so no one could track him down unless he wanted them to. He stayed in touch with a few high school classmates, two cousins from California, who he hadn't seen in person since his family's funeral, and a bunch of Army buddies who were scattered around the globe, but that was it.

"Oh my God, Nathan. Is that really you?" Willow asked in a husky, nearly breathless tone that sent a shiver down his spine. He hadn't gotten around to sending her a photograph of himself without all his gear on, so this was the first time she was really seeing him. He'd been worried that she wouldn't find him attractive, but her next words squashed that fear. "Holy crap, you're hot!" Her eyes widened in shock as she slapped a hand over her mouth for a moment. "Oh, shit. I didn't just say that out loud, did I? Please tell me I didn't. God, I'm such a babbling idiot." She groaned softly and sighed. "Shutting up now."

He smiled and chuckled at her. Damn, she was so cute. "You did say it out loud, but I promise I won't hold it against you. In fact, I'll say it right back at you. Holy crap, you're hot!" His grin grew as she giggled at him. "Actually, the words I really want to use are beautiful, stunning, captivating, beautiful . . ."

His voice trailed off as he watched a blush stain her cheeks. She was clearly flustered by his compliments.

"You—you said beautiful twice."

"It was worth mentioning twice." There was a long pause of silence between them as they studied each other, and then Nathan cleared his throat. He felt like he had the subtlety of a bull in a china shop, but this woman disarmed him completely. "Um, so I booked my flight for Saturday. I'll email you the itinerary later."

She smiled and sat up straighter. From the looks of it, she was on a couch, probably in her living room. He could see a painting of the ocean behind her on the wall, but the details were too hard to make out. "Great, I can't wait to show you around the metropolis known as Antelope Rock! The tour should take a whopping twenty minutes or so, but it's definitely worth it. And there'll be a quiz afterward," she added with a wink.

"I'll try to pay attention, but I'm sure I'll be distracted by the tour guide. What do I get if I pass the quiz?"

"Hmm. I'll have to get back to you on that. How was work today?"

As they chatted, he felt the earlier apprehensive tension in his shoulders subside. She was so easy to talk to—there was no room for nerves. "A lot better than it's been for the last eleven months. It feels amazing to be back on US soil doing mundane work and not have to worry about getting shot or blown up." His stomach dropped when she gaped at him in horror. "Shit, I shouldn't have said that. It—it wasn't that bad, Willow. There were just days that were worse than others. But I'm home safe and sound now, so there's nothing for you to worry about anymore."

She swallowed hard, and he could swear he saw her eyes well up, but no tears fell. "I-I tried not to think about what you were doing over there . . . what you were facing. I kept telling myself, whatever your job was, it didn't put you in any danger. It was scary to think otherwise and to know if something did happen to you, I'd probably never know other than your letters would have stopped coming."

He didn't tell her that he'd added a death letter to his footlocker over there after receiving her care package. It was the first letter he'd put in there since he'd ripped up the one for his parents and sister in his grief after they'd died. If he'd been killed or seriously injured in action, someone would've notified Willow for him and let her know how much he'd cherished her letters and friendship over the last several months. He hadn't wanted what she'd been worried about to happen. If his letters had stopped coming, she wouldn't have had to wonder if he'd been killed or so badly hurt that he couldn't write, as opposed to if he hadn't wanted to continue writing to her—which would have never happened. Those letters had been a lifeline for him, one he hadn't known he'd needed.

"I would've made sure someone had told you. I never would've left you hanging like that. But that's all the in past. Nothing to worry about anymore." Before she could dwell on the subject, he changed it. "So, how was *your* day?"

He was grateful when a smile reappeared on her face. "It was fantastic! I had another horseback riding lesson this morning, and I'm getting pretty good at it, if I do say so myself. We'll definitely have to go riding while you're here. But the best thing that happened was the phone call I got this afternoon. Do you remember the Brodericks? I told you they're the ones who own the alpaca farm I went to check out."

"Yeah, I remember."

"Well, they called to say someone they know in the alpaca community passed away last week. It's a small operation, but no one in the man's family wants to take it over, so they're looking to sell it! And the Brodericks immediately thought of me! Me!" Nathan suppressed a laugh at how animated she was with her hands as she spoke. The more excited she got, the more they flew around his computer screen. A buddy's wife was Italian, and it was a big joke among their friends that the woman couldn't think of a thing to say if they made her sit on her hands while she tried to talk.

"There's one male alpaca and eighteen females. The sale would also include all the equipment and some feed and other stuff. And the ranch's longtime foreman is willing to relocate to continue looking after the herd. According to Gail, the asking price is very reasonable and the foreman is a really nice guy. She's met him several times, and he does a great job with the animals. None of the farm owner's family lives locally anymore, except one nephew who's the executor of the will. He has no interest in the farm, so he just wants to get rid of everything as soon as possible."

"That's awesome, Willow. What do you have to do next?"

"Well, I have to go meet with the man's nephew. Since you're coming next Saturday, I was hoping you'd take a ride with me to check out the farm—maybe on Monday? It's only about an hour and a half from here. I mean, I can schedule it for after—"

"I'd love to go," he interrupted. "I don't know a damn thing about alpaca farming, but I can do some research before then, so I know what everyone is talking about."

"That would be great, but you don't have to do that. Trust me. I've been doing research all day, even though I did a lot before and after visiting the Brodericks. I've bookmarked so many websites, it's ridiculous. Gail also said, if I do buy the operation, I can call them anytime I need help or if I have questions. They'll also introduce me to people in the alpaca farming community. Apparently, there's a big, private group on Facebook, so it looks like I'll have to get back on that, at the very least."

"Well, when you do, send me a friend request. You can look me up by my email address, otherwise you won't find me because of the privacy settings."

"Great! I'll do it as soon as we hang up." Like the night before, they ended up talking for hours without realizing it. Five hours to be exact. When Nathan noted the time, he reluctantly told her he needed to get to sleep, since he had to report to duty at 0700. "Can I Skype you tomorrow night? Same time?"

The blush he loved on her cheeks rose to the surface again. "I'd like that, yes."

Lifting his hand to the screen, he traced her jawline with his fingers. "Goodnight, sweetheart."

He saw her breath hitch at the endearment, and her cheeks got even redder. "Goodnight, Nathan."

CHAPTER FIFTEEN

ZIPPING UP HIS COMPUTER BAG, Nathan waited his turn to deboard the plane. It felt like a thousand starlings had taken flight inside his gut, and not for the first time. He was so excited, yet nervous, to finally meet Willow in person. He just wondered if the feelings he'd developed for the woman on paper, the phone, and the internet would carry over to the living, breathing version. And would she feel the same for him?

It was great to be dressed like a civilian again and not have to shave every morning. He'd been like a teenage girl packing his luggage yesterday, trying to decide what clothes looked good on him to make a positive impression on Willow, yet not look like he'd put too much effort into it. He didn't know the first thing about seriously dating a woman. The past fourteen years in the Army hadn't left him much time for it, and when he did get a chance to spend time with someone, it never went beyond a night or two. He wasn't sure if the chemistry he felt between him and Willow would feel the same in-person, but he was determined to be optimistic and hope for the best.

He pulled his carry-on from the overhead compartment and followed the line of people off the plane. His palms were sweaty around the handles of his bags, and his stomach rolled with anticipation. He hadn't checked any luggage but still followed the signs to the baggage claim, as that was where they'd decided to meet. He wavered between wanting to run or drag his feet. What-if scenarios fought for supremacy in his head. *What if she doesn't like me? What if I don't like her? What if this is all just wishful thinking on both our parts? What if she's not really ready to date? What if she doesn't want to date a soldier who'll have to return to Kansas for the next five months before he's free to move wherever he wants? What if she found someone else during that time? A fellow rancher would be a better fit—a man who knew the land and what it took to live and work there.* He knew exactly dick about working on a ranch, beyond the ability to ride at a rudimentary level.

He mentally slapped himself and strode forward. What would be would be. He needed to have faith that the person in her letters, on the phone, and on Skype was who she really was.

The crowd in front of him cleared as they split in different directions, and then he saw her. She stood on her tiptoes, waving a large sign that read, "Pen Pal Extraordinaire!" She wore a bright pink t-shirt that showed off her inked sleeve, jeans, and pink Converse high-tops. Her rich brown hair barely brushed her shoulders and a giant smile lit up her face. She was so beautiful it staggered him, nearly stopping him in his tracks.

"Nathan!" she practically screamed, drawing the attention of everyone around them. He grinned and jogged to her. The sign fluttered to the floor, and her arms opened in welcome. He dropped his bags with a thump and not giving himself a moment to overthink it, gathered her into his arms. He tightened his embrace around her torso and lifted her while burying his face into her neck. Her hands clasped the back of his head, and her legs encircled his waist. He bit back a groan at the feel of her warm, soft body against his.

"You're really here," he murmured against her throat, breathing her delicious scent deep into his lungs, hoping to keep it there forever. "I'm sorry. I just . . . I couldn't not touch you. Holy hell, woman, you smell amazing."

She giggled in response, pulling back from him enough to cradle his cheeks in her hands. "So do you, and don't apologize." Her fingers were featherlight against his jaw where she stroked the stubble he was powerless to prevent after mid-day. "You can pick me up anytime you want." She kissed him softly on the cheek. "But for now, put me down, so we can get out of here, soldier."

"Yes, ma'am." His face felt hot and tight, and he made no attempt to temper his wide grin. Several people in the area were smiling at them, clearly thinking they were celebrating a long-overdue reunion.

Setting Willow back on to her feet, he picked up both of his bags, slinging one over his shoulder and holding the other so he could keep his right arm free. She grabbed the sign she'd dropped and rolled it up to carry. Unable to stop touching her, he slid his arm around her shoulders and tucked her against his side. "Is this, okay?"

"More than." She put her arm around his waist in response, squeezing slightly. "It should be awkward, right? But it's not."

Kissing the top of her head, he walked her out of the airport and into the parking lot where they stopped near a white F-350. "This is yours?" he asked in shock. "This is huge for you, isn't it?"

She stepped away from him and pulled keys from her pocket before unlocking the truck with a beep. "It was my father's and much newer than my own beat-up Chevy. I use mine on the ranch and this one for going anywhere I don't want to risk breaking down." She opened the crew cab door and gestured inside. "You can put your bags in here. It's supposed to start raining soon, and I wouldn't want them to get wet in the bed."

Following her instructions, he took care of his bags and climbed into the passenger seat. He watched in amusement as she had to use the running board *and* do a small hop to get herself into the driver's seat. Looking over at him, she narrowed her eyes. "You laughing at me, Nathan?" It reminded him of their first phone conversation when he'd said almost the exact same thing to her.

"Yup." Reaching toward her, he tucked a lock of her hair behind her ear. "You're adorable." Her tresses were like silk between his fingers, and he wanted nothing more than to bury both his hands in them and pull her into a kiss. But he hesitated. Was it too soon?

"What put that look on your face?" Her wide hazel eyes blinked at him in question.

"I was thinking about kissing you, but I wasn't sure if I should or not. I don't want to make you feel pressured." *Jesus, Casey, way to blurt it out.*

Grinning impishly, she scooted closer. "Well then, how about I kiss you?"

Before he could say anything in response, her lips were against his own, and his eyes fell shut as warm and tingling sensations exploded from his lips, racing to his chest and throughout the rest of his body. Licking the seam of his mouth, she silently asked for entrance, which he gladly granted. She tasted like cherry Chapstick and something spicy that had to be all Willow.

Giving in, he filled both his hands with her hair and took control of the kiss. Dragging her body closer to his own and angling her head the way he wanted it, he dove deeper and harder into her mouth with his tongue. He kissed her like a starving man as his cock hardened in his pants and his heart beat a frantic rhythm. He groaned at the feel of her in his arms and the taste of her on his lips drove his need to a critical point.

He forced his mouth away from hers, so he could pepper kisses down her neck, licking and softly sucking as he went. Letting go of her hair, he slid his hands down the sides of her throat, noting the rapid beat of her pulse, to her shoulders. Bypassing her tempting breasts, he rested his trembling hands above her hips. His chest heaved with his ragged breathing, and a tortured groan escaped him. "Willow . . ."

"Nathan, kiss me again," she whispered breathlessly from where her forehead rested against his shoulder.

Tipping her chin up with his hand, he gripped her jaw gently and gave her what she'd asked for. Never say he was a man to deny a lady anything. He swallowed her moans and soft whimpers, driving them both higher until he was sure he was about to come in his jeans.

"Baby, hang on." Pulling back from her, he attempted to catch his breath and calm both his racing heart and his painful hard-on. "I want you. More than I can put into words, but I don't want our first time to come with a charge of public indecency." With a final peck on her lips, he retreated to his side of the truck. He shifted his hips a little before putting on his seat belt, leaving enough room so as to not strangle his already throbbing cock. Trying to get his desire under control, he ran both hands down his face. "I guess my worries over a lack of physical chemistry between us are unfounded, huh?"

Smirking, she started the truck, which roared to life, vibrating the seat beneath him. That she was perfectly capable of handling the large vehicle was just another thing about her that turned him the fuck on. "Apparently so, Captain Obvious."

He barked out a startled laugh at her snark. "That's Staff Sergeant Obvious, Wannabe. Now, let's go before I forget where we are and finish what that kiss promised."

"You're gonna have to do better than that if you want to dissuade me, soldier." Despite her warning, she put the giant truck in reverse and backed out with ease.

"Fine then. How about this?" He placed his hand over hers on the gear shift, halting her movements. "The first time I make love to you, it's going to be in a bed, where I can spread you out and lick every inch of your delicious skin from your toes to your chin. Though, I'll be stopping at those perfect breasts of yours for a while." Her lust-filled gaze was glued to his own, and color dotted her cheeks. "I'll save the sweetness between your legs for last. I'm going to make you come on my tongue. I want your legs gripping my head and shaking, before I move and slide so deep inside you that you'll be sure you can feel my cock in your throat. We can fool around in this truck some other time, but I want to be in a bed the first time we're together, where I can spend hours exploring every inch of you. Understand?"

Willow swallowed, her throat bobbing, and he couldn't help but imagine those same muscles gulping him down and stroking the head of his dick.

"I, uh . . . I un-understand," she stammered as her fingers gripped the gear shift under his so tightly that her knuckles were white. Hazel eyes bore into his blue ones, seeming to look right into his soul.

A loud honk from behind the truck made them both jump. They'd been so lost in each other they'd forgotten she'd backed the vehicle out of the space, blocking both lanes of the parking lot.

"Let's get out of here. I'm hungry." Grinning wolfishly at

her, he made sure she understood he wasn't talking about food.

The expected rain began about three quarters of the way through the ninety-minute drive to Skyview Ranch. It wasn't long before it was coming down in buckets. Willow flicked the wipers on high and concentrated on the road. "Damn, I was hoping to get back to the ranch before the storm started."

"I missed the rain," Nathan said as he stared out the passenger window. The scenery was a blur amid the downpour. "And the snow too, though we did see it occasionally over there, especially in the mountains." He glanced over at her. "If they've never been there, most people don't realize the dessert gets damn cold at night and in the winter." His gaze fell on a flash of color on her left wrist—it was the bracelet he'd sent her. It was only a nylon thread strung with cheap glass beads in varying shades of amber, but seeing her wearing it and treasuring his gift thrilled him.

"I love rainstorms." Glancing at him, she smiled before turning her attention back to the road. "Driving in them? Not so much, but we're almost there. I haven't experienced winter here yet, but from what I understand, it comes early and stays late. That reminds me of another thing I need to get ready for—I don't have the kind of heavy winter clothes you need around here. Ginger, the girl who did my hair, was telling me that my normal lightweight hats and gloves won't cut it in temperatures that fall below zero on a regular basis. Not to mention a snow shovel and rock salt. In Philly, the city took care of the sidewalks—I didn't have to deal with it much. Now I have a whole driveway and paths to the barns to contend with." She bit her lip and rolled her eyes. "And now I'm talking about the weather like a total loser. You must be so impressed."

He grinned at her. "Hey, I'm the one who brought up the

rain and stuff, so it's my fault we're talking about the weather. And don't talk about yourself that way. You're not a loser. You just babble a bit when you're nervous, which is cute and totally fine because I'm nervous too."

"You didn't seem that way at the airport."

Laughing, he agreed, "I guess not. That was different because I'd thought of little else but kissing you for weeks now. Maybe you'll decide later that you don't like me too much after all and send me packing. This way, at least I got my kiss."

"The chances of that happening are very slim, soldier. I like you and your kisses just fine."

"Just fine? I'll have to try a little harder next time then, huh? If *just fine* is your impression."

She opened her mouth to say something but stopped before speaking. He didn't push her —the last thing he wanted to do was pressure her or make her uncomfortable— so instead, he changed the subject to the movie he'd watched on his iPad during the flight, asking her if she'd seen it before.

The rest of the drive passed uneventfully. They spoke of their plans to see the alpaca farm on Monday, what meals they'd like to cook during the week, and about horseback riding. While he had every intention of taking her out on that date he'd promised her, he didn't want to eat out every day. He wanted . . . no needed, to spend time getting to know her without the distraction of other diners around them. But that didn't mean he didn't want to meet some of the people she'd befriended in Antelope Rock.

"By the way, how the hell did they end up naming the town Antelope Rock? Aren't wild antelopes only in Africa or Asia?"

She smiled. "I thought the same thing when I got here, but according to Jeremiah, there are pronghorns that live in

Wyoming and the surrounding states. They aren't really in the antelope family, but they look similar, and many people call them American antelopes or pronghorn antelopes. So, I guess that's where they got the name for the town. Most of the people that live here just call it the Rock."

Willow turned down a long dirt lane—well, mud lane at the moment—and they passed under a rusted metal sign that read, "Skyview Ranch."

After pulling up to the house and putting the truck in park, she gazed out the windshield at her home, which was partially hidden by the pouring rain. "Here we are. Skyview Ranch. My home." Her nerves were obvious, and he tried to think of what he could do or say to put her at ease. The truth was, he was nervous as hell too.

"Willow?" He left the question hanging in the air, waiting for her to look at him.

Instead of answering him, she said, "Come on, let's make a run for it." Before he could stop her, she threw her door open and, as the rain pelted her, ran across the yard and up onto the covered porch.

Grabbing his bags, he quickly followed her, getting drenched in the process. She wouldn't meet his gaze when he stopped beside her, and his gut sank. Was she regretting this? Thinking back to the kiss at the airport, he had a lightbulb moment. Was she worried he'd want to jump her the minute they got inside? Maybe he'd given her that impression, but that hadn't been his intention. Yes, he wanted her, but he needed time to get to know her better first. She was special to him, and he didn't want to screw things up.

He followed her into the house and didn't take a moment to look around or do anything more than set his bags on the floor near the door. "Willow, hang on a second." Reaching out, he clasped her hand in his own, drew her close, and stared down at her. She tensed, and he knew then that his instincts were spot on.

"Yeah?" She swallowed nervously before looking down at her shoes.

"Let me clear something up here a second." Cupping her chin, he lifted it until her eyes met his. "I want you. Desperately."

Willow started to speak, but he placed two fingers over her lips. "Let me finish first, please?"

When she nodded her assent, he continued, "That being said, this is the first time we've met in person. I'm happy to sleep on the couch or wherever. As much as I'm looking forward to being intimate with you, I don't think either of us is ready for that yet. Okay? So, please, don't be nervous. I'm not pressuring you or expecting you to give me something you're not ready for." He carefully cradled her cheek with his free hand. "This thing between us feels too important for us to rush into bed."

CHAPTER SIXTEEN

WILLOW HEAVED A SIGH OF RELIEF. "Oh, thank God." Leaning forward, she let her head fall against Nathan's chest, ignoring the fact that his clothes were soaked more than her own. His arms came around her, and she embraced him in return. "Sorry, that probably sounded bad, but I was trying to figure out how to tell you that I fixed up the guest room for you." Snuggling into his warmth, she sighed again, this time in contentment. "You're amazing, do you know that? Most guys would be doing whatever they could to get into my pants."

When he tipped her face up again, Nathan's deep blue eyes shone down at her. "I'm not most men. That being said, can I kiss you again before you show me to the guest room? I'd like to wash off the airplane smell."

Smiling, she nodded. "Just sayin', if there is an airplane smell, I don't notice it. You smell positively edible."

"Flirting with me now, Wannabe?" He spoke softly, angling his head closer to her and nibbling on her jaw gently.

"Sure, flirting is fun." She gasped then moaned as he nipped her ear.

"Flirting with you is fun, that's true." He kissed her cheek and sought her mouth with his own. The kiss this time was different from the one at the airport. Gentle, less desperate, but still hot as hell. He licked one last quick swipe into her mouth before releasing her and retreating a step. "Bathroom?" He plucked his wet gray t-shirt away from his torso where it was stuck to his skin. She did her best not to stare at the defined chest the saturated fabric reveled.

"This way." Leading him through the living room and down the hallway to the guest room, she took the opportunity to get herself back under control. Opening the door, she stepped into the small bedroom. She'd bought a full-sized bed—the room wasn't big enough for a queen—and had added a chest of drawers and bedside table. A basic lamp was the only other furnishing. "It's not much, but the bed and linens are brand new. The bathroom you can use is across the hall—I have another bath off my room. Towels are in the closet in there. Um . . ." She paused, twisting her fingers together as she looked over the room she'd prepared for him. She'd decorated it with simple grey bedding that matched the darker grey curtains. She hadn't had time to find any artwork for the blank walls, which she was now kicking herself for. It was too plain. *Whatever*, she thought, *there's nothing you can do about it now*. "I guess I'll leave you to it. Are you hungry? It's a little early for dinner, but I can go get it started after I change out of these wet clothes. I was thinking spaghetti, if that's all right with you."

He ran a hand down her arm, caressing the skin under her ink. "Sweetheart, I haven't eaten a home-cooked meal, that I didn't prepare myself or have at a barbecue, in years. You could make literally anything, and I'd be happy with it. A shower won't take me long, then I'll come help you cook. Okay?"

Nodding, she backed out of the room. Determined to

chill the fuck out, she tried to stop acting like a total basket case. "Sounds good."

Leaving him to his shower, she retreated to her bedroom to change into dry clothes. A few minutes later, dressed in a clean pair of jeans, a vintage Go-Go's t-shirt, and the comfy, brown, slip-on moccasins she'd bought at Ducky's a few weeks ago, she shuffled into the kitchen. After filling the little cat dish by the backdoor with Ethel's kibble, she began pulling out the ingredients for the dinner she'd planned to make for Nathan. Locally sourced ground beef, homemade spaghetti sauce that was sold by a woman from Antelope Rock who grew her own tomatoes, pasta, and a few other items were placed on the island's countertop. She added a loaf of Italian bread she'd picked up at the bakery that morning, which had still been warm when she'd brought it home. The meal would be a simple one, but it would feature fresh, local ingredients and hopefully be the best pasta Nathan had ever eaten. She'd even splurged on fresh Parmesan to shave over the pasta. They said the way to a man's heart was through his stomach, and she was going to do her best to test that theory.

She'd just finished chopping an onion when Nathan ambled into the kitchen, carrying a bundle of gray fur cradled in his arms. "Look who found me."

Willow grinned at her pet who'd evidently already taken a shine to their visitor. "I was wondering where you were, Ethel. I'm surprised you didn't come running when I filled up your dish."

Nathan stopped beside her at the island where she was prepping the meal, and she was hit with the fresh clean scent of him. His short hair was still damp, and he'd changed into a blue Henley over black sweatpants. Clean, white socks were the only things on his feet. He hadn't shaved his stubble off, which she loved. Her mouth began to water for more than just dinner. Banishing the thought of what the skin on his neck tasted like fresh from the shower, she pushed a knife, a garlic press, and a bulb of garlic at him.

"Here, make yourself useful. Smash that up while I get the meat browning."

"Yes, ma'am," he replied, chuckling. He set Ethel on the floor, and as the kitten made a beeline for her food dish, Nathan washed his hands in the sink before getting to work. "It's good I'm used to taking orders, huh? How much garlic?"

"Shit, I'm sorry." Shaking her head, she added the ground beef to a pot on the stove. "I don't mean to be bossy. Two cloves should be good, please. Thank you."

"I don't mind. I know this is a little . . . awkward . . . for us both. We'll find our way. You just do you and everything will work out." He bumped her hip with his, the casual affection warming her heart. "Besides, I can appreciate a bossy woman."

"I have an idea." As she spoke, she added the chopped onion to the pot before breaking up the browning meat with a wooden spoon. "Let's play a game to get to know each other a little better. I know we talked about a lot of things in the letters and on the phone and Skype, but I feel like there's still a lot I don't know about you."

"All right, what do you have in mind?" Reaching around her, he added the garlic to the pot.

"A question for a question." After tapping the spoon on the side of the pot, she set it on a small dish next to the stove, and then turned around, crossing her arms over her chest and meeting his gaze. "I ask, you answer, and then you ask me something. If you don't want to answer, you forfeit your question."

"Okay. Who goes first?"

"Me, obviously. House rules, and ladies always come first."

He smirked and winked at her. "I'll do my best to ensure that."

Fighting a blush, she poked his bicep. "Smart ass. All right, favorite color?"

"Orange. You?"

"Orange? Really? I don't think I've ever met someone who answered orange for their favorite color. Mine is purple. Favorite song?"

"'Back in Black.'"

Rolling her eyes at him, she checked the meat mixture and saw it was cooked enough to drain. "That's such a typical guy answer."

"Maybe, maybe not, what's yours?"

"Are you going to keep asking me the same question I ask you?"

"It's not your turn to ask a question, Wannabe. I let it slide earlier, but this time you forfeited your turn."

Her mouth dropped open, and she teasingly smacked his arm. She wasn't normally so touchy-feely, but the man was a dream and she couldn't help it. "That's not fair!"

"Them be the rules. So, you owe me two answers. Favorite song and favorite flower."

"Fine, jerk," she huffed with a smile. "I'm not a huge fan of flowers, but I like succulents, and my favorite song is a toss-up between 'Break Stuff' by Limp Bizkit and 'Hurt' by Johnny Cash."

"Those are two very different songs. They're not even in the same genre." He let out a snort. "And what the fuck is a succulent?"

"Ah, ah. Not your turn to ask. I get two questions now." She shook her finger at him before opening the jar of sauce and adding it to the meat she'd drained. "Okay, let's see. Um, how do you take your coffee, and what's your favorite comfort food?" Putting a second pot into the sink, she began to fill it with water for the pasta.

"Black with a little sugar, and macaroni and cheese, nothing too exciting there."

"Nothing wrong with a classic. Unless it's AC/DC—there is such a thing as *too* classic."

"Blasphemy!" Shooing her aside, he lifted the heavy pot out of the sink and onto the stove for her before turning on the burner. "You're supposed to be letting me help, remember?"

"Yeah, but I'm perfectly capable of lifting a pot of water." She added salt to the water and then put the lid on, so it would boil faster.

"Of course you are. Just like you're perfectly capable of uprooting your life, moving cross-country, and starting over on a ranch. Doesn't mean I don't want to do things for you. My folks raised me to be a gentleman after all."

"Hopefully, not too much of a gentleman." The words were out of her mouth before she could censor herself. It was official, Nathan had broken what little filter she had. She slapped her hands over her mouth—something she seemed to be doing a lot with him.

He flashed what was quickly becoming his signature leering grin but said nothing as he stared down at her. Once again, his blue eyes seemed to bore into hers. Men like him weren't real, were they? When something seemed too good to be true, it usually was. Right? She liked him, *a lot,* and just hoped he was everything he seemed to be and wasn't just another illusion she'd regret down the road.

They finished making dinner together and sat down to enjoy the results of their labor. She admitted it was nice— more than nice actually—cooking with him and teasing and joking back and forth. They both relaxed more as the evening wore on, and Willow was struck by how natural it felt having him in her home. After cleaning up the dishes together and putting the leftovers away for lunch tomorrow, she took his hand and led him out to the side porch, grabbing the throw off the couch on the way. It was time to show Nathan one of her favorite things about living in Wyoming.

CHAPTER SEVENTEEN

NATHAN CLUNG to Willow's hand as she led him outside, a soft, dark-blue blanket over her other arm. "Where are we going?"

"The porch swing. It's getting cooler at night, that's why I grabbed the blanket."

"You want to snuggle on the porch swing?" He grinned in delight. He'd hoped this would be one of the things they'd do together this week, after she'd told him it was her favorite spot to sit and unwind. Giddy didn't cover how he was feeling about being with her right now.

"Of course." Glancing at him over her shoulder, she smiled sweetly, and his heart skipped a beat. This woman was something special, and he was the luckiest bastard on the planet, getting the chance to be here with her.

As she sat on the swing, his attention was drawn away from her to the multitude of colors painting the sky. Oranges, yellows, reds, deep blues, and white from a few clouds created one of the most spectacular sunsets he'd ever seen in his life. Stunned, he just stared a moment and the only word to pass his lips was, "Wow". It was obvious why they called this Big Sky country.

Willow tugged on his hand, urging him to sit next to her. "Didn't I tell you the sunsets here were to die for? I'd never seen one like this before moving here. It's one of the reasons I don't think I'll ever leave. Somehow this city girl became a wannabe rancher. Even if actual ranching turns out to not be for me, I don't think I could give up Skyview for anything now. I'd find something else to do with the land."

Settling in beside her, he put his arm around her shoulders as she spread the blanket over their laps. "I don't blame you. It's gorgeous."

They sat there in a comfortable silence for a little while, watching the ever-changing colors swirl around the sky as the sun seeped lower into the horizon, leaving dusk in its wake. The frogs and crickets serenaded them as the glow from hundreds of fireflies randomly illuminated their little corner of the universe. A gentle breeze caressed Nathan's skin, almost like a lover's touch. The balmy scents of clean air, hay, and wildflowers surrounded them.

It'd been a long time, if ever, since Nathan had felt such an incredible peace wrap around him. He could easily spend every evening of the rest of his life cuddling with Willow on the porch swing and never tire of it. His mind kept drifting back to the kiss they shared in the truck, to the intense need that'd flared between them. He'd had lovers in the past, but he'd never experienced that level of desire before. He knew they needed to take things slowly, but the acute yearning in his body was battling with the logic of his thoughts. Willow was the whole package. She engaged his mind with her sharp wit even while she made him desperate to bury himself inside her. He was falling for her hard while praying they wouldn't crash and burn.

WILLOW COULD STAY THERE all night, cuddled up to Nathan. Heck, she could stay there forever. The intense connection she felt to him should've frightened her, but it didn't. In fact, she was starting to understand why some couples said they'd found their soul mates. The righteousness she felt in Nathan's arms was something she couldn't explain if she tried. Something she hadn't even known she was missing was clicking into place.

Having followed them outside and gotten bored hunting grasshoppers and other insects, Ethel pounced on Nathan's foot, prompting him to pick her up and settle her on his lap. "So, where's the other half of this comedy team?"

"Fred comes to the back porch in the morning, usually around eight or nine o'clock." She snuggled closer to him. "Mmm. I could get used to this." Between the soft cotton of his shirt under her cheek and the comfort and warmth his body gave off, she could easily doze off right there in his arms.

"Me too."

"Is this weird for you?"

His chin dipped as he looked down at her. "Is what weird?"

"Being here with me? I wasn't expecting that first letter to develop into friendship, let alone more. Hell, I'm not even sure I expected a response from whoever got my letter."

He made a soft humming noise in his throat. "Honestly, it's not weird at all. Maybe it was a little at first, but . . ." his words trailed off, and she waited patiently for him to continue. "You know I don't have any family left. I have army buddies—ones who aren't in my unit that I don't see all the time—that I keep in touch with, but it's not like they write to me. Usually, it's just the occasional phone call, or email, or something. Deployment is lonely, even for people who have folks back home. I know I told you in one of my letters, but it bears repeating—you got me through being over there. If I didn't have your letters to look forward to and carry around with me, I don't think I'd be adjusting to being home as well as I am. It's hard to explain it to someone who's never served —especially in combat—but knowing you were back home, thinking about me? It was everything, Willow."

She stared up into his eyes that, even in the dark, were a brilliant blue that rivaled a cloudless afternoon sky. "I'm so glad I wrote that letter. This goes both ways, you know? I didn't have anyone either. My mom's dead. The father I never knew is also gone, and I'm an only child with no extended family. But I don't want you to think I'm here with you because there's no one else."

Tucking a lock of hair behind her ear, he gently kissed her forehead. She couldn't help but close her eyes and barely managed to keep her sigh of pleasure to herself. "I know that, Wannabe." He paused, then said, "Tell me about your mother."

"Well . . ." She smiled as she fondly recalled her mom. "She was so beautiful, even later after she got sick with diabetes. Growing up, I don't remember us having much money, and she worked a lot, but she was always there for me. Always pushing me to be the best I could be. She'd tell me that a person's worth couldn't be measured by their bank account but by the way they treated others. She came to every school event, even if it meant she had to work an extra shift later. I remember her being tired all the time, but she never took it out on me. We were a team, just her and me against the whole world. The only time we ever really argued was when I pressured her to tell me about my father. My friends in the neighborhood didn't all have a father figure at home, but they knew who their dads were at least. I would ask, and she'd look so sad and tell me that some things were best left unknown."

"She sounds amazing, I wish I could have met her."

Resting her cheek back against his broad shoulder, she said, "Yeah, she would have liked you." Inhaling deeply, she ran her hand up and down his chest, enjoying the feel of his warm flesh and firm muscles under the soft cotton. She traced the bumps and ridges of his defined pecs, noting the small nubs of his nipples.

"Willow?"

"Hmm?"

"What are you doing?"

"Touching you. I like the way you feel." Digging her fingernails in, she drew them down his chest lightly. He shivered, and she wondered how he would react if she clawed his bare back.

He put his hand over hers, halting her movements. "I like that you like it, and having your hands on me is amazing, but I thought we were going to take it slow?"

"Me touching you like this turns you on that much?" She giggled and grew bolder. "It's not like I've got my hand down your pants! And anyway, what's the point of sitting on a porch swing with a boy you like if you can't make out and feel each other up a little bit?"

Letting go of her, he gently lifted Ethel and set her down on the porch, making her yowl in protest. "Baby, there is no *boy* sitting here with you. I'm all man." In a sudden move, he picked her up, scooted to the middle of the cushioned seat, and deposited her onto his recently vacated lap, positioning her until she was straddling him. He gripped her hips to steady her and pushed his feet against the porch, rocking the swing back and forth gently. She could feel every considerable inch of him pressed against her. Her mind flashed to what it would be like to sit here like this but without the barrier of their clothes. She gripped his shoulders and held on while he rocked them. Each push and pull making the ever-present passion between them flare hotter than before.

"Oh my . . ." The chains supporting the swing squeaked and squealed with the back-and-forth motion, but all her attention was focused on the man under her. His thighs were solid between hers, and she could feel the heat of his groin penetrate the two layers of clothing separating them.

He grinned. "*Oh my* about covers it." Trailing his hands slowly up her back, he cupped her shoulders and pulled her fully against his chest. "Now, you said something about making out?" He bumped his hips up, showing her exactly how much she turned him on. The hard length of him hit her clit, and she ground down in response, swiveling her hips and drawing a groan from his throat. "Woman . . ."

"Shh. You're talking too much." He opened his mouth to protest, but she sealed her lips over his, kissing him into silence. She moaned against his mouth, rocked her hips down harder, and bit down on his bottom lip, drawing it gently between her teeth before licking away the sting. Pulling away slightly, she avoided him when he chased her mouth, instead kissing a path down his collarbone and sucked a bruise there. She hoped he wouldn't mind that she'd marked him. "God, you're so yummy, I want to taste you everywhere." She nibbled on his earlobe and relished the shudder it drew from him and how he thrust his pelvis up. Grinding her mound against his hardness, she used the swing's motion to build a rhythm. Soon, they were moving in sync, kissing, grasping, and caressing each other. They were as close as two people could be while still clothed.

"Willow . . . goddamn . . ." he moaned. Her core went liquid, and she knew her panties were soaked. It was taking more willpower than she wanted to admit to keep from ripping their clothes off and riding him into oblivion.

"Come here, I wasn't done kissing you." He grasped her hair with one hand and brought her mouth back to his, while his free hand squeezed her ass and kept her pressed tightly against him. His grip on her hair was firm but not painful, and she liked his forcefulness more than she'd ever imagined she would. His mouth and tongue continued their sensual assault, until her lips were swollen and sore, and they were both gasping for air. Neither wanted to stop long enough to breathe. They were making out and dry humping like teenagers, and she loved every second of it.

Her heart slammed against her chest, and she could feel her clit throbbing between her legs. "Nathan . . . fuck," she gasped, tearing her mouth free. "You're gonna make me come in my pants." She rested her forehead against his as she struggled to replenish the oxygen missing from her lungs. "I-I think I should get back to my own side of the swing."

"Mmm." He kissed her lightly on the nose. "My head says that's the smart thing to do, but my cock has other ideas."

Gaping at him, she blushed and ducked her face under his chin. "Nathan, honey, I swear you could get a nun into bed with just a smile and a wink, you're so delicious. But I don't have the fortitude of a nun."

"You like it when I talk dirty, huh?" Chuckling softly, he rubbed his hands up and down her back, soothing them both. "I'll remember that for later. Didn't mean to get carried away there, but you seem to have that effect on me."

"I think we have that effect on each other." Climbing off his lap, she reluctantly retreated to her own side of the swing as he shifted to the other end. She had to fold her hands in her lap to hide their trembling. As badly as her body wanted him, her heart and brain were telling her not to rush things. If Nathan was the man she believed he was, he wouldn't push her until she was ready to take their relationship to the next level. It was one of the many reasons she knew she was standing on the edge of a cliff, only one step away from falling madly in love with him.

"Come here." Wrapping his arm around her shoulders, he tugged her back up against his side. "I'll keep my hands to myself, for now anyway. Here's a subject change that is sure to kill my hard on, did you find anything else out about your dad?"

Laughing, she shook her head. "The boxes I've looked through so far were just full of junk. Nothing worth saving, and none of it told me anything other than the man was a miser. He squirreled away money, but let this place fall apart. I don't get it. I'd hoped for a journal or some photographs maybe, but so far it's been nothing but receipts and old newspapers, boring stuff like that."

"I can help you look through some of the other boxes, if you want?"

"That'd be great. Maybe you'll see something I'm missing. People in town seem to have very strong opinions about him, and I'm struggling to understand why." The breeze that'd been light over the past hour strengthened and blew across them, making her shiver. Noticing, Nathan bent down, picked up the blanket they'd both forgotten about, and draped it over them.

"I know you're chilly, baby, but are you okay staying out here a little longer?" Nathan asked as he tucked the soft material under her chin.

"When I have you to keep me warm? Absolutely." Sitting snugly against his side, she laid her head on his chest, feeling as if she'd been made to fit there. "Baby, huh?"

"Yeah, is that okay?"

Giggling and feeling happier than she could remember being in a long time, maybe ever, she poked his side. "Sure, you can call me baby—I don't mind. Not when it's you anyway."

"Damn right—no other man better call you baby either, whether I'm around or not."

Between the blanket and his body heat, she didn't notice when the temperature dropped a few degrees more. The sun had fully set, and the Milky Way had twinkled to life throughout the big Wyoming sky. She'd never seen so many stars before moving here—the urban pollution in Philly muted most of them. "I don't think I'll ever get over being able to see the stars like this."

"It really is spectacular, isn't it?"

They sat that way for a long time, holding each other close and listening to the sounds of the night. When a flash streaked across the heavens, Willow pointed and exclaimed, "Look! Did you see? It was a shooting star. You have to make a wish."

"Nah, I have everything I could wish for right here." He kissed the top of her head and kept staring up at the vast, inky black sky peppered with sparkling lights from other galaxies.

Beside him, Willow sighed in complete and utter happiness. It was a feeling she wasn't familiar with, but she wasn't going to squander or question it.

CHAPTER EIGHTEEN

THE NEXT MORNING, Willow groaned as she rolled over. She briefly nestled back under her fluffy down comforter before the memories of yesterday came flooding into her mind.

Nathan was here.

In her house.

Right now.

And she was laying around in bed like a lazy asshole.

Checking the time, she saw it was just shy of eight. Hoping he was still sleeping, she rose and stepped into her slippers. After a quick stop at the bathroom, she headed down the hallway, intent on brewing a pot of coffee before making breakfast, but she halted in her tracks in the kitchen doorway.

Nathan was at the sink, rinsing out the carafe and refilling it with water. Scratch that. A better way to say it was a shirtless, *half-naked*, gorgeous hunk of a man was standing barefoot in her kitchen making coffee. She didn't bother to stop herself from dragging her gaze along every inch of exposed skin. *Holy mother of God!* She couldn't take her eyes off him. Up his sinewy arms, over the tattoo on his shoulder blade, and down his muscled back. She took a few extra moments to admire where gray sweatpants rode low on his hips, revealing two dimples on the small of his back that she was dying to see if they tasted as good as they looked. The sun shone in through the windows and colored his skin in a soft warm glow. She was about to start drooling on herself any second now. Had she died and gone to heaven? Because that was the only reason her muddled brain could come up with for why there was a golden-skinned god standing in her kitchen.

Glancing down at herself, she noted her very un-sexy outfit of ratty, old sweats and a too big slouchy t-shirt that read, "Wyoming Girls Do It Better."

Shit. Should she go change? That would be dumb though, right?

"You look your fill yet, Wannabe?" Peeking over his shoulder at her, he smiled warmly. "Mornin', sweetheart. Sleep, okay?"

"Ug . . . um." Clearing her throat, she tried again. "Er. Yes. Y-you?"

"I slept like the dead," he said before scooping coffee grinds into the filter basket. "I gave Ethel fresh water and topped off her food dish. Was that all right?" He poured the water into the reservoir, set the coffee pot on the warmer, and then hit the button to start it brewing. Turning around to face her, he crossed his arms over his impressive chest. His bare arms were just as drool worthy as the rest of him. Since when were arms sexy?

The few brain cells she'd managed to rally fled. His front was even sexier than his back. Dark hair covered his pecs and trailed down his defined abs into a narrow line that disappeared into his pants. She'd never really liked hairy guys before, but she was officially a convert. Her fingers itched to scratch through the coarse strands and dig into the muscles underneath. What would the hair feel like against her palms? Her cheek? Her nipples? She shifted her thighs together, surprised at the ache that'd developed so quickly just from the sight of him shirtless.

Her gaze kept roaming downward, noting the snug fit at the crotch of his pants, and she snapped her eyes back to his face. Jesus, she'd been blatantly checking out his package. Twisting her fingers together behind her back, she forced herself to look at his face and not keep ogling him like a total ho. But, oh my God, the man was sex on a stick.

"Fine. It's fine. Feeding the cat is . . . is totally fine. Just fine." *Great, good job, Willow. You can't even speak!*

"Are you all right?" He stalked toward her. Suddenly nervous, she backed away from him, and his eyebrows furrowed. "Willow?"

Her butt hit the wall, and she gulped. Literally gulped like an idiot. "F-fine. Everything is just . . . just fine." God, could she say the word fine a half dozen times within a thirty-second time span? Apparently so.

The corners of his mouth twitched. "You don't seem *fine.*" He stepped even closer, his body heat warming her even through her clothes. Yeah, just *her* clothes, because he was hardly wearing any.

"You're . . . um . . . you don't have a shirt on."

"No. I get pretty warm when I sleep." He lightly traced his knuckles down her cheek. "Does that make you . . ." His fingers brushed down her neck and along her collarbone that was exposed by the loose collar of her shirt. ". . . uncomfortable?" His touch raised goosebumps down her arms in a rush, and she shivered.

"It makes me uncomfortable in my pants." Her mouth fell open, and her face heated so fast she was surprised she didn't pass out. "Oh, fuck me, I said that out loud, didn't I?"

The shock on his face quickly morphed into amusement

as laughter burst from him. "Holy shit, woman, you make me uncomfortable in my pants too. This is certainly one way to start the day, huh? Who needs caffeine when I have you?" He slipped his arms around her waist and hauled her up against his chest. "Now, come here and give me a good morning kiss. Then we'll have a lazy Sunday breakfast. Just you, me, Fred, and Ethel. How does that sound?"

"Perfect, Nathan, that sounds absolutely perfect." Wrapping her arms around his neck, her only thought as he devoured her mouth was she was damn glad she'd taken a moment to brush her teeth. After that, all thoughts fled, and she only knew the burning desire and need he brought out in her.

This is going to be the best week ever . . .

NATHAN COULDN'T HAVE ASKED for a better day as he and Willow got out of her truck to wander around the small town. The sun was shining, with only a few fluffy white clouds in the sky. The temperature was a comfortable sixty-eight degrees, accompanied by a slight breeze. From Willow's descriptions and photographs, Antelope Rock looked exactly as he'd imagined it would. It reminded him of Foxborough, Colorado, where he'd grown up.

Willow had a list of things she needed to get or do while they were in town. Since the main street was only five blocks long, they'd parked at one end, in front of Ducky's Feed & Supply, intending to run most of their errands on foot. Earlier, after a delicious breakfast, including fresh-from-the-coop eggs, they'd sat on her back porch and waited for Fred to show up. When the little critter had finally made an appearance, Nathan had watched in awe as the prairie dog and Ethel interacted with each other as if they were both part of the same species.

As he'd sat there with Willow, discussing their plans for the day, a sense of rightness and belonging had flowed over him. Not once since his family had been killed had Nathan felt . . . well, content and at peace. He could've stayed on that porch swing with Willow for the rest of his life and never want for anything more. Well, that wasn't exactly true. He wanted her in his bed, or on the kitchen table, or in the barn, or any other flat surface they could find, but he was willing to take things at a snail's pace if necessary. They'd get there, he was sure of that, but she was worth his patience.

Willow fascinated him in a way no other woman ever had. She was such a contradiction of terms—soft yet tough, quiet yet vocal, beautiful yet down-to-earth, shy but brave. He didn't know many people who would uproot themselves from a city they'd grown up in and travel halfway across the country to become a rancher without any prior knowledge or experience. But while they'd sipped their coffee that morning, as she'd explained to him about the alpaca operation they'd be going to look at, it'd been obvious she'd done plenty of research on her pending new career.

Now, as they strolled down the sidewalk, several townsfolk nodded hello as they passed by the couple, while others didn't bother to acknowledge their existence. One thing Nathan did notice was that he and Willow were garnering a bit of attention. Fourteen years in the army had given him a sixth sense concerning his surroundings. More than a few residents were watching them, although some were trying not to be obvious about it.

He squeezed Willow's hand to get her attention before asking, "Why are people staring at us?"

Willow snorted. "I've discovered there are two types of people in this town. The first type is staring at us, trying to figure out who you are and what you're doing with Satan's spawn. They'll be praying for your soul in hopes you don't follow the divorced, tattooed chick with the nose stud into Hell."

"Seriously?" Aghast, he couldn't believe anyone would treat Willow so callously. Didn't they see what an amazing person she was?

"Yup. I ignore that bunch for the most part, but my Philly snark comes out every once in a while to put them in their place. Now, the other type is trying to figure out who you are, if you're my boyfriend, and if you're good enough for me."

Nathan burst out laughing. "The second type sounds like my kind of people."

"Good, because you're about to meet one of them." She gestured to a man who'd just come out of the small post office and was heading toward them. He wasn't scary looking, but his keen gaze was pinned on Nathan. Clearly, he intended to have a little chat with the man currently holding Willow's hand. He was about five foot eleven and lean, but it was obvious the man was corded with muscle. Red hair brushed his shirt collar from under a straw cowboy hat, and he strode forward with graceful confidence.

When the three met in the middle of the sidewalk, Willow pointed a finger at the older man before he had a chance to say anything. She also gave him an evil glare. "Be nice."

The man rolled his eyes. "I was just going to tell him if he hurts you, I'm gonna hurt him. You already knew I was going to say that, so why'd you have to go and ruin it? You're no fun, dammit."

Willow sighed heavily, but a warm smile still spread across her face. "Nathan, this is Jeremiah Urban, my local guard dog. Jeremiah, this is Nathan Casey. Be nice," she repeated to her neighbor.

"What? I'm always nice!" Jeremiah joked. "Come here, give me some sugar."

Not waiting for Willow to close the distance between them, he scooped her up in a hug that lifted her feet from the ground. Jealousy coursed through Nathan before he remembered the other man was gay—even if he was in the closet. If it was anyone else, Nathan would have a serious issue with another man putting his hands on her in such a familiar way. He paused, recalling when Willow had told him how she'd pulled a shotgun on her ex. Even though she didn't need him to be her knight in shining armor—she was more than capable of taking care of herself—it still didn't mean Nathan would let anyone hurt her or come between them.

"Put me down, you overgrown child," Willow chided.

Jeremiah obeyed her with a grin, then turned his attention to Nathan and held out his hand. "It's a pleasure to finally meet you, son. Your girl here has told me a lot about you. Let me just say thank you for your service, and I'm glad you came home in one piece."

Nathan wasn't offended, nor surprised, when the other man called him "son". Even though there was only about a five- to seven-year difference in their ages, Jeremiah seemed like an old soul. He undoubtedly used the word with affection, and that's how it was taken. Nathan shook the proffered hand. "Thank you. I appreciate that. Willow's told me a lot about you too. Thank you for befriending her and helping her out with everything. Knowing she has a friend like you here eases my mind when I'm in Kansas."

"It's been my pleasure. She's a breath of fresh air in this stuffy town."

Nathan chuckled at that. "I'm sure she is. And don't worry, hurting her is the last thing I'd ever do."

"Glad to hear it."

Willow shook her head at both of them. "I knew you'd get

along with each other. Anyway, I'm actually glad we ran into you, Jeremiah, I was going to call you later. Would you mind taking a ride with us tomorrow to see the alpaca farm? I know there's a pretty big difference between cattle and alpacas, but they're still animals being raised on a ranch. I thought maybe you'd come up with some questions or observations I might totally miss."

The man winked at her. "I'd love to help you out—you should know that by now. And that's the great thing about having a foreman and a bunch of ranch hands—the boss gets to take off almost whenever he wants. What time do you want to leave?"

"I told the guy's nephew we'd be there at ten, and it's over in Redworth."

"I know where that is. Better pick me up by eight—we'll probably hit some traffic on the interstate."

"Eight it is. I'll bring the coffee. Thank you so much."

"My pleasure." He clapped his hands once. "Now that that's settled, why don't you two head on over to my place around five tonight? One of my ranch hands, Ethan, got engaged to his girlfriend the other night, and we're having a small barbecue to celebrate." His gaze darted to Nathan. "Willow's already met all my workers, and like her, I'm sure you'll fit right in."

Nathan was liking Willow's friend more and more, especially knowing the man had zero romantic or sexual interest in her, and honestly even if he did, Jeremiah still seemed like a hell of a guy. He shrugged and looked at Willow. "I'm game if you are, sweetheart."

She nodded her assent before turning back to Jeremiah. "What can we bring?"

"If you have a specific beer you'd like, bring that. Food will be more than covered. Oh," he said, snapping his fingers. "Camp chairs. We never have enough to go around."

"Sure? I'd feel bad not bringing something more than that."

"I'm sure, Willow-girl. However, the chance to grill your new man is going to be more than enough for me."

"Bring it on. There's nothing you can ask or say that'll scare me off of this one." Nathan pulled her closer to his side, kissing the top of her head.

"You two are so sweet you're making my teeth ache. On that note, I'm gonna get going. I'll see you later, kiddies!"

"Oh, you're a riot, you know that, Jeremiah?" Willow shouted at his back as he walked away. "I can't wait until you meet someone––I'm going to bust your balls so hard, dude!" The man just took his hat off, waved it in the air, and laughed as he strode to his truck.

Willow tugged on Nathan's hand. "Well, come on. Looks like we have to go buy some beer and camp chairs after we run the other errands."

"Lead the way, baby." He really meant that. He'd follow this woman anywhere. How was he feeling so much for her in such a short time? He felt like he'd stepped onto the set of a Hallmark movie or some damn thing. He still didn't understand how this amazing woman wanted to be with him, but he wasn't about to look a gift horse in the mouth. He was one lucky bastard, that was for sure. Grinning to himself, he followed Willow toward the entrance to the feed & supply store, making no attempt to stop from watching her perfectly round ass wiggle as she walked in front of him.

Damn, he sure did love watching her walk.

CHAPTER NINETEEN

When they got back to the house, they had several hours to kill, so Nathan suggested they go through a few of the remaining boxes filled with her father's papers and other things. He really wanted her to find something positive about the man who'd never been part of her life until after his death.

Nathan followed as Willow led him down the short hallway to the overhead door to the attic. "When Jeremiah and his ranch hands helped me clean this place out, there was stuff everywhere. It was too much to go through all at once to see what was worth keeping and what wasn't. They packed up all the papers, and anything that looked like it might be worth saving, into boxes and put them up here for me." She pulled the string that released the stairs and stepped back as they unfolded. "I managed to get through most of them, but there are still a few left. Let's carry them down and go through everything in the front room where we'll have the most space."

"Lead the way, my lady. Your pack horse awaits." He teasingly slapped her ass and followed her up the steps before ducking his head to avoid the low beams. He was hoping they didn't need to spend too much time in the cramped space-—he wasn't looking forward to braining himself, which was bound to happen if he was up there too long.

"Pack horse. Ha ha. Soldier boy got jokes, huh?" She pointed to a stack of five large, plastic storage boxes that looked pristine compared to their dusty cardboard counterparts that'd been stored up there for what had to have been decades. "I think these are all of them. Eventually, I'll go through the rest of this shit that was already up here when I moved in." Waving her hand around to encompass the attic, which was overflowing with faded boxes held together with yellowed tape, broken pieces of furniture, and two mattress and box spring sets, she sighed.

"Soldier boy? Really? You know we don't like that, right?" Gently elbowing her aside, he hefted one box up against his chest and carefully made his way to the ladder.

"Sorry. I didn't mean anything by it." The warmth of her palm running down his back soothed him even as it heated his blood.

"I know, baby, it's okay." His gaze shifted to something behind her. "Who's that? He looks too old to be your father."

She glanced over her shoulder to the large portrait of an older man. "Oh, that was hanging over the living room fireplace when I moved in. According to Jeremiah, that's my father's great-uncle, Simon Hillcrest. He owned the ranch when Jason came to live with him and left it to him when he died. Simon never married and didn't have any kids. It's a creepy picture—his eyes seem to follow you when you move —but I felt funny throwing it out, since he's technically a relative, so I just stuck it up here."

Nathan took several steps to his left and then to the right. "Holy shit—you're right. His eyes do follow you. Ugh, that gives me the chills." He shook his arms and shoulders in an exaggerated move before gesturing to the group of boxes. "All right. Grab one of those and let's get this done."

Two trips later, they sat on the floor of the living room, dust floating around them as they began sorting papers.

"What are you looking for exactly?" Nathan asked, setting aside what appeared to be copies of property taxes from almost thirty years ago.

"I don't really know—just anything that looks different. Not records or receipts. I mean, I get cattle operations need to keep logs of births and everything, but all the cattle are gone. I don't need any of that. I'm hoping to find something more personal. Something that tells me more about who my father was."

"Okay, I'll just put aside anything I think you need to look at and throw out the stuff I know is junk."

"Thanks." Craning her neck to the left, she shouted, "Alexa, play eighties rock!"

"The station, eighties rock, on Amazon Music," the electronic voice replied before the opening cords for "Welcome to the Jungle" filled the air.

"Just another thing I really like about you, Willow," Nathan said as he put aside more papers for the trash after determining they were logs from the 1995 calving season. "You have excellent taste in music."

"Hmm. What else do you like about me?" she asked, with a smirk on her lips and a twinkle in her eye.

"I'm not going to tell you—what fun would that be? I'd much rather show you." Winking, he sifted through another stack of calving logs in the box in front of him, and his hand bumped against something hard near the bottom. "Hang on a second, I think I've got something." Pulling the papers out, he found a small wooden chest beneath them. It was made from rich dark wood, mahogany perhaps, and inlaid with cherry blossoms. It was about an inch or two longer than the length of a legal-size envelope and maybe four inches thick. Lifting it from the cardboard box, he handed it over to Willow's eager hands.

"What the?" she mumbled to herself, turning it over in her hands. Her eyes narrowed. "How does it open? I don't see a latch."

"Let me see it a sec." She gave the chest back to him, and he examined each of the six sides from every angle. Something inside rattled and shifted, but it didn't sound broken. He ran his fingertips across the inlaid flowers, noticing they weren't perfectly smooth. "Hmm."

"What?" Willow scooted closer to him—her thigh pressed tightly against his as she watched him fiddle with the box.

"I think . . . hang on." He pushed down firmly on the largest of the flowers, surprised when a soft click sounded and the lid popped open. "It's a puzzle box." Not opening it any further, he passed it to Willow.

She studied it in awe. "That is so cool. What was so important to him that he had to keep it in a puzzle box?" Her fingers gripped the lid, but then she paused, as if almost afraid to look inside.

"Open it and see," he encouraged her. "If I had secrets to keep, this looks like a good place to stash them." He was nervous for her. She'd been searching for answers, and it looked like she might find them within the keepsake. Would they be everything she'd hoped for? He didn't know, but he was willing to be by her side while she figured it out.

WILLOW STARED at the gorgeous but mysterious box as her heart pounded and her hands shook. "I don't know why I'm so afraid."

Nathan set a reassuring hand on her trembling arm. "Don't be so hard on yourself. It's okay to feel what you're feeling."

Nodding, she took a deep breath then lifted the lid the rest of the way. Inside she found a stack of letters tied together with a simple piece of baling twine. Trust a rancher to use whatever was practical. That more than anything told her these were left there by her father. A woman would never use baling twine to tie something important together like that. She pulled the packet of letters free and handed the box to Nathan without even looking at him. Her eyes were glued to the front of the top letter.

Cheryl Crawford.

No address, just her mother's name, handwritten in black ink.

"Is that your mom?" Nathan wrapped his arm around her, pulling her fully against his side.

"Y-yeah." She swallowed what felt like a lump the size of a boulder. Scraping her nail down the twine, she looked up at him. "Will you think it terrible of me if I said I wanted to look at these alone?"

"Of course not, baby. How about I go start some lunch for us? Come find me when you're ready." He kissed her softly and put the box beside her knee before rising and leaving the room.

Slipping the twine free, she selected the top envelope and put the rest of the stack back into the box. When she pulled out the letter, a photo fluttered out, landing softly on her lap. It was small and faded with age. A tall, young man stood behind her even younger looking mother, holding her flush against his body. A black Flyers ball cap shaded his face, but his grin was a mile wide and was matched by the bright smile on her mom's face. Willow knew that cap—had even worn it several times since moving there and finding it in the hall closet.

Her mother couldn't have been more than sixteen in the picture. Thinking back, Willow realized she'd never seen any pictures of her mom from when she'd been a pregnant teen. There'd only been photos of her mother when she'd been much younger or after Willow had been born. There certainly had never been pictures of her with this man —Jason.

After gently putting the picture with the other letters, she unfolded the pages in her hand. She took a deep breath, feeling as if she was balanced on a precipice. She knew, intrinsically, that everything she ever knew about her mother, and everything she *didn't* know about her father, was about to change.

May 29

My Beloved Cherry,

As I write this, knowing that I will never send it, I question my sanity. Why am I torturing myself this way? Though I don't suppose it makes much of a difference. The memory of you lives so strong within me, I know that for the rest of my days, you'll be the only woman I'll ever love. Yes. Woman. No matter what our families say, you are a woman. My woman. Just as I am your man. It will always be so, even as the miles between us stretch on forever, you're in my heart and I can only pray that I'm in yours as well.

Leaving you behind today was the hardest thing I've ever done. I will never get the image of your tear-stained face from my mind. Your sorrow slayed me and broke my heart into a million pieces. Even streaked with tears, with red, swollen eyes, you're still the most gorgeous thing I've ever laid eyes on.

I know your heart is shattered, just as mine is. I know you'll probably blame me for not fighting harder for us. Love shouldn't come with conditions. As pure as my feelings for you are, your family is right in some ways. I'm too old for you. You have your whole life ahead of you, and you don't need a poor bastard like me hanging like a load-stone around your pretty neck. While part of me knows that, the other part is unwilling to let you go forever.

My parents insisted I go to my uncle's ranch in Antelope Rock, Wyoming, where I can work for him. I'm on my way there now, since I have nowhere else to go. Can you imagine? A south Philly boy like me living in Wyoming? I've visited him there before. It's been a few years though, but I mostly know what to expect. I don't think it'll be a bad life, other than living there without you. But, Cherry baby, you know if I tried to stay with you, I'd be in jail and you'd still be alone. I care nothing for myself, but I can't let you live with that guilt.

They're calling my bus. I have to go. I love you, Cherry, always and forever, until the stars burn out and the sky falls, my heart will beat for you.

Always yours,
J

🦌

WILLOW CAREFULLY RE-FOLDED the letter and returned it to its envelope. Her movements were precise and careful. She was positive if she moved too quickly, she'd splinter into minuscule pieces, never to be the same. Something wet splashed against the back of her hand, and she realized she was crying. Helpless under the onslaught of her emotions, she gave up fighting and allowed herself to feel every iota of injustice, rage, and grief. Sobs tore painfully from her throat as she gasped for air.

"Willow!" Nathan shouted, and his heavy footfalls ran toward her.

Within seconds, she was gathered tightly in his embrace as her heart broke for the love her parents had and were denied. It all made sense now. Well, maybe not all, but a few things were clearer to her now. Others were still a mystery. Her father hadn't mentioned the pregnancy—had he not known?

"Willow, baby?" The concern in Nathan's voice just made her cry harder. It wasn't fair! Her parents had been torn apart by *their* parents. Instead of letting Willow, her mother, and Jason be a family, they hadn't given them any choice.

"J-just . . ." She hiccupped, then managed to get the rest of her plea out. "Don't let me go."

"Never, baby, that's never going to happen." He pulled her fully into his lap and rocked her gently while running his fingers through her hair and kissing her temple. "I've got you, shh. It's okay."

Clutching fistfuls of his shirt, she let herself cry in a way she hadn't since she'd been a child. Her chest ached with the force of it, and her head was starting to pound, but still the tears flowed.

She didn't know how much time passed as he held her, but neither moved until her gasping sobs slowed and finally stopped. Nathan's shirt was soaked under her cheek, but she made no effort to leave his comforting embrace. "I'm sorry," she whispered in a hoarse voice.

He ran a hand up and down her back in a soothing manner. "Nothing to be sorry for, Wannabe. Come on—up you go. I want you to drink a glass of water, take some Tylenol, and get into bed. When you wake up, you can tell me all about it."

Willow allowed him to pull her to her feet, and she followed each of his instructions, downing an ice-cold glass of water and two white pills. He led her into her bedroom where he closed the blinds on the windows before carefully stripping her of her shoes and jeans. There was nothing even remotely sexual about his actions—he was caring for her on the most basic of levels.

Once her head hit the pillow, he pulled the blanket up to her chin, dropped a kiss on her forehead, and turned to leave.

"Wait," she said, grabbing his hand. "Stay with me. Please?"

Wordlessly nodding his ascent, he kicked off his shoes and climbed onto the bed behind her. Pulling her close, he shifted them both around until they were spooned together. His warmth seemed to settle into her very bones and her muscles finally relaxed.

"Sleep, baby, I'll be right here when you wake up." Nathan pressed his lips to the sensitive spot behind her ear. "Rest. I've got you."

She drifted off with the rich scent of him thick in her nose and a cocoon of utter contentment surrounding her.

CHAPTER TWENTY

WILLOW WOKE to the heat and hard press of a man at her back. Momentarily disoriented, it took her a second to remember she'd fallen asleep in Nathan's arms. He must have dozed off with her. She hadn't shared a bed with a man since her divorce, and even during her marriage, there were many nights where one of them would pass out on the couch, leaving the other to sleep alone. She didn't remember having someone else in her bed ever feeling this nice.

Wiggling backward, she rubbed her ass against his groin, eliciting a groan and a shift of his hips in return. "Willow, what are you doing?" he murmured.

"Getting comfortable." She held the arm he had around her chest tighter against herself, clutching at him like a security blanket. "I don't want to think for a few minutes, so just go with it."

"Okay, baby. Whatever you need. Just, maybe keep the ass wiggles to a minimum, hmm? You're all warm and soft from sleep, and it's sexy as hell. I'm trying to be a gentleman here."

She couldn't restrain her soft laughter, and of course, a little poking the bear was in order. She rubbed her ass firmly against his crotch. "Is that a gun in your pocket, cowboy, or are you just happy to see me?"

He tugged his arm from her grasp and moved it down to her hips, before tightening his hold and halting her teasing. "I know what you're doing."

"Yeah, I thought it was pretty obvious. About as obvious as how happy you are to be spooning me." She tried to wiggle again but wasn't able to get as much movement as before due to his hold. "Very, very happy."

"Aside from that, you're distracting yourself from talking about what you read in that letter. Which is just fine, of course, but I don't want you to push us both into something physical as a distraction from your feelings. Like I told you, the first time I make love to you, I will not be rushed, nor will I be coaxed into it. Would I mind being an emotional band-aid in the future? No. But not right now."

Huffing out a breath, she scooched forward to give him some space. "I'm sorry." Feeling like a heel, she started to get up, only to be jerked back down.

"Nope. Not happening. I didn't say I minded you rubbing that sweet little ass all over my cock. I just meant that it wasn't going to go any further than that at the moment. Now, get back here where you belong and talk to me." He settled her against him once more.

She hesitated for a few seconds while searching for the right words to say to him. "I'm sorry I fell apart on you like that. That's not me. I'm not a crier."

"Nothing to be sorry about. You needed it. Can you tell me about it?"

She marveled at this man. He was patient and kind, sure and true. Men like him didn't exist in real life, at least not in her experience. With a few simple words, he'd just stolen another piece of her heart. It wouldn't be long before he possessed the whole thing. She waited for the fear that thought should bring, but it never arrived. Huh, imagine that —after all she'd been through in her life, she wasn't afraid of the consequences of falling for this man.

"Wannabe?" Nathan prompted her.

"As you probably already figured out, it was a letter from my father to my mother. Only, he never sent it to her. He didn't go into a lot of detail, but it seemed like their match wasn't approved by her family because he was much older than her. I don't think his family was happy about it either. Like I told you before, my mom was fifteen when she got pregnant with me and sixteen when I was born. My father was twenty-two at the time. He'd just turned fifty-six before he died. In the letter, he said something about being put in jail, so I'm assuming statutory rape charges." Rolling over to face Nathan, she continued, "He loved her so much. You'll have to read the letter for yourself to fully see that. It just broke my heart. My whole life, my mom was alone, but the entire time there was a man here who loved her beyond sense, but they were forbidden to be together? Why didn't he come find her later?"

Sweeping a few loose strands of her hair off her face, Nathan kissed her softly. "I don't know, but I bet the answers are in the rest of those letters."

"I don't think I have the guts to read another one right now. Maybe tomorrow." She brushed her mouth over his chin, enjoying the feel of his stubble against her lips. She wanted to trail kisses down his neck, drag his clothes off, and keep working her way down until his cock was buried in her throat. The desire surprised her. Normally she wasn't one to initiate blow jobs or enjoy giving them too much, but the thought of making this strong man come undone under her hands and mouth turned her crank like nobody's business.

"Come on, let's have a light lunch, since we'll be eating at the barbecue later." Nathan patted her ass softly and rolled away from her.

"Then what?" she asked as she stood and stepped around the foot of the bed.

He took her hand in his. "How about a walk? I'd love to see the rest of the property and what needs to be fixed if you're getting the alpacas soon. I can do a few things for you while I'm here."

"Nathan, you don't have to work while you're here. I don't—"

Cupping her chin, he cut her off. His voice was low and husky. "Sweetheart, I want to help you out with whatever I can. Please let me."

His blue eyes bore into hers, setting her heart galloping in her chest. His intense gaze told her he wasn't extending the offer for any other reason than he cared about her. He wasn't trying to impress her nor did he think doing some work would get him into her pants. He really didn't mind helping with some chores around her place, and he wouldn't think less of her for asking for his assistance. Hell, she'd let him bulldoze the barn in that moment if he'd wanted to.

Going up on her tiptoes, she kissed him softly on the lips. "You're a good man, Nathan Casey. Let me feed you and then I'll show you around Skyview."

His smile was the best reward for accepting his offer that she could ever receive.

WILLOW PULLED up to the drive-thru window and passed the coffee cup carrier the clerk handed her over to Nathan. Jeremiah was in the back seat, happily chattering away as if all three of them weren't suffering from massive hangovers.

"How the fuck are you so chipper, Jeremiah? Goddammit,

my head feels like it's going to split open, and you're running at the mouth with no issue." Nathan was grumpy as hell today, and Willow struggled not to find it slightly adorable.

Jeremiah snorted. "I thought a soldier like you would be more familiar with working through a hangover. First time?"

"Fuck off, and no, it's not," he responded without any heat behind his words. "I'm just out of practice. I don't pull this shit anymore."

Chuckling, Willow tried her best to ignore her own pounding head while she waited for the Tylenol she'd taken to finally kick in. The barbecue last night had quickly evolved into a party filled with line-dancing lessons, shot contests, and some dumb-ass hay bale-tossing challenge that Nathan had somehow won. She admitted to herself with zero shame that watching a shirtless, tipsy Nathan toss bales of hay by firelight had been one of the best things she'd ever seen. She hadn't missed the appreciative glances Jeremiah had snuck at Nathan either, but she wouldn't hold it against him.

"Shut up, both of you, and drink your coffee," she ordered good-naturedly.

"She's bossy, ain't she?" Jeremiah griped, poking Nathan in the shoulder, almost causing him to spill his coffee. "That your kind of thing? I could give you some tips if she's super toppy."

"Goddammit, poke me again, and I'm going to snap your hand off and feed it to you. And what the fuck would you know about a toppy woman?" Willow had already confessed to Jeremiah that Nathan was aware of his secret. For his part, Nathan had assured her friend that he had no issues with the man's sexual orientation, and he would remain mum about it when others were around. Willow liked how that knowledge gave Jeremiah the freedom to be who he really was with them, without having to worry about saying the wrong thing or being ridiculed. In fact, the two men acted as if they'd been friends for years, the way they joked around and gave each other shit, since shortly after Willow and Nathan had arrived at the JP Ranch yesterday.

"Maybe not a toppy woman, but I know about bossy tops and just how to handle them. That's all I'm saying."

"She isn't a top! What, you think she's wearing a strap-on and bending me over the couch, dammit? Fuck me, I can't believe I'm having this conversation." As they hit the road, Nathan kept up a steady stream of back-and-forth bitching with Jeremiah until Willow had enough. Reaching forward, she cranked the radio, blasting rock loud enough to shake the windows. It made her head feel like it was going to split like a melon, but it stopped their bickering mid-bicker. They both screeched and moaned as Nathan lunged forward to turn the music down while glaring at her.

Willow pointed at him and then Jeremiah. "Both of you, shut your fool mouths, drink your coffee, and keep your hands to yourself. Fuck me, it's like driving with a couple kids. If you can't get along, I'll leave you both right here on the side of the damn road and go to the farm myself. Understand?"

"Yes, ma'am," they replied in near unison, although both appeared to be trying to hide grins. Blessed silence filled the cab of the truck, and Willow sighed in relief.

The rest of the drive passed uneventfully, with any further conversation being quite tame if not hushed. When they arrived at Birchwood Farm, their hangovers had faded to a tolerable level and both Nathan and Jeremiah had calmed down. Willow pulled her truck to a stop near a row of other vehicles and a livestock trailer.

Grabbing her sunglasses and pulling the brim of her father's Flyers hat farther down on her forehead, Willow hopped out. While her headache had subsided, the bright sun was killing her eyes, threatening to bring back the pounding.

She waited by the hood of her truck for Nathan and Jeremiah to join her. The latter was scoping the place out with a practiced eye.

"Looks like a good setup. Clean and in good repair, which bodes well for the state of the animals. Poorly maintained ranches usually equal sub-par quality livestock. Speaks to the character of the owners as well." Gone was the joking goofball, and in his place was a multi-generational rancher. Even Nathan seemed to notice the change.

"Speak for yourself, cowboy. Appearances can be deceiving—sometimes it's the hired help that keeps everything afloat. You shouldn't judge a book by its cover, as they say."

The deep voice coming from behind them startled Willow. Turning, she saw the source was one of the biggest men she'd ever seen. Standing at least six foot four, he was built like a brick shithouse. Broad shouldered, with short-cropped dark hair and tanned skin, he was handsome enough to stop traffic. His thick arms were crossed over his equally large chest as he stared at them with frank suspicion. His tree-trunk legs were shoulder-width apart, as if he was bracing himself on the deck of a ship on rolling seas and not hard, stable earth. Dressed in jeans, a work shirt with the sleeves rolled up, and a black cowboy hat, he looked every inch a native Wyomingite.

"Hello, sorry about that. I'm Willow Crawford. I'm here to see Jeffrey Faulkner about buying some alpacas and equipment?"

When the man didn't respond right away, Willow glanced at Jeremiah and saw he was frozen in place, his mouth slightly open. His eyes were glued to the other man, and a flush colored his cheeks, making his freckles stand out in stark contrast against his otherwise pale skin.

Finally, the stranger spoke. "I'm Dale Harris, the foreman here. Sorry about the wary greeting, but I wasn't expecting you for another hour."

When Willow's brow furrowed, as she wondered if she'd messed up the appointment time, the man held up a hand. "I highly doubt it was your fault—most likely I was given the wrong time. Anyway, Mr. Faulkner is up in the house on the phone. He asked me to give you a rundown of the operation, since he doesn't know his ass from his elbow."

Okay, obviously he didn't think much of the nephew of his deceased boss, Carl Faulkner. Willow wondered if Dale had gotten along with the elder Faulkner at all, but then she recalled Gail Broderick saying the man had been the foreman here for years and was well-liked and respected in the alpaca farming community.

Dale continued, "I understand you might also want me to come work for you." His eyes slid sideways to Jeremiah and quickly returned to hers, clearly dismissing the other man. Jeremiah's back snapped straight at the slight, and she spoke as he began to step forward.

"Maybe," she responded, not wanting to commit until she managed to get a better read on the man. The glowing recommendations carried a lot of weight with her, but she was the one who'd be dealing with him on an everyday basis. "This is Nathan Casey and Jeremiah Urban. Nathan is my . . . um, my boyfriend." Why had she hesitated on the word? "Jeremiah is my neighbor who owns a cattle operation, the JP Ranch. I'm very new to ranching of any variety, so he's here to advise me."

"Fair enough. Come on then, tour starts now."

Dale was gruff and stoic, and Willow wasn't sure what to think of him. As she followed the bigger man, she noticed

Jeremiah had his eyes glued to Dale's ass. She whacked him on the arm and hissed, "Stop it!"

"What?" he whispered back. "Do you see that thing? How can I not stare at it?"

Oh geez. This day was definitely not going as she'd planned. The last thing she needed was her best friend to start waving the rainbow flag for the first time in his life and in front of a man who might just deck him.

Sigh.

CHAPTER TWENTY-ONE

Making sure the foreman couldn't hear her, Willow glared at Jeremiah and quietly admonished him. "Can you not sexually harass the man I'm hoping to hire?"

"Knock it off, both of you," Nathan interjected, keeping his voice as low as theirs. He nodded his head toward where Dale had stopped by the open door of a barn and was waiting for them, with his arms crossed again over his massive chest and a scowl on his face. "You have an audience."

"Everything okay?" Dale asked, eyeing them shrewdly as they caught up to him.

"Yup. Totally . . . fine." Jeremiah said. "Don't worry about us. Lead on."

Dale cocked an eyebrow in Jeremiah's direction, shook his head, and then led the trio into a small corral that was attached to a medium-sized barn. Loud barks greeted them as they drew closer. "Those are the herd's guard dogs— Johnny and June. They're siblings and a mix of Great Pyrenees and Maremma sheepdogs. They're trained to guard the alpacas from predators, sleeping most of the day and patrolling the barns and corrals at night. They also serve double duty as midwives and nannies. If a cria is in trouble, they'll take it and hide it. One time, we had one that wasn't doing well, and the mother wouldn't have anything to do with the little guy. June tucked that cria so deep into a pile of hay, it took me an hour to find it."

"That is so cool! Do they come with the alpacas if I purchase the herd?" Willow asked with delight, seeing the two giant, white and grey dogs standing on their back legs with their front paws on the fence. They were majestic, but their size was definitely intimidating.

"Yes, they do. I raised them from pups—they're more mine than Faulkner's. He wants to get rid of them. If you don't want them, I'll keep them myself. Make sure that gate closes behind you. I'm not about to be chasing alpacas across the field today." Jeremiah opened his mouth to respond, but Willow glared a warning at him.

"Johnny, June. Down." Dale followed the command with a sharp hand gesture. Obeying immediately, the dogs dropped down, settling on a pile of hay in the corner of the barn.

The threesome followed the foreman through the set of gates before closing them. A sharp tang of ammonia hit Willow's nose, and she recognized the light aroma of urine. The odor was very different from horses, but not as bad as other animals could be. In fact, it reminded her a little bit of Ethel's litter box.

They stepped over a pile of manure and followed Dale across the hay-strewn corral. There were two large metal troughs full of water, but otherwise the area was empty of any equipment.

"Normally this time of year the alpacas stay outside, even sleeping out here when it's not raining—they hate the rain. Otherwise, they'll only go into the barn if they need to get out of the sun or away from each other a bit. They've very social animals, but like people, they have distinct personalities and fight on occasion—especially when the babies are around. The mothers are very protective of their young, and they operate as family units. You'll learn which ones get along, which ones avoid each other, and how they're related to one another, which is very important when it comes time for breeding. No one wants inbred alpacas."

The trio followed Dale deeper into the fenced area and around the side of the barn. Standing together in the shade of a metal canopy was a group of about eighteen alpacas, huddled around a pile of hay on the ground, taking turns eating. They were all different colors ranging from pure white to golden yellow to black and brown.

"Holy crap, they're bigger in person." Nathan blurted out. Willow couldn't blame him for being surprised, since she had a similar reaction during her first meeting at the Brodericks' farm. The alpacas all stood at over six feet tall, easily. With long necks and big eyes, they were strange-looking animals but in an adorable sort of way.

"That's what he said," Jeremiah mumbled under his breath, earning another glare from her.

Ignoring him, she asked Dale, "How many are for sale again?"

"The eighteen females that you see here—five of them are pregnant and due next May or June. Then there's the one male that's kept separate from the others."

"Why separate?" Nathan asked, eyeing the creatures just as warily as they did him.

"Unless you're ready for them to breed, you keep the males apart from the females. Plus, they tend to be more aggressive and disrupt the herd. Juvenile males are okay with the group until they mature, but then they should be separated."

"It's the same with cattle—lets you control when calving begins," Jeremiah added, not hesitating a moment and walking closer to the herd. He bent and picked up a handful of hay and cautiously, but with complete confidence, strode to the group of animals. "Here now, ladies, looks like you missed some hay."

As he spoke to them, he kept his voice calm and held out the hay, patiently waiting for one to approach him. They seemed very curious about him and only slightly nervous. A large, ebony-colored one seemed to be the bravest and stepped forward, bent her head, and ate the proffered fodder from Jeremiah's hand. "Aren't you a lovely girl, huh?"

"He makes that look easy," Nathan grumbled.

"It is," Dale replied. "They aren't anything to be afraid of. As long as you respect them and treat them well, they'll do the same for you." He leaned down, grabbed some hay, and waved Nathan and Willow forward. "Come meet them and you can decide if this is what you really want. Grab some hay and do what your cattle rancher just did."

Jeremiah scowled at Dale but refrained from retorting. Meanwhile, the foreman handed some hay to Willow, then Nathan before offering a few straws to an alpaca standing next to him, which eagerly accepted the food.

Following Dale's lead, Nathan did as he suggested, looking sideways at Willow a little nervously. "I feel dumb. If horses don't weird me out, why should alpacas?"

"It's okay, just do what they're doing." Passably familiar with the animals from her earlier visit to the Brodericks' farm, she stayed still as she held the hay out, not retreating when two of them bumped against each other in their rush to get to her. A pure-white one reached her first but stopped before getting too close. Willow froze. The alpaca's big eyes were ice blue, and with the large white sclera surrounding them, it made her look blind. It was freaky as hell.

"Is she blind?" Willow asked in alarm.

"No, ma'am, that's just her eye color," Dale replied. "It

may look odd, but she's totally fine, I assure you. Her name is Fannie Mae."

"Aww, what a cute name." She held the hay out farther. "Here you go, Fannie." The animal stretched her long neck down, gently reaching for the hay in Willow's hand with her mouth. The fine fibers around Fannie's jaw tickled Willow's palm.

"What's wrong with her mouth?" Nathan pointed with his free hand to where Fannie's lips were split into two sections.

Dale let out a laugh and actually smiled, transforming his already handsome face to something that reminded her of a Roman god. It was obvious Jeremiah noticed it too because his jaw dropped, but Dale didn't pay him any mind as he explained, "Their mouths are normally split like that and are very dexterous—they use them like fingers and each lip operates independently of the other. Go on, she won't bite you. They only have bottom teeth in the front anyway."

The weird finger-like lips of the alpaca gently plucked the hay from Willow's hands, brushing her fingertips. Fannie's mouth was soft as velvet and seemed incredibly delicate. "Feels like a horse, huh, Nathan?"

"Yeah, it's similar." Nathan replied, relaxing now that it was obvious the animals weren't going to charge or bite. He lifted the hay he was still holding and offered it to another nearby alpaca.

"Just keep your hand flat and still," Dale instructed.

With her other hand, Willow carefully patted Fannie's neck and stroked her hand downward. Her fur, or hair rather, was soft as cotton and twice as fluffy. Grinning, she kept petting Fannie until the animal lost interest and walked away, her place quickly taken by another curious alpaca looking for fodder or an ear scratch. Willow gave her both.

All four of them kept feeding the herd until the hay was gone. Dale then showed them around inside the barn, explaining the minimal tack that was required for their care. Lead ropes and harnesses were about the extent of it. He pointed out the dried corn and grain mixture the animals were fed in addition to the hay, explaining that it was infused with additional minerals they needed. Willow had learned from the Brodericks that maintaining an alpaca herd was pretty straightforward. The real work came when it was time to shear them—a task that was often best hired out to professionals.

"There's another barn where we keep three horses and two goats, Lucy and Desi. They're also up for sale, along with two ATVs. Faulkner can't operate an ATV to save his life and has no interest in the horses. If you don't want them, I'm sure we can find another buyer. The horses are good, sturdy animals—gentle too, if you're a less-experienced rider—and I keep the ATVs well-maintained. You should be able to negotiate a good deal for them, including all the tack and the three saddles we have for the horses as well. One-stop shopping, you could say."

"That's a lot more animals than I was originally looking for right now. It's just me on the ranch, and even with your help, that seems like a lot of work. Though two goats named Lucy and Desi really feels like fate." At Dale's confused look, she explained, "Ethel is the name of my cat, and a prairie dog that loves to visit me every morning is Fred."

The man chuckled. "Fate. Gotcha."

Turning her head, Willow smiled and met Nathan's eyes. He was only going to be at the ranch for a few more days and then she'd be alone again. They hadn't yet talked about what his plans were after he retired from the Army, and it was an awfully big assumption on her part to think he would want to move to Wyoming to be a rancher with her.

"Willow, this is your decision. Do whatever you think is best," Nathan said, resting his hand on the small of her back.

"It's what you were thinking about, getting a couple of horses eventually, right? It's just happening sooner than you'd planned."

"It *is* a lot of effort to run a successful ranch, no matter what type," Dale chimed in. "But if I come work for you, taking care of all the equipment, the animals, and their tack and feed, will be my job—that's what you'll be paying me for. It'll be the same amount of work I do now, just at a different location. I was Carl Faulkner's foreman for the past six years, but I can get you some more references."

Willow shook her head. "That won't be necessary. The Brodericks already gave you a glowing recommendation. Also, the fact that Mr. Faulkner employed you for all that time, and the barn and the animals look well cared for, are testaments to how good you are at your job. If I go through with this, the foreman position is yours, if you want it."

He nodded his assent before she glanced around the property. "An alpaca herd, three horses, and two goats. I'll need to make some fast renovations on the smaller barn." There was fencing that needed to be fixed as well, among other things, but one of the pastures was in good enough condition to start with.

"Yes, the alpacas and horses have to be housed separately from each other because the alpacas are more sensitive to parasites that horses aren't bothered by. The goats can go in the same barn as the herd though."

"Lucky for you, Willow-girl," Jeremiah chimed in with a wink, "you know people who can help with the renovations, not to mention sell you hay at a reasonable price. But if you find that the horses are too much work and expense for you, I might be interested in buying them. They're fine quarter horses—good for cutting cattle and ranch work. As for your labor concerns, I know Ethan's cousin has been looking for a new job as a hand. He made the mistake of dating his boss's daughter, and now that they've broken up, he'd rather cut all ties. He's a good worker though, and if I had an opening for him at my place, I would've already offered him a job. If you want, I'll hook you up with him during the week for an interview. Between a foreman, yourself, and one hand, you should be able to get plenty of work done. I can even loan you a few of my hands for those fast renovations, now that we're done with cuttin' hay."

Willow nodded but didn't reply. Her mind was whirring with the possibilities. Did she really want this? It wasn't only the hard work that gave her pause—it was a lot of responsibility, both financially and to the animals.

"So, what do you think?" Dale asked, brushing loose hay from his hands.

"I don't have the experience to handle all this on my own, and it wouldn't be fair to the animals for me to try, but since you're willing to stay on as my foreman, I can't think of a reason to say no." Over the course of the tour, Willow had warmed to the man and could see that his gruff exterior hid a caring nature. Any man who was as kind and considerate to animals as he seemed to be earned her approval. "I don't have an apartment or bunkhouse available for you yet, but Jeremiah has offered the use of one of his empty bunks for anyone I hired until I could arrange for quarters at Skyview."

Dale crossed his arms, as he seemed to do every time he eyed Jeremiah, and shook his head. "Not necessary. I have a fifth-wheel trailer and can live in that, provided you have a safe place to park it and hookups for power and such."

"I think that can be arranged easily enough. Would you require an employment contract in writing or are you comfortable with a verbal agreement?"

"I'd like it in writing, if it's all the same to you. No offense intended, but we've just met, and it's a big commitment." Dale leaned back against the wall of the barn, looking like the quintessential Marlboro man from their vintage advertising campaigns. Jeremiah couldn't keep his eyes to himself, and Willow was afraid if he didn't cool it, he'd end up with a split lip—or worse. It was clear to her that, although Dale had warmed up to her and Nathan, he had a different opinion about her neighbor.

Subtly stepping in front of Jeremiah, blocking his view of Dale, she offered her hand to the foreman. "I can respect that. As long as Mr. Faulkner and I can reach an agreement on the sale, I'd be happy to have you. I'll contact my attorney as soon as the sale is underway and have the papers drawn up for you."

He shook her hand, his grip firm and his large palm thickly calloused from years of labor-intensive ranch work. "That'll be fine, Ms. Crawford."

"Willow, please."

"Willow it is." He pulled a small piece of paper out of his shirt pocket. "Here's my cell number and email address if you have any other questions or concerns. Carl's nephew knows nothing about the animals or the operation, but I'll be able to give you accurate information and straight answers."

She took the paper. "I appreciate that, thank you."

After saying their goodbyes, the trio turned toward the house where a man in his fifties stood on the back porch, watching them approach—Jeffery Faulkner. City-slicker was the immediate description that popped into Willow's head at the sight of him, with his designer clothes, greased-back hair, and a Bluetooth earbud in place. She smiled to herself, *city-slicker* was definitely not something she ever thought she'd be calling someone else, yet here she was.

"Ms. Crawford, I presume? I'm Jeffery Faulkner." The oh-too-confidant-looking man descended the porch steps, with his hand extended. His self-important tone was the same one he'd used when Willow had spoken to him on the phone while making the appointment to see the animals. If she hadn't already told him she was the one interested in purchasing the animals, he probably would've written her off as the "little woman" and opted to do business with one of the two men with her.

"Yes, it's a pleasure to meet you, Mr. Faulkner," she fudged while subtly wiping her palm on her jeans after shaking his sweaty hand. She hadn't realized Dale had followed them, but he now stood off to the side, his arms crossed as he wore his disapproval of Faulkner plain as day. Another thing in favor of Dale––he didn't pull any punches.

"I assume you're still interested in purchasing the alpacas and all the stuff that goes with them. I'm sure a lovely lady such as yourself and I can come to an agreeable arrangement." His smile made her skin crawl as he ignored the others. The man was a slug and that was an insult to the species.

Willow's eyes narrowed, and her bullshit meter was pinging at a ten. The guy was a real piece of work. "I'm sure two business owners, such as ourselves, can come to an equitable sale agreement, yes." She may be a girl from Philly, but she was no idiot. This guy was going to try and fleece her. Best to nip that in the bud right now. "Allow me to introduce you to Nathan Casey and Jeremiah Urban. Jeremiah is the owner of JP Ranch and is here as my friend and advisor. Nathan is my partner." She was deliberately vague––let the jerk think she had a financial backer.

He shook both men's hands and gestured to the house. "Please, won't you come in, and we'll discuss this like civilized people. Dale, I'm sure there's something else you could be doing." His icy tone and glare directed at the foreman told Willow all she needed to know. This man didn't respect the people who worked for him or the jobs they performed that lined his pockets. She decided then and there that she was going to low-ball the negotiations. She didn't see any reason to give this asshole any more money than absolutely necessary.

Nathan and Jeremiah both let her lead the conversation, only interjecting something when she asked them for their opinion. Jeremiah had a talent for reading the room that would've been welcome in any boardroom. A dumb cowboy, he was not. By the sweat on Mr. Faulkner's brow, it was obvious he realized too late that he'd underestimated her and her companions and was in way over his head.

Yup, she'd come a long way in the months since moving to Antelope Rock, and it was definitely for the better.

CHAPTER TWENTY-TWO

Before leaving her bedroom, Willow checked her
reflection one more time in the mirror. After dropping off
Jeremiah and arriving home, Nathan had told her to go get
dressed, because he was taking her out on the date he'd
promised her. Dinner and a movie, with the man she was
growing to deeply care about, sounded just about perfect
after the long but successful day.

Following the tour Dale had given them, they'd spent the
next two hours in negotiations with Jeffery Faulkner. If he'd
thought she was going to be an easy mark, she'd shut that
shit down from the get-go. Even Nathan and Jeremiah had
commented during the drive home they'd been impressed
with her shark-like negotiation skills. She'd gotten the
alpacas, equipment, and remaining feed for a reasonable
price and well below her budget. She owed some thanks for
that to the Brodericks who'd given her a list of what things
should cost new, versus used and the value of the animals.
They'd known Carl Faulkner well enough to know the
quality of his herd and had given her a maximum price per
head to stay under. She'd even managed to get the three

horses and their tack, the two goats, and the two ATVs thrown into the final agreement. Once the lawyers for both sides did their thing and the sale was final, Dale had said he would organize the transportation of the animals and everything else to Skyview. But Jeremiah had jumped in at that point and said, with his livestock trailer and the one she was purchasing with the herd, there was no need to pay a company to do it. Her new foreman hadn't looked thrilled with the prospect of working with the other man, but he'd still agreed with him.

On the way home, Willow had contacted Howard Smith to give him the information he needed to get started on all the paperwork, including the employment contract for Dale.

Speaking of Dale, Jeremiah seemed to have developed an infatuation/hatred of the man. He'd bitched about him for the first twenty minutes of the trip home, until Nathan had reached over and cranked up the radio when AC/DC's "Dirty Deeds Done Dirt Cheap" had come on. Willow hoped there wouldn't be a problem between her friend and her new employee once the latter moved onto her property. She'd have enough on her plate without also dealing with the two men sniping at each other.

"You ready yet, woman?" Nathan called down the hall to her. "I promise, you're gorgeous just the way you are—no need to spend time getting dolled up for me."

"Hold your horses, soldier. I'm coming." After searching her bedroom closet for something nice to wear, she'd opted for a mid-length, flowy, white skirt that made her feel romantic. She'd then paired it with new, black dress boots—yes, those were a thing apparently—and a black, long-sleeved, button-up blouse with the top three clear crystal snaps undone. This was Wyoming after all, and a little bling equaled dressy.

Walking down the hall, she met Nathan in the living

room. His eyes widened at her appearance, and he stood straighter as his gaze roamed her from head to toe and back up again. He was so handsome it stopped her in her tracks. If she'd thought he was gorgeous shirtless, that was nothing compared to the man dressed up. He wore fitted black jeans and a button up shirt the same ocean blue of his eyes. With no tie and the top two buttons of his shirt undone, showing her a glimpse of his dark chest hair, she was practically drooling on her boots. He still hadn't shaved his scruff off which just added to the appeal.

"Holy sex on a stick Batman, you look amazing." And there went her filter again. Her cheeks flamed hot with embarrassment.

Laughing, Nathan stepped closer to her and gathered her into a hug. "Good Lord, woman, I love it when you speak your mind like that." Keeping one arm tight around her waist, he cupped her cheek with his other hand before leaning down and kissing her softly. "You look pretty amazing yourself, Wannabe." He brushed his lips across hers in the gentlest of caresses. "Before I throw caution to the wind, and you into your bed, let's go. I want to wine and dine my girl while I have the chance."

Her heart clenched at the thought of him leaving, but she forced the uncomfortable feeling aside. Tonight was about them—being together and enjoying each other's company. She wasn't going to ruin it by dwelling on the fact that his visit would be over in a few days and then he'd be back in Kansas, ten hours away. She'd become so attached to him in such a short period of time. How was she going to let him go?

Nathan had her truck keys, and when she reached to take them from him, he pulled his hand away. "Nope. I can't pick you up at your door, but I *will* do the driving. This is a date. Let me show you I can be a gentleman."

"You know, have you ever heard the saying that a gentleman ruins a lady's lipstick, not her mascara? Or the other one, a gentleman opens doors for a lady, so he can smack her ass as she walks through?" Grinning wickedly, Willow fiddled with the buttons on his shirt, blinking up at him with a look of such false innocence, he didn't know if he wanted to laugh or kiss her again. He easily settled on the latter.

"Hmm . . ." He lifted his head, licking his lips. "You don't seem to be wearing any lipstick."

"Not a speck. No mascara either." Smacking a loud peck on his mouth, she swatted his ass. "Let's go—I'm hungry. Wouldn't want me to lose it and eat you, now would we?"

"Oh, but what a way to go . . ." Rolling his eyes at her antics, but loving every second of them, he led her outside and drove them into town. He'd picked Jeremiah's brain earlier and taken his advice. There was only one special, date night-worthy restaurant in town—Bella Mia. It served classic Italian food and good wine, according to Jeremiah anyway.

When they arrived, Nathan missed keeping her from jumping out of the truck again. He wanted to open the door for her, like his father had taught him to do, but the damn stubborn woman kept ruining his plans. He loved her independence, but there were just some things he wanted to do for her for no other reason than it gave him pleasure to treat her the way she deserved.

Inside the charming restaurant, Willow's eyes lit up when she noticed a young man, about seventeen or eighteen, dressed in black jeans, a white shirt, and a black bow tie behind the hostess stand. "Cody! I didn't know you worked here too," she exclaimed, giving him a swift hug before stepping back to Nathan.

The kid's face turned beet red, but he quickly paled and glanced away from Willow's enticing cleavage when he noticed Nathan glaring at him. "Um, yup, I . . . um . . . work here sometimes when I'm not at the store. Usually, I just bus tables, but the regular hostess is sick. They call me in when they're short-staffed. I'm trying to save for college and that tattoo I told you about." He seemed to realize he was babbling and snapped his mouth shut.

Undoubtedly oblivious to the kid's crush on her, Willow set her hand on Nathan's arm. "Nathan, this is Cody Moore. He was one of the first people to be nice to me after I moved here. His sister is my new hairdresser. Cody, this is . . . um . . ."

It was Willow's turn to blush, and Nathan recalled how she'd hesitated earlier in the day when introducing him to Dale. It was clear she was worried about putting a label on their relationship, and he decided to stake his claim once and for all. Holding a hand out to Cody, he said, "Hi, I'm Willow's boyfriend, Nathan Casey."

He wasn't sure who was shocked more, the kid or Willow, but Cody recovered first and shook his hand. "Um . . . hi. It's . . . uh . . . nice to meet you. Let me . . . um . . . . where would you like to sit?"

"Do you have a table that's a little more private than the others?" Nathan asked, resting his hand on the small of her back. He could feel the heat of her skin through her blouse, and he groaned inwardly. God, this woman fired his blood.

"Um, yeah, we do." Avoiding eye contact with both of them, Cody grabbed two menus and led the way past several tables—some of which were occupied, while others sat empty. He stopped by a cozy booth in the back that was a good distance away from the other diners. The round candlelit table was covered with a starched, black cloth and set with elegant white china, silverware, and glasses. Burgundy napkins rested atop the plates and matched the trim around the soft beige walls. Black-and-white prints of Italian landmarks, music playing softly in the background, and low-lit sconces all added to the appealing atmosphere. While the décor wasn't original, it was romantic.

Putting the menus on the table, the teen stepped back. "Your server will be with you in a few minutes to take your drink orders. Please enjoy your date, um, I mean, meal." Blushing again, he swiftly retreated back towards the front door.

"The kid has got it bad for you," Nathan observed, as they sat at opposite ends of the booth's curved, black, leather-covered bench, then scooched in until they were sitting beside each other.

"What? No way! He's just a sweet kid who likes to talk to me about tattoos when I run into him at the store." Opening her menu, she scanned the selections while also hiding her pink cheeks with the leather-bound folder. A teenage busboy set a basket with fresh bread and dish of herbed olive oil on the table, then quickly filled their water glasses before disappearing again.

Nathan grinned at her sudden bashfulness but waited until they were alone again before explaining his earlier observation. "Nope. He might like your tattoos, but he's definitely got a crush on you. Not that I can blame him at all —you're a ten. Scratch that—you're an eleven. If it was anyone other than a teenage kid still in high school, I might have to have words with him in the parking lot for looking down your shirt, but it's pretty cute."

"Cute? You think having your thirty-three-old girlfriend crushed on by someone practically half her age is *cute*?" She glared at him over the top of her menu, making him chuckle.

"Yes. And so are you when you're trying to be all . . ." he waved his hand at her, " . . . what you're doing right now." *Which is making my dick hard.* But he didn't say that. Even acknowledging it to himself was bad enough. He shifted in his seat, trying to get some relief from the throbbing bulge in his pants. Fat chance of that—the woman made him crazy without even trying. God help him if she ever put her mind to it, he'd be toast. Burnt toast with a raging erection.

"You realize you're not making any sense, right?" Smiling, she took a sip of her water.

"You scramble my brains, Wannabe. Give a man a break, here."

Leaning across the table, she pecked a kiss onto his lips, retreating before he had a chance to deepen it into something more.

"Anyway, Cody's a good kid. Like I said, his sister, Ginger, is my new hairdresser. We met at the drunken Jenga night. We're taking Cody and his friend, Bubba—yes, that's his real nickname—to get tattoos next week. Bubba got a really bad tribal one a few months ago that he wants to get covered up with an eagle. Cody had to wait until he turned eighteen a few weeks ago to get one. His mother wouldn't let him do it before then. He wants this really cool one he saw on the shop's website—it'll look like the skin of his upper arm is splitting open, and instead of seeing blood, muscle, and bone, there'll be an American flag behind the opening. I'll show you a picture of it when we go home. Cody's been asking me for my input ever since he saw mine and wanted me to go with them to make sure the artist is talented and has sterile conditions. He's heard too many horror stories, including Bubba's."

He was about to ask her if she would be adding to her own ink, but then he realized they were no longer alone again. A female server had stepped up to their table.

"Hello, and welcome to Bella Mia. I'm Chasity––one of the owners. I apologize in advance, but we're a little short-staffed, so I'll be helping out tonight. Can I get you started with some drinks? Maybe a glass of wine? The house Chianti is wonderful."

Nathan's gaze met the eyes of a short, older woman. Her face framed by bouncing curls that looked bleached blonde. Her hands rested on the small of her back, and she was dressed professionally in the same attire as Cody. However, her face was heavily made up, and instead of making her look younger, it aged her further—he guessed she was around sixty, and that was being generous.

"Sure, wine sounds lovely," Willow said, smiling pleasantly at the server. "The Chianti would be great."

"Excellent. And for you, sir?"

"Whatever IPA you have on draft is fine." He reached over and entwined Willow's fingers with his, wishing the server would disappear, so he could get back to his date.

"I'm sorry," the woman continued, her bright white teeth flashing from behind her painted red lips. "I know this might be a little forward, but I know just about everybody who lives here. Did you just move to the Rock or are you just visiting?"

"I moved here, yes," Willow responded. "A few months ago, but this is the first time I've been here. My father passed away and left me his ranch."

The server's mouth dropped open as her complexion went fish-belly white under her foundation. "That—that wouldn't happen to be Skyview Ranch, now would it?" Her tone had become frigid, and all pretense of politeness had disappeared. "You're Willow Crawford aren't you, Jason Hillcrest's *illegitimate daughter*?" The way she'd said the last two words was as if they disgusted her.

Beside him, Willow stiffened. "Yes, I am. Is that a *problem* for you?" It was her turn to spit icicles. Her hands clenched into fists, and the blood drained from her knuckles.

Oh shit, she's pissed, he thought before he decided to put a stop to this before it ruined their evening.

"Look, Chasity, was it?" Nathan interrupted, not wanting the conversation to go any further south than it already had. "I understand people around here didn't have the best feelings about Mr. Hillcrest, but we're here on our first official date. Could this maybe wait until another time? We'd really just like to order and enjoy our evening." He kept a tight leash on his temper, not willing to let small-town gossip about a dead man mar their evening. He didn't know what the woman's beef was with Willow's father, and honestly, he didn't much care.

"Sure." Chasity bit the word out with venom, spun on her heel, and marched off like someone had stuck a hot poker up her ass.

"That was so ridiculous. What the hell is her problem?" Willow asked. "I'm so sick of this. It's not the first time someone has held my father's less than favorable reputation against me. The man is dead—let him rest in peace. For Christ's sake, I never even met him, so why bitch to me? Why do people have to be so . . . so . . . damn rude?"

"I don't know baby, but let's not allow her to ruin our date." Lifting her hand, he kissed her knuckles, happy to see their normal color had returned. "We still have a movie to get to."

With a somber expression, she studied their joined hands. It killed him to see her feeling even a moment of sadness. "I'm sorry, Nathan. I know I shouldn't let it get to me, but you're right. I'm not going to let anyone spoil our night. But would you mind if we just kept it to dinner this time? We can go to a movie later in the week. Let's eat and then hang out at home. I think I've had just about enough of the Rock for one night."

Home. He liked the sound of that. "Anything you want, Wannabe."

A few minutes later, a different server arrived with their drinks and took their dinner orders. Willow didn't mention the rude woman again, and Nathan followed her lead, putting everything out of his mind but getting to know this amazing woman even more. With the candlelight reflecting off the natural highlights in her hair, her lyrical laugh, and sharp wit while verbally sparring with him, she was the most beautiful woman he'd ever known. If he wasn't in love with her yet, he was well on his way.

CHAPTER TWENTY-THREE

June 18

My Beloved Cherry,

I can't believe it's been three weeks since I last saw you and held you in my arms. I miss you more with every minute, hour, and day that passes. I remember a phrase from when I had to read Romeo and Juliet in high school. Star-crossed lovers. That's what we are—wrong side of the tracks, different upbringing, even our religions don't match up, with me being Catholic and you being Protestant. I just pray we don't meet the same fate. Even if your parents never change their mind about me, I'll find a way for us to be together again. Unfortunately, that might take longer than I'd hoped.

I keep remembering our first date. The only thing I should've done differently would've been to pick you up at your house like a gentleman, bring you flowers, and shake your father's hand. As it is, seeing you waiting for me outside the movie theater, the lights reflecting off your gorgeous hair, is still burned into my brain. You looked so beautiful that I couldn't believe that a woman like you would be interested in a man like me. Never in my life would I have thought to go see The Great Gatsby, but that was the film you'd wanted to see, and that was all that'd mattered to me—I still have our ticket stubs. You let me put my arm around you, and I don't think I watched any of the movie because I was way too busy staring at you. My heart just about exploded when you let me hold your hand afterward as we walked to the restaurant. I still remember the red and white checkered tablecloths and little candles. I realized then that you were even more stunning by candlelight. You'd said it was so romantic. I fell in love with you on that date, my sweet Cherry.

I never found our age difference to be an issue, and I know you didn't either, but our parents and others saw things differently than you and me. If I'd only waited a few more weeks, none of this would've been an issue. But a love like ours couldn't be contained. While I don't regret making love to you, I'm so, so sorry your folks found out, and it ultimately resulted in us being torn apart instead of bringing us closer together like we'd dreamed.

I did some research, and the statute of limitations on the statutory rape charge your father threatened me with is twelve years in PA. Even without your cooperation, he can still persuade the law to pursue charges against me. That's why I can't send these letters to you—he would use any attempt to contact you as an excuse to have me arrested. You begged me to take you with me, but if you came here to live with me—or anywhere else—I could still be arrested and extradited to PA. I want you to finish school and go to college to be a teacher like you always wanted to. I don't want to be the cause of your dreams not coming true. I could never be so selfish to take that from you.

So the only way we can be safe, and for you to get the education you deserve, is to wait the twelve long years. I know that sounds like forever—it would feel like it too—but I'd wait a lifetime if I had to. You mean the world to me, and someday, I'll make my way back to you. I just pray that when I get there, some other man hasn't stolen your heart.

I've been working my ass off here on my uncle's ranch, and I'm so tired by the end of the day, I'm asleep before my head hits the pillow. That's actually a good thing, because then I get to see you again in my dreams.

My great-uncle Simon is a grumpy bastard, but as long as I keep doing a good job, he doesn't bother me. I've learned a lot about ranching over the past few weeks, and despite the hard work, I have to say I'm starting to enjoy it. I'm even learning how to ride a horse.

Living in a small town sure is different than living in Philly. The movie theater is really small and only shows one movie at a time. And everything is slower here. No one is in a hurry, and if you try to rush them, they tell you to stop and smell the roses or some shit like that. The air is so much cleaner—no smog or industrial smells. It does take some getting used to the stench of manure though.

You'd love it here, Cherry. The sunsets are amazing, like a painting, only a hundred times better. Then when the stars come out, there are so many of them that you could spend a lifetime counting them and still not come close to getting them all. I saw a shooting star last night, and I don't have to tell you what my wish was—I'm sure you can guess. I'll just keep making the same wish every time I see one until it comes true. I just have to keep having faith that, one day, I'll get to hold you in my arms again and tell you how much I love you.

Well, it's late, and I have to be up at the crack of dawn, so I'll end this letter. Even though I can't send it, I'll add it to the other one I wrote, and when we're together again, you can read about how my thoughts were always with you.

Love,
J

FOLDING THE LETTER, Willow tucked it back into its envelope, then rested her head on Nathan's shoulder. After dinner, they'd gotten their dessert to go and returned home. With the weird way the owner had reacted to Willow's presence, they hadn't lingered over their meal, opting instead to share a serving of molten-lava cake on the porch swing. As they sat there, she'd let him see the first letter from her father's secret stash before reading the second one aloud to him.

As he used his foot to gently rock the swing back and forth, Nathan placed his arm around her shoulders, gave her a squeeze. "So, they were like Romeo and Juliet—like he said. Her parents, and probably his, weren't happy about the relationship. A few years older and their age difference wouldn't have been an issue. The religious differences I can't comment on, since I've never understood that."

"It doesn't explain why my mother never wanted to talk about him and why he never came back for her. She never married, although she did get engaged once when I was around seven, but it ended a few months later when she found out he was cheating on her. She didn't go to college either, even though she got her GED after I was born."

"Hm. I wonder why she didn't go to college. I mean, I know there was a time when teenage pregnancy was something to be hidden and only talked about in hushed tones. But obviously your grandparents didn't make her give you up for adoption even though she was sixteen when she had you. If they were helping her out, she could've easily gone to school at night, right?"

"I don't know." Willow shrugged. "Hell, I didn't even know she'd wanted to be a teacher when she was younger."

"What were your grandparents like? Did they help her care for you or was she on her own?"

"They didn't kick her out or make her give me up, but I know they resented me—especially my grandfather. We were never close. My grandmother grew to love me, I guess, in her own way, but I think she was always disappointed my mother had to give up her dreams for me—although she never said that around me. My grandfather was the complete opposite—he reminded my mother quite often of all she could've had and done if she hadn't kept me. He worked in the city's sewer system—far from a glorious job. If my mom had actually gone to college, she would've been the first one in the family."

"Did you go to college?" he asked before taking a sip from his beer bottle.

"I went to the community college and got my associates

in liberal arts, not that I really did anything with it, but it made my mom happy."

"What about your grandparents? Were they happy you went to college?"

"At that point, they'd already passed. My grandfather died of a heart attack when I was thirteen, and my grandmother passed away two years later from a stroke. After that, it was just me and my mom. She didn't have any siblings and hadn't stayed close with any of her cousins or aunts and uncles."

"And after she passed away, you were on your own. Just like me. Maybe that's why Fate brought us together."

She lifted her head from his shoulder and looked at him. "You believe in Fate?"

He paused a moment, rubbing his free hand over his short hair, as if gathering his thoughts. "Yeah, I do. We may not always be happy with what Fate sends our way, but a lot of good comes out of it. Think of all the 'what ifs' that had to happen before we got to this moment. What if your father decided you were better off never knowing who he was? What if you'd just told the lawyer to sell the place and send you the money because you wanted to stay in Philadelphia? What if you got here and decided it wasn't for you and still ended up selling it and moving on? What if you never spotted that flyer and sent a letter to Any Soldier. What if, out of all the units your letter could've gone to, it ended up in a different soldier's hand instead of mine? And it's gotta be Fate, don't you think? I know some people say there's no such thing as a coincidence, but I wouldn't have found you without a whole lot of them."

He leaned down and brushed his lips across hers. Willow couldn't help the whimper that escaped her as Nathan deepened the kiss. Fate. Coincidence. God. A being from another universe telepathically manipulating the strange humans on Earth. It didn't matter to her how she'd ended up in Nathan's arms, she was just grateful she had.

Pushing gently on his chest, she withdrew from him and stood, holding out a hand to him. When he took it, she silently led him into the house and down the hall to her bedroom, knowing she'd fallen completely and irrevocably in love with her soul mate.

CHAPTER TWENTY-FOUR

WILLOW SHUT her bedroom door behind them with a soft click. She loved this man, even if she wasn't willing to say the words yet, she was ready to show him. The talk of Fate had made her realize she was no longer willing to wait. If Fate had brought them here, then she was going to take everything Nathan had to offer and give it in return.

Urging him toward the bed, she pulled off her boots and socks, throwing them aside. "I want you," she said before reaching for his belt.

"Hang on." Gripping her fingers, he halted her attempt at undressing him, although he did toe off his sneakers and pull off his socks. "I told you, for our first time together, I was going to take my time with you. That I was going to kiss and lick every inch of your skin. That starts now." He dipped his index finger into the open vee of her shirt and pulled on the material. "Take off your clothes."

Willow's heart was beating like a drum and her panties were soaked, and he hadn't even done more than kiss her. She took a step closer to him and ran a finger down his sternum, wishing there wasn't a shirt between his flesh and hers. "Bossy, much?"

"Oh, baby, you have no idea. I've wanted you for a long time. I have a list." He sat on the queen-size bed, reclining on his elbows. His feet sticking out from the legs of his faded blue jeans drew her gaze. Why did she suddenly think a man's bare feet were sexy? It made no sense—they were just feet, and as a rule, they weren't supposed to be sexy, but somehow, he managed it. "A man on deployment has a lot of time to think about his woman back home, and I thought of little else."

"A-a list?" she stuttered, fiddling with the hem of her blouse. Why was she suddenly so on edge? She wanted this— she wanted him, more than she could express with words. She'd been the one to pull him down the hall and now she was hesitating. Why? Maybe because her feelings for him had hit her all at once and making love with him mattered. It *really* mattered to her, and it meant more than just connecting with another human connection and getting off. It felt momentous and precious, and she didn't want to screw it up.

"Yes, but we'll come back to that. It's long, and I don't plan on checking off all the items tonight. Why are you nervous?"

"I don't know." She shrugged, looking at her feet, wiggling her bare toes into the rug. "I was just trying to figure that out myself. I mean, it's not like I've never had sex before." But even though she wasn't a virgin by any means, in this moment, he made her feel like one. It was the first time intimacy had meant so much more than just the physical aspect, but she wasn't sure she was brave enough to tell him that. Sex was easy, emotions were not.

He growled. "Rule number one—I don't want to hear

about any other man who's been with you. As far as I'm concerned, I'm the first."

She laughed, and some of her anxiety eased. "Come on. Really?"

"Really." Standing, he closed the distance between them and cupped her face in his big, warm, calloused hands. "Logic says, of course you've been with others, but even the thought of another man having the pleasure of touching you . . ." His right hand trailed down her face to her throat, before going further and clasping her breast. He squeezed gently then flicked his thumb across her nipple. "Tasting you . . ." Bending his head, he kissed her throat, making her moan, before licking a stripe up to her ear, where he bit on the lobe. She cried out as shivers wracked her body. "Or sliding deep inside you makes me crazy. I've never been a jealous man, but you make me feel things I never have before."

"Oh God . . ." She ran her hands over his soft, cropped hair, as his mouth left her ear and found her lips. His kissed her like a starving man, and she was a buffet. His mouth was hot and his lips soft. His tongue slid along hers, seeking and stroking. His hands seemed to be everywhere at once, pulling her closer, grabbing her ass, and hauling her up against his hardness. "Nathan . . ." Gasping, she tilted her head to the side as he nuzzled her neck. "What are you doing to me?"

"I have a list, remember? The first thing is to see you naked." Gripping her shirt, he pulled it up and over her head, tossing it over his shoulder. He stared down at her black lace bra for a long moment, before raising his head and meeting her gaze. His blue eyes blazed with desire and need. "You're so beautiful," he whispered, before cupping both hands under her full breasts, hefting their weight in his palms. His thumbs found her nipples again, and she gasped as pleasure zinged straight to her clit. He froze, and his eyes grew wide at his discovery. "Willow? Are these what I think they are?"

Confusion mixed with lust in her muddled brain. "Breasts? Um, yes. They're boobs. I'm sure you've seen some before."

He jerked both bra cups down, tumbling her breasts free and revealing her to the light. "No, smart ass. These." He tugged gently on both her tiny nipple rings, forcing another desperate moan and gasp from her. "You have your nipples pierced."

"Y-yes." *Please don't let that be a turn-off for him*, she thought to herself.

"Fuck, that's so sexy." He latched his mouth on to her right nipple, tugging at the jewelry with his teeth before switching sides and doing the same on the left. Every pull, every suck coursed through her nervous system, and down her belly until they reached her throbbing clit. A whimper escaped her, and he released the piercing. "Does it hurt when I do that?" He didn't give her a chance to answer before he pressed her breasts together and buried his face in her cleavage. "Goddamn woman, I'm about to come in my jeans."

"No, no, it doesn't hurt. It feels really good." Wrapping both arms around his head, she held him to her chest, threw her head back, and reveled in the pleasure he gave her. "So good."

"Yeah?" He lifted his head, keeping his eyes locked onto hers as he slid his palm down her side, gathering her skirt into his fist. He raised it and slipped his hand underneath. Pressing his palm between her legs, over the material of her underwear, he groaned. "Holy shit, your panties are soaked."

"Uh-huh." Pushing his hand out of the way, she tugged on his shirt. "Take this off."

Reaching behind his head, he dragged the garment up and off, letting it fall to the floor at their feet. Willow kissed the tattoo over his heart, once then twice, while tracing her index finger down his cock where it was straining against the confines of his jeans. He canted his hips forward, but she reversed the direction of her finger and ran it up the dark swathe of hair covering his abdomen. When he snaked his arms out to grab her around her waist, she sidestepped him, and he groaned. "Tease."

Sometime during the last few minutes, her nerves had fled—his evident need and desire for her made her feel sexy and powerful. There wasn't room for doubts or second-guessing, not with this heat flaring between them. And fuck, she wanted to burn with him. She unceremoniously unclasped her bra, throwing it aside, before unzipping her skirt, pushing it down, and stepping free of the billowy, white fabric. She stood before him in nothing but flesh-colored cotton panties. His hands twitched at his sides as his hungry gaze roamed every inch of her exposed skin.

"Who's teasing, soldier?" Stepping closer to him, she slowly dropped to her knees at his feet. His hands immediately went to her hair, tilting her head back and meeting her gaze with his own.

"What are you doing?" His voice was gruff and rumbling, low and intense—carnal.

"Don't you know better than to question a woman when she's on her knees in front of you?" She scratched her nails up the denim covering his sinewy thighs, causing the muscles to quiver under her touch. Unclasping his belt, she popped the button on his jeans free and carefully lowered the zipper before tugging his pants down to his ankles. He wore black boxer briefs, the tight material clinging to every inch and ridge of his impressive length. Placing her palm over him, she rubbed up and down firmly, learning his shape. His cock was thick and hard, the broad head pushing out against his boxers as if seeking her touch.

"Willow . . . I don't know . . . shit." He gasped and moaned as she fitted her mouth over his cock, wetting the fabric of his underwear. She could taste the salty essence of his precum where it'd leaked through the material. Resting her face against his thigh, she glanced up at him while rubbing her cheek against his coarse leg hair. His cheeks were flushed, and his chest rose and fell with rapid breaths. Smiling, she kissed his groin again, inhaling deeply and loving the smell of him—a little musky, but warm and all male.

"If you keep putting your mouth on me like that, this is going to be over much sooner than I'd like. I haven't . . ." He paused to gulp, and Willow watched in odd fascination as his Adam's apple moved up and down. "I haven't been with anyone since before my deployment."

"Then you'll have more than one in you." Smirking, she pulled his boxers down, pushing them down to join his pants at his ankles. Once released from its confines, his cock slapped against his lower belly. She gripped his length and pumped a few times, loving the feel of the silky-smooth hardness of his flesh under her hand. Meeting his gaze, she licked him from root to tip, before humming as she softly sucked the wide head between her lips.

"Willow . . . baby, please." His head fell back as she held his cock by the base and drew him into her mouth as far as she could. Her lips stretched around him, and she worked him deeper into her mouth. When the head of his cock hit the back of her throat, she breathed through her nose and swallowed, letting the muscles of her throat close around the tip. Nathan spat out a reverent curse, and his hand in her hair tightened almost to the point of pain. All that did was spur her on.

Drawing back, she bobbed her head, matching the rhythm of her mouth with strokes of her hand. Moaning as his spiciness tantalized her taste buds, she popped her mouth free and licked a bead of precum from the tip. "You taste good."

"Come here." He let out a sexy growl while tucking his hands under her arms and lifting her up to stand. Kicking free from the last of his clothes, he took two steps forward and pushed Willow onto the bed. She landed on her back and bounced, giggling. Her smile disappeared at his intense stare before he stripped her panties from her body, adding them to the pile of clothes on the floor. Nathan crawled over her, settling some of his weight against her. He rubbed his chest against her nipples, forcing a gasp from her lips. Reaching between them, he ran his fingers down her slit, testing her wetness before slipping one, then two fingers inside her. Her body naturally yielded to his invasion. While he stretched and finger-fucked her, he alternated between kissing her and sucking on her pierced nipples. "I love these. I could play with them all day," he said, before tugging on one of the silver rings. "They're so pretty. It's all I can do to keep my hands off you."

"Ah! Please, Nathan, shit! They're so sensitive." Writhing beneath him, she didn't know if she wanted to get closer to him or further away. He was driving her mad with his clever fingers and wicked tongue.

Just as she was sure she was going to come, he retreated, propping himself up on his hands on either side of her head. She glared at him. "W-what? Why are you stopping?" Out of breath and out of her mind with want for him, she was two seconds from flipping him onto his back and taking matters into her own hands, so to speak.

He brushed his mouth across hers. "I don't have a condom on. We should have talked about this earlier."

Biting her lip, she looked down their bodies. Seeing the physical evidence of his desire heated her blood even more. "I'm . . . um . . . I'm on the shot, and I haven't been with anyone since the last time I got tested—which was well over a year ago. I'm clean, if you don't want to use them."

"Willow, are you sure?" His gaze searched her face for any sign of uncertainty, and she was touched he wasn't tossing the important discussion aside after her disclosure. "The army tests us regularly, and I haven't been with anyone since before my last physical, but this is a big deal." He brushed a few strands of her hair away from her cheek before kissing her lips softly.

"I'm sure. I've never been more sure about anything. I want to feel you—all of you."

Taking her at her word, he reached down, lining himself up with her entrance. He rubbed the head of his cock up and down her cleft, spreading her wetness over himself before easing inside her slowly, thrusting shallowly a few times, stopping before he was all the way inside her. "Oh fuck," His body stilled. "You feel like heaven and I'm trying really hard not to embarrass myself here." He drew a noticeably deep breath before continuing.

When he was finally buried to the hilt, they clung to each other, marveling at the feeling of being joined in the most intimate way. It was more intense . . . more everything. Her brain overloaded on pleasure, to the point she couldn't form coherent thoughts. He was thick and filled her to capacity, stretching her in the most delicious way. She clenched around him, and he hissed, resting his forehead against hers.

"Nathan . . . please move. I need you."

"Holy shit, baby. You feel better than I ever imagined." He withdrew and surged forward again, then began alternating between slow, long drags that made her beg and short shallow thrusts that made her gasp and dig her nails into his shoulders. His pace increased and became almost frantic. "I know I said I'd take my time with you, but I can't. You're just . . . too . . . *shit*. . . so . . .wet . . . and warm . . . fuck!"

Tilting her hips, she met him thrust for thrust and after that, there were no more words. Their bodies did their talking for them. Together, they climbed higher and higher. Willow lost all perception of time. Her senses were full of Nathan.

The heady, masculine smell of his skin.

The zesty taste of him on her tongue.

The sounds of pure pleasure erupting from him.

The hedonistic expression she saw on his face.

The feel of him driving deep inside her, hitting the spot that had her begging him to send her over the edge.

She was drowning in him and loved every second of it. She'd had sex before, but she now understood that was all it had been during those encounters . . . just sex. But with Nathan, she was making love. They were two completely different things when you were with the right person and emotions were involved. The only sounds in the room were their gasps and moans of pleasure and the slap of flesh against flesh.

Willow's climax hit her out of nowhere, bowing her back with the force of it. Digging her fingers into his shoulders, she cried out, jerking with the shredding force of her release. Nathan plunged into her once, twice more and held himself deep inside her as he followed her into a sea of sheer bliss. His head fell against her shoulder as the warmth of his release bathed her insides. That was a first for her, and she treasured the feelings, knowing he was closer to her than anyone else had ever been.

The waves of her orgasm crashed over her and seemed to go on forever before releasing her from the turbulent riptide. Panting and sweating, Willow lay beneath Nathan and tried to catch her breath. "I'm . . . pretty sure . . . you killed some of my brain cells."

"Well, the feeling . . . is mutual." They stayed joined

together until their lungs replenished their loss of oxygen. Gently pulling out of her, making them both wince at the oversensitivity, Nathan flopped onto his back beside her and gathered her close. "I'll get a cloth to clean us up in a second, as soon as I'm sure my legs will hold me."

"No rush. I get it. I *sooo* get it." In fact, her legs gave a violent twitch, and she giggled in pure delight. "See? Aftershocks, because you rocked my world."

Lifting her chin, she met his eyes, and they both dissolved into laughter until their sides hurt.

"Baby, can I just say . . ." Nathan laced his fingers through hers and brought her hand to his mouth, kissing her knuckles. "You amaze me, and not just because making love to you blows my damn mind."

"Blows other things too." She grinned, pinching his side with her free hand.

"Ouch!" Swatting her away playfully. "Minx! Anyway," he continued. "I can't remember ever laughing after sex before. You're . . ." Rolling to his side so he was facing her, he tucked a piece of her hair behind her ear. It was a move he'd done often over the past few days, and it never failed to make her insides melt a little. "You're everything. I don't want to ever let you go."

"So don't." Leaning forward, she kissed him, sweeping her tongue deep into his mouth. She was desperate for him again already. Rolling him over, she straddled his hips and showed him exactly how well she'd learned to ride.

CHAPTER TWENTY-FIVE

THURSDAY MORNING, they worked side-by-side, repairing fence around the pasture. It was hard, monotonous work—pulling the old wire off, replacing the broken and rotted posts, then stringing new wire, all while trying not to cut themselves to ribbons. Heavy work gloves protected their hands but did nothing for their exposed forearms. Willow only had a few more weeks left of warmer weather to get things done outside, and Nathan had wanted to help her as much he could. She was grateful but still felt bad he was working during his time off.

"I bet this isn't the way you thought you'd spend your leave. Fixing a stupid fence," Willow grumbled, angry at her father for letting the ranch settle into such a state of disrepair.

"No, but I will say it's still a hell of a lot better than being in Iraq. No burn pits, no RPGs or rockets going off, and no gunfire. I'll take fixing fences all day over that. Plus, you're here." Winking at her, he pulled the wire taut, holding it fast against the new post while Willow nailed it into place.

"I don't like to think about it. You being in danger like that, I mean."

"Then don't, it's over. I don't have to go back. Just a few more months, and I'll be out of the Army for good and free to go wherever I want."

She bit her tongue, knowing it was way too soon for her to ask him to move there to be with her. He'd probably think she was either desperate or insane if she suggested it now. Determined to change the subject, she said, "I was thinking, do you want to go out tonight? After we finish the fencing, I know I'm going to be too tired to cook. How do burgers and beer sound?"

"Burgers and beer sound perfect." Smiling at her, he moved onto the next post. Pulling the leaning and rotting wood from the ground, he tossed it into the back of her old truck before installing a new one. They worked in sync for several more hours, replacing the damaged fence line around what would be the alpaca pasture. Willow hadn't been able to stop imagining them working side by side like that for the rest of their lives, raising alpacas and, maybe someday, a few kids. She could even envision what they would look like—a little boy, with Nathan's blue eyes and dark hair, and a little girl, in brown pigtails with hot pink on the tips.

She jerked back on the reins of her imagination. *Slow your roll, psycho.* They were so not at that point yet. They were, technically, only a few days into a relationship—thinking about kids now made her into that crazy lady that talks about the wedding on the first date.

🦌

THAT EVENING, after showering together, which led to a very satisfying orgasm for them both, Willow finished getting dressed. She slipped her black, Johnny Cash t-shirt over her head, pairing it with faded blue jeans and her favorite bright pink Chuck Taylors. She might be living in Wyoming now, and even own two pairs of cowboy boots, but that didn't mean she had to give up her favorite things from her life in Philly. A spritz of perfume and she was ready to go.

Joining Nathan in the living room, she found him dressed similarly in jeans and a dark red t-shirt. The color looked amazing with his dark hair and tanned skin tone. Heavy black boots completed his outfit.

"I don't know, we might need to stay home," she said, eyeing him from head to toe.

Concern immediately darkened his features. "Oh? Why? You okay?"

"Oh, I'm great. But when the women in town catch sight of you, I'm sure I'm going to have to let loose my Philly fighting skills. Or bring my gun . . ."

Laughing, he gathered her close. "Don't worry, Wannabe, you're the only woman I see. The only one I *want* to see." After kissing her soundly, he let her go and grabbed his wallet and the truck keys. "Don't even bother trying to bring any money. ID only. I'm paying. And driving."

Rolling her eyes but deciding not to argue, Willow pulled her father's Flyers ball cap down on her head, slipped her ID into her back pocket, and led the way to her truck. She'd called Jeremiah earlier to see if he wanted to join them, but he'd said he was beat and would catch up with them tomorrow.

Arriving at the Spur & Bull, Nathan parked her truck in the last available spot. Several people were milling about, talking and smoking, while Lynyrd Skynyrd flowed from the open front door of the bar. "Why is it so busy? Holy shit, it's a Thursday. Don't people have work in the morning?"

"Tonight's ten-cent wings and free pool." Willow pointed to a poster in the window by the door. "Every weeknight, it's something different. I've been here maybe three or four times. The food is great. They have a deejay and live bands on the weekends a lot too. Though I avoid the line dancing—that is so *not* my thing. I've got two left feet."

"That makes two of us, but the rest I can go for. Stay right there a sec, Wannabe." She narrowed her eyes at him but didn't move. It took her a moment to realize why he'd issued the order. After climbing from the truck and rounding the hood, he opened her door, took her hand, and helped her down before leading her inside. No doubt he was staking his claim publicly from the start. She smiled at the thought. She could really get into possessive Nathan, as much as she liked bossy-in-the-bedroom Nathan. With any other guy, those traits would probably have been turn-offs.

Inside, where the music was even louder, they were assaulted by the smell of beer and fries and the distinctive *clack* of pool balls breaking. The rumble of conversation rose and fell all around them. The place was packed with men in cowboy hats and women in rhinestone embellished jeans.

"What, no mechanical bull?" Nathan joked, towing her around the long U-shaped bar to the far side where they, surprisingly, found two stools opening up. They would be sitting with their backs to the dance floor and the two pool tables, which Willow didn't prefer, but choices were limited. Even the scattered tables were filled.

"Nope. Sorry to disappoint. I realize the name might be a little misleading." Pointing around the bar, she continued, "But the décor speaks for itself." Horns of all shapes and sizes lined the walls. Longhorns, ram horns, deer antlers, and everything in between. Many of them had pairs of spurs dangling from them. From rusty and old to brand new and shiny, the décor was eclectic and original. One whole wall, behind the pool tables, was filled with photos of varying sizes of past and present customers. Some were of people celebrating different milestones, like birthdays, anniversaries, and at least one shotgun wedding, while others were of friends just having a good time on a night out on the small town. Several were taken at rodeos, with chap wearing cowboys and rodeo queens holding up shiny buckles.

When Nathan and Willow took their seats, Maddie Carmichael immediately came over and leaned across the bar to hug her. "Willow! It's so good to see you, honey. And who is this handsome devil?" Maddie winked at Nathan, flipping her waist-length dirty-blonde hair back off her face. "Is this the spicy piece of man meat you told us about at Jenga night?"

Man meat? Nathan mouthed at her, while her face flamed red with embarrassment. "Maddie, I thought anything said at Jenga nights was sacred and never to be repeated. And yes, this is Nathan Casey, my . . . uh . . . he's . . . mine."

Giggling madly, Maddie reached over the bar and shook Nathan's hand. "Oh, yes, any fool with eyes can see he's all yours. Got any friends?" she asked him with a twinkle in her eyes.

"Actually, yes." Grinning, Nathan slid his hand onto the top of Willow's thigh, squeezing and massaging it. "My buddy, Zach Ramsey, would probably get along with you just fine. I'll have to get him up here sometime. He's getting out of the Army next summer. "

"Zach Ramsey, huh?" Maddie purred, her flirty personality coming to the forefront. She was always a little wilder when she bartended—she said it helped with tips. "I like the sound of that just fine. I'm going to hold you to that introduction. Now, what can I get you two kids tonight?"

"I'll have an IPA, and Willow?" Nathan raised his brow at her in question, as he handed over his debit card for their tab.

"Jack and Coke, please. It feels like a whiskey kinda night."

"Coming right up. One beer that tastes like dirty feet and a glass of bad decisions in the making." Maddie slapped the bar top with her hand and then sashayed over to the other end to draw his beer and mix Willow's drink.

"Dirty feet? Bad decisions?" Nathan flexed his fingers where he was still gripping her thigh, and the intimate touch stirred her desire again. "Ramsey would love her—he likes his women sassy. She sure knows how to sell this place, huh?"

She shivered and shifted in her seat, as memories of the previous night's sex marathon they'd shared flashed in her mind. "Something like that. Maddie is a riot when she lets loose."

"Apparently, so are you. *Spicy man meat*? Care to explain that, Wannabe?"

Willow used the distraction of Maddie delivering their drinks and food menus to avoid the question. They quickly decided on their dinners, wings for Nathan and a burger and fries for her.

"I'm waiting." Nathan nudged her with his elbow after Maddie left them again to put their orders into the kitchen.

She shrugged. "What can I say? I was drunk. What was said can't be held against me." After swirling the straw around in her drink, she took a long draw on it and swallowed while avoiding his gaze.

"Nice try, woman." Leaning closer, he kissed her neck before licking a path to her ear, where he nibbled on her ear lobe and whispered softly, "I think, you were thinking an awful lot about my *man meat* back when this fire between us was just on paper. I'm *thinking* . . ." He kissed her jaw, turning her face with his hand, so he could reach her mouth. Speaking against her lips, he continued, ". . . you like me a whole awful lot, Wannabe, and I'm *thinking* you need another taste of how much I like you in return."

"Umm hmm. That sounds good. Yup. Let's do that," Willow mumbled before kissing him. She couldn't get enough of the man, his rough kisses and gentle hands. She'd never wanted someone this desperately before. She was a stranger to this level of need, but she'd decided to embrace it with both hands.

"Now, Willow, are you going to introduce me to the man before you suck his face off in public? This town does have laws about that, you know."

Jerking back, Willow looked over Nathan's shoulder to see Sheriff Grady Minor grinning at her. "Erm." She was pretty sure her cheeks were hot enough to fry an egg on. Clearing her throat, she tried again. "Um, Nathan, this is Grady Minor, the local sheriff."

"Pleased to meet you, Sheriff," Nathan said as he stood and offered his hand. "Willow told me about the trouble she had, and I'm grateful to you for your help." After they shook, he added, "Please have a seat. Can I buy you a beer?"

"I was just doing my duty, as you know all about from personal experience. And I don't mind if I do. Please, call me Grady—I've got the night off."

Nathan moved to stand behind Willow, holding his beer in one hand and keeping his other wrapped possessively around her shoulders. "Duty or not, I still appreciate it. Though the way Willow here told the story, she had it well in hand."

"Very true." Chuckling, Grady accepted his beer from Maddie, who'd brought it over without being asked.

"Put that on my tab, please," Nathan told her before turning his attention back to the sheriff. "I still feel better knowing you're around to look out for her when I can't be here. That ex of hers has a reckoning coming if he shows his face again."

"I'll tell you the same thing I told Annie Oakley over here, make sure it's justified, but I'd prefer if you didn't kill him. The paperwork for that is a bitch." He gave Willow a wink. "Care for a shot, girl? I remember you seemed to like them well enough last time."

Groaning, she covered her face with her hands and replied through her fingers, "No. Never again will I do shots with you, or Maddie or Jeremiah for that matter. It took me two days to recover from the last time."

"Willow! What else aren't you telling me?!" Nathan sounded appalled, but the grin on his face and amusement in his eyes belied his tone. "You got drunk with the *sheriff*?"

"Ugh, yeah. And Maddie and Jeremiah and a bunch of other people. After I shot at . . . I mean, *near*," she emphasized, looking pointedly at the lawman, "my ex, Grady told me it's like a rite of passage for Wyomingites to get drunk after they shoot at . . . *near* someone. So, I believed him. I mean, why would a sheriff lie, right? Jeremiah drove me here, and I swear, after Grady told everyone the story, half the bar bought me drinks. I had no bar bill that night, but the headache lasted for days. If anyone brings Fireball anywhere near me tonight, I might just puke on you—fair warning." In reality the evening had turned into an impromptu party, with the local ranchers welcoming her into the fold, so to speak. Some were still salty about her father, but most of them had put that aside. The problems she still encountered around town seemed to be from a group of church ladies and anyone related to the Jenkins family.

It was a bit weird how she'd been shy, with few friends back in Philly, where her tattoos, pink hair, and nose stud had fit in. But in the Rock, where none of those things were common, she was coming out of her shell and having more fun than she'd had in years, if ever.

When their food arrived, Grady excused himself to let them eat, inviting Nathan to shoot a game of pool when they finished. Maddie's shift was about to end too, and she said she'd keep Willow company while Nathan and Grady played.

Three hours later, Willow stood with her back against the wall, drinking a soda, and laughing at a drunk Nathan. If the man was a charming rogue when sober, he turned into a Casanova after he got a good buzz going. When not taking his turn at pool, he couldn't keep his hands off her—to the amusement and delight of the entire bar. After his fifth beer, and the two shots they'd done with Grady, she'd switched to straight Coke and managed to sneak the truck keys from his pocket, earning a nod of approval from the lawman.

"Listen h-here, Sheriff—" Nathan began before he was interrupted by his own loud hiccup. He mumbled an apology and pointed at the older man with his pool cue. "All this country music isn't good for the soul. I mean, it's so damn *sad. So* sad. Who the hell wants to be sad all the fuckin' time? Not me. Not that I am. Look at that gorgeous woman over there." Winking at her, he leaned forward and lined up his shot. "She makes me so damn happy, and this sad-ass, cryin'-in-my-beer, my-dog-died-and-took-my-truck, country twang bullshit ruins that for me." Grady opened his mouth to respond, but Nathan kept going. "Or is it my wife died and took my truck? No, it's definitely my dog died. Right? Whatever, it doesn't matter. It all sucks."

"Nathan, my friend, you're not going to change many minds around here. Sure, we listen to rock and such, but country music holds our soul and that won't be changing anytime soon." They'd been arguing good-naturedly about the pros and cons of country music for a while now.

Flapping his hand in dismissal, Nathan finally took his

shot. And missed. Again. He really was terrible at pool and got worse as his buzz got better. "What the fuck? I swear this table is crook'd."

"Baby, the table is fine. It's you who's crooked." Willow pointed down to Nathan's feet, noting he couldn't stand still and was swaying widely from side-to-side.

"Oh." He looked down and carefully, and very slowly, moved his feet to shoulder-width apart, bracing himself like he was standing on the rolling deck of a ship instead of a barroom floor. "You're right, Wannabe. Look at that!" Mumbling to himself, he moved to take another shot, even though it wasn't his turn, and stumbled again.

Handing her unfinished drink to Maddie, who nodded and shooed her off, she stepped over to her very drunk boyfriend and wrapped an arm around his waist. "Come on, soldier boy, time to get you to bed."

"Soldier boy? Try s-soldier man!" She laughed when he leaned down and sniffed her hair loudly. "Goddamn, Wannabe, you smell so fuckin' good. How come you always smell so nice? I could just eat you up. Hmm . . . now that, *that* is a fine idea. Let's go. See ya, Sheriff!" Waving, Nathan led the way. She guessed when he decided he was ready to go, he was ready. Not that he'd be eating anything when they got home, except maybe a sandwich to soak up more of the alcohol in his gut.

Grady and most of the other patrons laughed loudly and waved goodbye in return, accompanied by shouts, catcalls, and shrill whistles. Nathan spun around, almost tripping over Willow, and took a bow to the crowd. Grabbing his arm and waist, she barely kept him from face-planting. "Come on, Nathan, you're going home to bed."

"Not without you, I'm not. I have plannnssss." He drew the word out as if it had ten syllables instead of one.

"Of course you do, and you can feel free to tell me all about them. In the morning."

Sure enough, Nathan was snoring half-way home. He was passed out cold, with his face smashed against the window and his mouth hanging wide open. Willow smiled and was tempted to pull over just so she could take a picture of him with her phone.

After she got them back to Skyview and parked the truck, Nathan woke up just enough to stumble his way inside and into her bed with her assistance. Willow stripped him of his boots and clothes, evading his wandering hands and ignoring his begging the entire time. She couldn't help but laugh at his pout when she tucked him in, leaving a glass of water and pain reliever on the bedside table.

"Go to sleep. I have to take care of the chickens and check on Ethel, and then I'll be back."

"'Kay," he mumbled into his pillow, already falling back asleep. "'Ov you."

Her heart seemed to skip a beat as she froze for a moment, not sure if he'd really just said what she thought he had. Pushing the ridiculous notion aside, she did her evening chores quickly before undressing and climbing into bed beside him. He muttered something before rolling over and wrapping her up into his arms, sighing heavily into her hair. "Mmm . . ."

She drifted off, her mind and heart full of possibilities of their future. She was afraid to hope for too much, but the man holding her was breaking all her barriers and making it impossible not to.

CHAPTER TWENTY-SIX

"Ready, soldier?" Willow asked, putting on the cowboy hat she'd apparently bought after her first riding lesson, before grabbing the truck keys and a denim jacket for later when the temperature was expected to drop.

They hadn't done much yesterday, besides binging on the *Fast & Furious* series while pigging out on junk food, mainly because of Nathan's massive hangover. It'd been a while since he'd gotten that intoxicated—well over a year—but Willow had insisted she hadn't minded. In fact, she'd called him a cute drunkard.

"Sure thing, Wannabe. I haven't been to a rodeo since I was a teenager. I'm really looking forward to it." Hell, even if he wasn't, he'd go anywhere and do anything as long as it was with her. She had him wrapped around her little finger and didn't even realize it. It was a place he was very happy to be.

"Well, I've *never* been to a rodeo, except the ones in my bedroom the past few nights." Laughing, she winked and smacked his ass, making him yelp and jump, before following him out the door. He caught her around the waist and kissed her senseless, wanting to savor every moment with her. The timing of the local event they were going to, that had apparently drawn entries from all over the state, couldn't have been better. He was leaving tomorrow and desperately needed a distraction from the fact. He'd never considered going AWOL before, but being with her made the idea tempting.

When he finally let her go, and they descended the front steps, Willow continued, "Jeremiah and one of his ranch hands are competing, and I promised I'd cheer them on. Plus, it's for charity. It was in the newspaper, and there've been posters and flyers about it all over town for a few weeks now. All the proceeds from today go to the Chriscos, a family from Butterfield, which is the next town over. Their son suffered a severe TBI in Afghanistan, and they need remodeling done on their house to accommodate his wheelchair and things."

"An even better reason to go. We'll make sure to make a donation too." Stopping beside the truck, Nathan couldn't help himself—he grabbed her again and stole another deep kiss, bending her backward over his arm. Every time he touched her, she fired his blood and turned his cock hard as a post. He didn't know what he was going to do after he had to say goodbye to her tomorrow and return to his lonely apartment in Kansas—probably cry himself to sleep like a little bitch. The week had flown by, and he was already counting the days until he could get leave again and come back.

Refusing to think about it anymore until tomorrow, he promised himself he would enjoy the day and the remaining time he had with Willow.

They arrived at the county fairgrounds in Butterfield to a scene of controlled chaos. In the huge parking area, rows of livestock trailers mixed with campers and trucks. Tailgaters were aplenty as people played cornhole, caught up with friends and family, and enjoyed their day off work. It was loud, dusty, and smelled of sweat, manure, beer, and barbecue.

"Holy shit," Willow murmured. "This is awesome."

Laughing at her surprise, and happy he could experience her first rodeo with her, he draped his arm over her shoulders and followed a line of people past a row of vendors, toward the main entrance. After buying their tickets at a booth, he led her through the doors to the main arena while keeping a hand on her at all times. There were quite a few cowboys shooting appreciative glances her way. He couldn't blame them—she looked hot in her tight jeans, cowboy boots, and snug, vintage Van Halen t-shirt. But Willow was his, and if he had to keep her plastered to his side all day, well, that was just fine with him.

Like outside, there were people inside selling everything from event t-shirts and western apparel to toys for kids. Booths offered a variety of carnival food and ice cream. Spotting a beer kiosk, he tugged her along by the hand. "Want a beer?"

"I never say no to cold beer and the company of a sexy-as-sin man." She smirked when he shot her a look over his shoulder and raised a questioning brow.

"You, of course." She ogled him from head to toe and back up again, gesturing to his fine physique. "I mean, the company of *this* sexy-as sin-man."

"Nope, she meant me." Willow's hand was pulled free from Nathan's, and he spun around to see Jeremiah embrace her and lift until her feet left the ground. If it'd been any other man, that would've been the start of a brawl, but he'd grown fond of her neighbor who treated Willow like she was his kid sister instead of just a friend.

"Good try, but she's taken." While they greeted each other, Nathan paid for his and Willow's beer. Jeremiah was wearing chaps, a protective vest, and had a contestant number affixed to his back. His usual tan hat had been replaced with a black Stetson. Spurs on his boots jangled with every step.

Smiling, Nathan took a sip of his beer, before licking foam off his upper lip and nodding at the other man. "Check you out. You look like a real cowboy and everything. Who'd you steal the snazzy outfit from?"

"Ha. Boy's got jokes, huh? I'd like to see you throw yourself off a horse and rope a steer. It'd be hilarious. Or better yet, get that ass on the back of two-thousand pounds of pissed-off bull."

"Nah, I give him all the rides he needs," Willow snarked at Jeremiah as she took the cup of beer Nathan held out to her. She lowered her voice before adding, "But here you are, riding smelly livestock instead of your own hot man."

Nathan snorted, offering her a high-five. "Nicely done, baby."

"You guys are fucking assholes," Jeremiah grumbled good-naturally as an announcement blared loudly, declaring the start of the events. "That's me—gotta go." He kissed Willow's cheek swiftly and jogged off, spurs clicking and the fringe on his chaps slapping against his thighs.

Pivoting in the opposite direction, Nathan and Willow headed for the stands to find good seats. Country music played loud enough to be felt through the soles of their feet, and Willow was so excited, he couldn't help but be infected by it.

As they weaved their way through the crowd, a woman stepped in front of them, stopping them in their tracks. She was wearing black jeans, cowboy boots, a brown cattleman hat, a blue western shirt with "Event Staff" embroidered on the left side of her chest, and a broad smile. "Hi, I'm Tina Malcolm, one of the rodeo organizers, and I noticed your shirt," she said, gesturing to Nathan's green t-shirt, with "US Army" in large lettering on it, that he was wearing over a pair of faded jeans. "Are you a veteran or still serving?"

Caught off guard, it took him a second to respond. "Um . . . I'm . . . um, still serving. Got a few months left before my discharge is final."

The woman held out her hand for him to shake, which he accepted. "Thank you for your service. I'd like to invite you to join other current members of the military and some veterans in the center of the arena for the national anthem. We wanted to honor as many service members that are attending the rodeo as we could."

"Uh . . ." He glanced at Willow, then back at Tina. "Thanks, but I don't want to leave Willow alone."

"No worries. She's more than welcome to stand with you. There will be several significant others and kids out there. Please, we'd be honored if you joined them."

When he looked at Willow again, she smiled and nodded at him. If he wanted to do this, she was clearly giving him her support. He squeezed her hand, proud to have her at his side. "Uh, sure. We'd love to. Thank you."

"It's my pleasure," Tina replied. "If you come with me, I'll take you to where everyone is lining up behind the honor guard. When you're done, we've roped off a section of the best seats for you and the others."

Less than ten minutes later, after shaking hands with about a dozen members of the military, both active duty and veterans, along with their family members, Nathan and Willow walked out into the center of the dirt arena with everyone. The group was led by three teenage girls, dressed in fancy western shirts covered in sequins, riding horses. Each of the girls carried a pole with a flag to honor America, the state of Wyoming, and those who'd served and were POW or MIA. They stopped in the middle of the arena as the spotlights made their countless sequins sparkle.

Willow and Nathan stood between a Vietnam veteran, who'd served in the Navy, and his two grandchildren, and a Marine, who'd lost a leg in the early days of Operation Iraqi Freedom, and his wife.

"Please rise for the national anthem," the male announcer said over the loudspeaker. The crowd stood, removed their hats, and placed their right hands over their hearts. Nathan barely kept himself from saluting, since he wasn't in uniform. It would be a hard habit to break when he became a civilian again.

"Joining us in the center ring with the honor guard are veterans and current members of the United States military and their families. Please give them a round of applause to acknowledge their service and thank them." A roar went up in the crowd as everyone clapped and whistled. Many in the group they were honoring waved and tipped their hats. After a few moments, when the din had died down, the announcer continued, "Today, the anthem will be sung by Isabella Chrisco, sister of Private First Class 'Big' Jim Chrisco, who we're all here to support today. The entire Chrisco family thanks you for your attendance."

A tall, pretty woman in her early twenties stepped up to a microphone that'd been placed in front of the honor guard. "O, say can you see . . ."

Nathan's heart beat faster, swelling with pride, same as it did every single time he stood for the colors and anthem. He loved being a soldier and serving his country, but his enlistment was almost up, and he couldn't wait to start the next chapter of his life. Hopefully, with Willow at his side. It was the first time since he'd lost his family that he truly looked forward to something—a lifetime of somethings.

As the song finished, the crowd broke into loud applause again before resuming their seats. The honor guard rode off to the gate they'd all entered from, while several event staff members directed Nathan, Willow, and the others to the reserved section of seats, where they'd be front and center for all the rodeo action.

The first competition was the women's barrel racing, which had Willow's eyes popping out of their sockets. The competitors thundering around the stationary barrels had enthralled her. Dirt clods flew through the air, kicked up by the hooves of the horses galloping like the wind. When a new best time was posted, Willow shook her head. "Crap! I'll never be able to ride a horse that fast."

Nathan put his arm around her. "Maybe not fast enough for competition, but you'll get there, baby. You did great when we went riding the other day." While she still needed more practice when it came to cantering and galloping, she'd done well with trotting when they'd gone on a trail ride through a local wildlife park with her instructor the other day. It'd been a lot of fun, but Nathan had paid for it the next day. Like he'd told Willow, it'd been years since he'd ridden a horse, and his ass and thighs had painfully reminded him of that fact. Thankfully, Willow had offered to apply a healthy dose of arnica gel to his aching body parts. The massage she'd given him had been fantastic, almost as amazing as the sex that'd followed.

Up next was the calf roping competition, which was Jeremiah's event. While Willow's neighbor had posted an impressive time, he'd lost out on winning the event when the last roper took the lead.

After his ranch hand, Ethan Rivers, had placed third in steer wrestling, or bulldogging as it was also called, Jeremiah had taken off his chaps and spurs and managed to track down Willow and Nathan in the crowd. Luckily, there'd been an empty seat for him next to Willow. Nathan flagged down a beer vendor to buy Jeremiah and himself a round to toast his second-place award.

It wasn't until Nathan handed the other man the aluminum beer bottle that he noticed the guy looked pissed about something—and he didn't think it was because Jeremiah had lost the first-place buckle. He was about to ask him if he was okay, but the announcer called out the name of the lead-off competitor in the next event. "Our first bronc rider of the day is Dale Harris."

Nathan furrowed his brow at Willow. "Isn't that your new foreman's name?"

"It is. Think it's the same guy?" she asked.

"It's the same fucker all right—I saw him down in the chutes," Jeremiah grumbled just loud enough for Nathan and Willow to hear him.

"You saw him? What happened, Jeremiah? Please don't tell me you got into an argument or something with him. He's going to be living on my ranch and working for me in a few weeks."

A snort was his reply followed by, "Don't worry, Willow-girl. I'll be more than happy to avoid the pompous ass from now on." He mumbled a few more choice insults under his breath.

Willow looked at Nathan and rolled her eyes. "Well, isn't that just fucking peachy."

Nathan didn't think Jeremiah could get more pissy than he already was at Dale, until after the guy won his event. As he stood in the center of the arena and accepted his prize, his gaze seemed to zero in on Jeremiah out of the hundreds of people there. Nathan's eyes nearly bugged out when Dale blew a kiss Jeremiah's way. No one else beside him, Willow, and Jeremiah could probably figure out who the man had been looking at when he'd made the gesture, but Jeremiah's face blooming beet red and his expression turning thunderous was all the confirmation Nathan needed. Clearly something had happened between the two men, and Willow's friend wasn't one bit happy about it.

Before Nathan and Willow could ask Jeremiah what in the hell was going on, the man excused himself and left the stands. Willow stared after him and then shook her head. "Yup, this is going to be a riot."

Putting his arm around her shoulders, Nathan pulled her close and kissed her temple. "Just another day at the rodeo, Wannabe. As for those two, they're men, they'll settle it. Probably with fists, but you need to leave them to it." Although, after that blown kiss, Nathan wondered if they'd be using other body parts to settle things. Either way, it was none of his business.

"Boys are so dumb sometimes." Rolling her eyes, Willow added, "And yes, I meant *boys*—at least when it comes to those two acting like children."

Laughing, he kissed her again. "You're not wrong, baby, you're not wrong. I was at least smart enough to know a good thing when I saw it."

Her blush charmed him. He loved that he could make the rosy glow appear on her skin. Though he'd much rather they were in private, where he could watch the color spread down her chest. Those damn nipple rings of hers drove him crazy, and he got half-hard just thinking about them.

The events concluded, with the winners keeping their buckles and ribbons and donating their cash prizes to the Chrisco family. Nathan loved hearing that. It was the same thing the people in his hometown would've done too.

Full of fried foods and beer, Nathan and Willow strolled out with the crowd to the parking lot. It'd been a long but fun day.

Arriving back at the ranch, they quickly locked the chickens in for the night before heading into the house and collapsing onto the couch together. Ethel found her way into Nathan's lap, as was becoming her custom.

"I don't know what she's going to do without you tomorrow. Probably be really sad and cry a lot." Willow spoke softly while stroking the feline's fur rhythmically. Ethel purred in response, oblivious to the tension creeping between the couple.

Knowing they weren't really talking about the cat, he decided to play along anyway. "I'll be sad too. I'll miss her like crazy. But I hope she's not too sad. She knows I'm going to be back just as soon as I can manage it."

"Really?" Willow looked up at him, her eyes so big and wide—full of hope.

"Of course, baby. I wanna be in Wyoming. It's where my girls are." He winked at her. "And Fred too—can't forget about him."

Shifting over and shooing away Ethel, who gave her an indignant glare, Willow straddled Nathan's lap, wrapped her arms around his shoulders, and sighed. "Good, because we want you here too."

Returning her embrace, he buried his face in her hair, inhaling deeply. He wished he could put her in his pocket, take her with him, and keep her beside him always. It should've been too soon to be feeling so strongly, but there was no stopping the freight train of emotions barreling through him. This woman was it for him. He knew it to the depths of his soul. He just needed to find the balls to tell her and hope like hell that she felt the same way.

CHAPTER TWENTY-SEVEN

WILLOW MANAGED to control her tears until she'd driven all the way home and parked her truck in the driveway. As soon as the engine shut off, there was no holding them back. Sobs ripped from her throat, as she rested her head against the steering wheel.

She felt like her heart was splitting in two——half was here with her and the other half just boarded a plane for Kansas. She knew she'd see him again——hell, he'd promised to Skype that night——but now that she'd had him in her home and in her bed, she wanted him there always.

She cried until her head was pounding and her face throbbed. Her chest ached, both with physical and emotional pain. If Nathan knew she'd broken down like this, he'd be as devastated for that as she was over him leaving. Her one comfort was knowing their separation was temporary. He wasn't going overseas again, and as soon as his exit paperwork was finished, he'd be done with the Army. She hadn't been brave enough to ask him to live here with her, a decision she was regretting now.

The truck was still running, and the radio began to play

"Here Without You" by 3 Doors Down. Screeching in frustration, she smashed the buttons until the song stopped.

"Now, darlin', is that really how you should be treating this fine truck?"

"Ack!" Yelping in surprise, Willow clutched her chest. Jeremiah stood outside her open window with his hat tipped back on his head and his thumbs tucked into the pockets of his Wranglers. He looked like a gay ginger extra from a John Wayne film.

"Fuck right off! Holy shit you scared me!"

He snorted. "I'm not surprised. You were sitting there with the radio blasting, crying like your dog died. A herd of elephants could be stomping through here with a high school marching band and the naked cast of *Magic Mike*, and you wouldn't have noticed a damn thing. And not noticing the strippers would've been a sin, by the way, darlin'." Stepping forward, he rested his forearms on the door, leaning down so he could look her in the eyes. "He went back today."

It wasn't a question, but she nodded anyway. Just thinking about Nathan being gone made her tears well up again.

"Come on, Willow-girl. What you need is a distraction. And I've got just the thing." Opening the truck door, he didn't wait for her to climb down. He just grabbed her hand and pulled her from the vehicle and into his arms for a brief hug. "You have horses and those fluffy things arriving soon, and I'm here to help figure out what renovations we need to do to the barns. I even have a notebook." He pulled a battered, black-and-white composition book from his back pocket. He'd folded it in half to get it into the tight spot, but from the state of the deeply creased cover, that was a regular occurrence.

"Jesus, what did you do to that poor thing?" She looked at

it aghast, offended that he'd treat a book that way, even one that was meant to be written in.

Glancing down at the book and then back up at her, his brow furrowed in confusion. "What? I have to fold it, otherwise it won't fit in my damn pocket. It's not like I've got a free hand to be carrying it around. Book in one pocket, work gloves in the other." Shrugging, he dismissed the subject and looped his arm through hers. "Come on, rancher woman. We've got a barn renovation to plan. Lucky for you, you've already got two barns. This would be a bitch if we had to build one too."

He drew a laugh from her against her will, and it was then that she realized he'd planned this, knowing she'd be upset after dropping Nathan off at the airport. Walking along with him to the smaller of the two barns, she was grateful to have him in her life and told him so. "I'm so glad I met you. I don't know where I'd be without you right now. The ranch, everything." He stopped in his tracks and met her gaze, the apples of his cheeks stained with a deep blush. Rising on her toes, she pecked a kiss on his stubbled cheek. "Thanks."

"Now, now, Willow-girl, you know I like boys," he jested, before getting them moving again.

Laughing, she bumped his hip with hers. "Make that one boy in particular. You couldn't keep your eyes off a certain foreman the other day. Even if he did piss you off at the rodeo."

She didn't think it was possible, but his blush deepened further. "You're seeing things––your lust–addled brain is making you hallucinate."

"Sure, I hallucinated you looking at his ass like it was a side of beef and you were craving a steak." Rolling her eyes, she added, "Just admit it. You're here to distract me and cheer me up, right? Well, I'll be distracted by talking about your crush on Dale. I don't blame you by the way. God was having a good day when he sculpted that man."

They'd reached the barn, and he pulled open the pedestrian door, waving for her to enter before him. "Like I told you when we first sorted through everything, all the basics are here. But you'll need to pour concrete, add stalls, a tack room, better lighting, and radiant heat. You'll also need a contractor to double-check the roof and supports on the loft. You'll be storing hay, alfalfa, and grain up there for the horses, and it's gotta be kept dry—don't want any mold creepin' in."

"Hmph. You're changing the subject. Fine, fine, I'll let it go for now, lover-boy." Following him as he strolled through the gloomy barn, she took a good look around. When she'd first moved to the ranch, she'd done a walk-through but deemed this building as a future project and not a priority. It'd previously been used for storage, housing tractors, broken farming equipment, and in general, junk. Jeremiah and his ranch hands had cleaned out everything that wouldn't be of use to her, which had been most of it, and had it hauled away for scrap metal. Now, the building stood empty yet filthy. Cobwebs hung in long swaths from the rafters, and dirt and animal droppings covered the hard-packed floor.

"If we pour concrete, won't we need to install drains too?" She kicked the toe of her boot through a clod of dirt, breaking it apart.

"Sure, but that's easy enough. You'll need to hire out the concrete, that's not something we can do, but my hands and I can add in stalls here, here, and here." He kept talking and pointing, pausing only to jot down notes in his book. She hadn't noticed the tape measure on his belt until he pulled it free and told her to hold one end while he began to measure and take even more notes.

"You're good at this," she commented.

"Sure. It's a necessary skill. Easier and cheaper to build or repair it yourself on the ranch, instead of hiring people every time you need something done. I've been fixing fence and building decks and barns my whole life. This ain't nothin'." He waved a hand, encompassing the space around them. "Once the concrete is down, we'll have this barn ready for horses and feed in two days, tops."

"Why aren't you a carpenter then, if you enjoy it so much?" Willow asked, releasing the end of the tape measure at his nod. She knew he liked to whittle and had a wood-working shop in one of the several barns on his property where he'd make and fix things. Not that he'd ever allowed her, or anyone for that matter, inside it.

"Well, I never thought about it. I come from a long line of ranchers. It's in my blood. It's like . . ." he paused, writing something else down before continuing, "just because you love reading, doesn't mean you want to be a librarian, right? It's a hobby––one I enjoy––but ranching is my life. It's in my soul."

She smiled at him, placing her hand over her heart. "You, Jeremiah, secretly have the soul of a poet. Dale is sure going to appreciate that when you're having pillow talk."

His face flamed bright red, and Willow laughed until her stomach hurt. Every time she thought she could get it under control, one look at his admonishing expression had her in hysterics again. Bending double, holding her sides, she roared until tears streamed down her face, and she was sure she was going to pee her pants any second. Gasping for air, she straightened and wiped her tears. "Oh God, Jeremiah, I do adore you. I needed that. You should have seen your face!"

"You are a wicked, wicked, evil woman, Willow Crawford." He tried to sound angry, but his smile spoiled it. "Fine, yes, Dale is sexy as fuck, and I wanna ride him like

Seabiscuit. Probably after I punch him in his stupid, handsome face. Does that make you feel better?"

"Ha! Yes!" Offering her hand, she gave her best friend a high-five, and her heart felt lighter than it had since before she'd stood at the airport watching her soul mate walk away.

The sound of a car engine coming down the drive drew her attention. Walking out of the barn, she was surprised to see a florist delivery van, painted bright blue with flowers all over it, with the name, Pickin' Peonies, in curling pink script on the side. The Rock's only flower shop was located in a small nursery on the way out of town heading toward Butterfield. The driver had to be lost or have the wrong address.

Waving a greeting, she strode closer to the colorful van as a young woman got out, hurried around to the back of it, and opened the hatch.

"Afternoon!" Willow called. "Can I help you?"

"Are you Willow 'Wannabe' Crawford?" the delivery woman asked, after glancing at a piece of paper she then stuffed into the back pocket of her jeans. "I know this is Skyview Ranch—I just didn't know anyone was out here these days."

Confused, but with a racing heart, Willow replied, "Yes, that's me." *Did he really do this?*

"Nice to meet you—I'm Jesse Powell. I have a delivery for you—just a moment." Reaching into the open cargo area of the van, the woman retrieved a small potted plant. Stepping closer, she handed it to Willow. "Now if you're not familiar with succulents, just remember they don't need a lot of water. They're easy care."

Staring down at the small plant, her eyes blurred with tears that weren't from laughter this time. "Is there . . ." She cleared her throat. "Is there a card?"

"Oh yes! I'm sorry, I almost forgot." Handing over a letter-sized envelope she continued, "That's some fella you got there. He called yesterday and made the arrangements for the delivery. He had Jeremiah back there deliver the letter to us too." She waved over Willow's shoulder. "Hi, Jeremiah!"

Willow glanced back to see her friend tip his hat at Jesse from where he stood in the open barn door. "Hey, Jesse."

The woman directed her attention back to Willow. "He wanted to be sure you got it with the plant. Poor guy had no idea what a succulent was, but he was positive you'd love it. I had to take a bunch of photos of the ones we had and text them to him. This is the one he liked best."

Willow nodded as her gaze dropped to the plant again. Without even knowing it, he'd sent her favorite—a baby rubberplant. "I do. I really really do. Thank you, so much. It's really beautiful."

"Don't thank me—thank that man of yours." Shutting the van's rear hatch, Jesse climbed back in the delivery vehicle. "You two have a good day, now," she called out the open window as she drove away.

"You too," Willow and Jeremiah replied in unison.

As she cradled the note and the plant carefully in one hand, Willow waved goodbye to the florist with the other. Heading back into the barn, she set the little green plant down on an old wooden bench and opened the letter.

Wannabe,

I miss you already. We managed the date, but I didn't get to do flowers, then I remembered you're not a flower kind of girl anyway. Thank God for florists, since I had no clue what a succulent was. I hope you like the one I picked out, and I look forward to sending you many more.

Yours,

Nathan

"I couldn't believe it when he called me and asked me where he could get you a succulent." Jeremiah laughed from behind her, glancing at the note. "He's such a sap. That man has got it *bad* for you, Willow-girl."

"Trust me, the feeling is entirely mutual." Smiling, she carefully touched a leaf on the plant, knowing just where she was going to put it—on her desk in the bedroom, in the same place she'd written to him. Was it corny as all hell? Yes. Did she care? Not even a little.

After a relaxing dinner together, with a few beers and more laughs than she could count, Jeremiah had gone home to tend his own animals. After putting the chickens to bed and feeding Ethel, Willow went to her bedroom, with the kitten on her heels, and retrieved the box containing her father's letters from where it sat atop her dresser. Sitting on the edge of her bed, she caught a trace of Nathan's scent. Of them. She knew she should wash the sheets, but she couldn't bring herself to lose that connection with him yet. Glancing at the bedside clock, she saw she had an hour until their planned Skype call.

When she pushed on the carved cherry blossom, the lid popped open with a soft click. Picking up the next letter, she set the box on the bed beside her and began to read.

August 23rd

My Beloved Cherry,

It's been two months since I've had time to sit down and write to you. We've been cutting hay for what feels like forever. It's hot, dirty, back-breaking work from sunup until sundown. At the end of the day, I shower off the dust and grime and collapse into bed, too tired to even dream. Which means I don't get to see you.

Yesterday, we finished the last of it, and so today, after we did the basic chores, we took the rest of the afternoon and evening off. I caught up on sleep and finally saw you again. I dreamed of when we made love that first time. Your skin glowing in the moonlight, your eyes open and so full of love it nearly stopped my heart. You didn't know, but I was so nervous that night. I was so desperate for you, but I didn't want to hurt you. I was a fool to worry. What we have transcends the physical. Making love with you wasn't just a joining of the flesh, it united our souls. I can never regret it. Not as long as I live. I know maybe I should, but I can't bring myself to think poorly of something so magical. Holy, even. I burn for you even now. I think I always will.

These past few months have felt like a lifetime, and I pray that I have the strength to wait the twelve years before I can hold you in my arms again. My heart is locked in a prison without you. The only relief I get is the sun, the fresh air, and the exhaustion hard work brings me. This ranch is saving my sanity, my life. I know if I wasn't here, I'd be running back to you as fast as I could, and it would ruin both our lives.

My soul bleeds for you. I find myself sniping at my uncle and the other hands. They glare and tell me I'm being an asshole, but I can't stop the venom. It shames me, the way I talk to people sometimes, but I hurt so much, all the time, and it's hard to keep it inside.

I wonder, are you happy? Are your parents treating you okay? Is school going well? I ask myself all these things that

*I would give anything to know and come up empty. I don't
know how many times a person can survive their heart
being broken, but mine snaps in two every time I wake from
a dream and you're not beside me, in my bed and in my
arms where you belong.*

*Tonight, there's a dance and party in town to celebrate the
end of hay season. My uncle is making me go, saying I need
to get off the ranch and be around people instead of just
him, the other hands, and the damn cows for a few hours.
Maybe he's right. These years will pass too slowly if all I do
is sit in this room, thinking of you, and working myself
until I collapse.*

*Uncle Simon is calling me——it's time to go. I love you, with
all my heart, always and forever.*

J

WILLOW HAD NO TEARS LEFT. Admittedly, even though this
letter was as heartbreaking as the others, she was becoming
used to the emotions her father's words evoked. They were
beautiful, and she mourned the man he was that the world
never knew.

Checking the time, she saw she had fifteen minutes to
shower and make herself presentable before Nathan Skyped
her. She didn't want him to see the evidence of her tears. Not
to mention, she was dirty and probably still had a few
cobwebs in her hair from the barn.

Anticipation bolstering her, she carefully put the letters
away before stripping and walking into the bathroom. As she
turned on the water in the shower to let it warm up, she

wondered what Nathan would think and do if she answered his Skype call buck naked. Grinning now, with happiness bubbling in her stomach, she stepped into the tub under the spray, looking forward to the surprise on her man's face when he found her sitting in front of him wearing nothing but her skin.

CHAPTER TWENTY-EIGHT

WILLOW CLEARED her throat as she prepared to read the next letter aloud to Nathan during another one of their nightly Skype sessions after he'd returned to Kansas. While they spoke every day, either over the phone or internet, Willow needed time to recover after reading each of her father's letters, so she only tackled one every other day. The emotions they evoked drained her.

Jason—she still couldn't allow herself to call him her *dad* —was a completely different person on paper than the people of Antelope Rock ever knew. He'd been a soulful man, passionately in love with the young woman he couldn't be with, and every letter left Willow gutted and in tears. The time frame between letters she'd read so far was as little as two days and as much as several months. There were only a few left. Some had only been a short paragraph or two, while others had been longer, but all of them were of him professing his love to her mother. A few letters detailed the goings-on around the ranch and town and what his plans were for building a life there with the woman he loved when they were finally able to be together again.

October 15th

My beloved Cherry,

I'm in such shock, my hand is shaking as I write this. A baby? You're pregnant with my child? At first I thought my cousin Aaron was joking when he called a few hours ago to tell me the news, but he convinced me he was serious. Sweetheart, oh how I wish I could be there for you. From my estimate, you're about eight months along. I'm trying to picture your rounded belly, and the image I have in my head is beautiful, though I'm sure my imagination can't do the reality justice.

I thought my heart was broken before, but knowing you're pregnant with our child and I'm not there by your side . . . I don't have words for what I'm feeling right now. Rage, hurt, and sorrow to the very pit of my soul. I still don't regret making love to you, but knowing you're carrying a piece of us both elates me even as it slays me. I feel dead inside sometimes, Cherry. Can a man die of heartbreak? I don't know, but the only thing keeping me going is thinking of you—even though thoughts of you bring me more pain.

While trying to concentrate on finishing my work, I had a daydream about you like I always do, only this time, you cursed me. You stood before me, swollen with child, and instead of love in your eyes, it was hate. Is that our future? Will you grow to despise me? Will our child?

I'm so lonely without you, Cherry. So very lonely. Uncle Simon introduced me to a girl at a church function the other day. I'd call her a woman, since she's my age, but she doesn't act like one. Her name is Chasity Jenkins. She's tiny, blonde, and giggles at everything I say, even when I'm not trying to be funny. She doesn't hold a candle to you, in either the beauty or brains department. Uncle Simon wants me to date her—apparently her parents approve of me too— but I can't bring myself to even think of someone else that way. To have someone who isn't you in my bed would be a betrayal of everything I feel for you. Even now, when I'm so scared my stomach is in knots.

I hate this. I HATE it. I need to be there with you, with our family. I need to support you and hold you. I'm a bastard, and I wouldn't blame you if you never forgave me, but if I came back to Philly to be with you, I'd be thrown in jail. The baby is all the proof they'd need to toss away the key.

I'm a coward. I should send this letter. You need to know you're not alone, even if I can only be there is spirit. You need to know I still love you. I still want you, and now, our child, in my life.

I can't write anymore. Not tonight and maybe not for a while. It hurts too much.

J

WILLOW PUT the letter back and took out the next one. No tears came this time, but her heart ached for both Jason and her mother. It was so unfair. She also now had an inkling of why the restaurant owner had been so hostile to her while Willow and Nathan had been on their date. Either her father hadn't gone through with dating Chasity, or he'd started a relationship with her and it'd ended badly. Willow had meant to ask Jeremiah about the woman, but then forgot with all the work that'd needed to be done to prepare for the arrival of her new animals and foreman.

Instead of stopping after just one letter this time, curiosity won out over her feelings, and she opened the next envelope. It would be the first time she'd be reading them back-to-back, but she suddenly needed to know what happened next in her father's life. "I'm going to keep going, okay?"

"I'm here, Wannabe." Nathan's steady calm presence grounded her, even if he was on the other side of the computer screen.

December 1st

Dearest Cherry,

Have you forgotten me? Did you have our baby yet? Is it a boy or girl? Did you scream my name as the labor pains became unbearable? Did you think of me when you named our child? Were you forced to give him or her up? I wish I could've had the courage to be there for you and that Fate hadn't been so cruel as to keep me away from you.

I love you, but I don't deserve you. I doubt I ever did. I'm sorry, my sweet Cherry.

J

November 9th

Cherry,

It's been seven years since I've written to you. Seven very long years. I had to put you out of my mind. I had to. I was drowning in memories, swallowed up by grief. I forced myself to focus on my work and building a life here. If I dwelled on you and our child, I would've lost my mind. I was going crazy. For a while there, my work had suffered, and Uncle Simon and I had argued over it, until words were no longer enough. There were punches thrown and tears shed, but he finally set me straight. You are there and I am here. Nothing was going to change that. I was so naive. Who can wait twelve years for the love of their life? Twelve years is a lifetime.

Aaron called me today. I haven't spoken to him in a long time, but he told me about Willow, our daughter. I have a daughter! I bet she's as beautiful as you. But he also told me about your engagement. It hurt. After all this time, it still feels worse than I can describe.

Uncle Simon passed away about eighteen months ago, leaving me the sole heir to his cattle ranch. This will be my legacy now—this and Willow. I'm not worthy of either of them, but at least I'll be able to nurture one.

I've made a choice. I can't pine for you forever, especially since you've moved on. I'm going to ask Chasity Jenkins to marry me. She'll make a good ranch wife. She knows what to expect. I don't love her, but I care about her enough to marry her. Mostly, I'm lonely. And I'm tired of being lonely.

Goodbye, Cherry.

J

May 29th

Dearest Cherry,

Chasity left me today—ironically, eleven years to the day I had to leave you. I came in from checking the cattle and found her standing in front of the fireplace, holding the cigar box I keep my letters to you in. She'd already burned the movie ticket stubs and all but one of the pictures I still had of you and I, after she'd read the last letter I'd written you. She screamed at me and threw things. Thankfully, I grabbed the letters before they ended up in ashes too—like my marriage—like everything I touch besides this damn ranch.

I feel bad for hurting her, but it's probably better this way, for her to know the truth—I have a daughter, and my heart has always belonged to another, and always will. I hate to say it, but I was never a good husband to her. In fact, I haven't been a good man all these years without you. Between my mean streak and my refusal to father any children with her, and now this—she had her fill of me. I let her go without a fight. You were the only woman for me, and no substitute, no matter how pretty and sweet, will ever fill the void you left in my heart and soul.

I hope you've found happiness. Aaron moved to California a long time ago, and my folks have been in Florida for the past eight years. I don't know anyone in Philly anymore—at least not someone I can call up out of the blue and ask about you. It's better not to know I think. This way, I can imagine you and our daughter laughing and happy. We missed our chance, Cherry baby, but I still don't regret the time I had with you. Those memories will have to carry me forward through the rest of my days.

Always yours, forever,

J

THERE WAS ONLY one letter remaining in the box. Lifting it free, Willow noticed the envelope was different from the others, newer, and scrawled on the front, in the now familiar script of her father, was *Willow Crawford (Hillcrest).*

She dropped it like it had burned her. "No way am I doing this right now! Fuck that. Fuck this. Nope. All the nopes!"

She didn't have the emotional fortitude to open that envelope.

"Baby, talk to me." Clearly worried, Nathan leaned closer to the screen, as if he could crawl through and gather her into his arms.

Shaking her head, she closed the box. "There isn't anything to say. His last letter is addressed to me, and I'm not reading it. Not now, maybe never." Meeting his eyes, she wished with all her heart he was with her. In that second, she knew she would fight for him, for them. The next time he was here, she wasn't going to let fear and doubts rule her, she was going to tell him how she felt and ask him to move to the ranch when his time in the army was complete. She wanted to ask him in person though—not when he was hundreds of miles away. "Nathan? When can you come back to Wyoming?"

CHAPTER TWENTY-NINE

IT'D BEEN two weeks since Nathan had returned to Kansas, and Willow was finally falling back into a normal routine. Jeremiah had been her rock, streamlining the renovations of the horse barn and making certain the larger barn was ready for the alpacas. They'd gotten the concrete floor installed last week, just before the weather began dropping below freezing after the sun went down. The first snowfall had come last night, and she'd woken up to find the fields covered in a sparkling blanket of white. It looked like a beautiful postcard, far different from the slush and dirty snow she had been used to in Philadelphia. Today felt like a new beginning—fresh, clean, and inspiring—which fit, because the alpacas and horses would be arriving any minute.

It was just after noon, as she stood on the front porch, with her hands buried deep in her coat pockets, a bright pink beanie on her head. Jeremiah had laughed when he'd seen her shoveling the porches and walkways that morning when he'd stopped by to plow her lane. He was dressed in Carhart work pants, boots, and a shearling lined coat, topped off with his tan, everyday cowboy hat. She'd smirked and said, "Not all of us can look like Wyoming fashion plates. I'm still just a girl from Philly." Shoveling and salting the walkways around the house and over to the barn had been a lesson she hadn't known she'd be getting. In Philly, the city workers cleared the snow away. She hadn't even owned a snow shovel until a week ago when she'd heard the news of the pending storm, and she'd gone to Ducky's to get one. Thankfully, the snow had stopped coming down just before dawn. Her shoulders and arms ached, and she hated that she'd felt freezing cold even as she was sweating. What she wouldn't give right now to be sitting on her couch with Nathan, warming themselves in front of a roaring fire. Last week, she'd arranged to have several cords of cut firewood delivered at Jeremiah's suggestion. She needed extra logs available in case she ever lost electricity and had to stay warm during the colder months until it came back on.

The roar of an engine broke the silence, and she grinned at the sight of a huge black truck hauling a livestock trailer, led by Jeremiah in her own white truck, pulling a second trailer. She hadn't made the trip with him because she'd needed to stay behind and get the barns warm and lay down straw bedding which Jeremiah's ranch hands had delivered early that morning. After the alpacas, goats, and horses were settled, Willow and Jeremiah would go back with Dale to pick up the fifth-wheel, the ATVs, and the feed.

Stepping off the porch and into the snow, she walked down the freshly shoveled path, to the alpaca barn, anxious to see her new herd. The larger pasture was for the females, and a second, smaller one for the male was directly adjacent to it. That way, the animals could socialize as they were accustomed to, but their breeding could still be controlled. When they did the renovations to the horse barn, they'd also added a second, separate entrance to the alpaca barn, so the male could go in and out while remaining apart from the females.

Dale made a wide turn and then backed up the trailer to the barn with the ease of life-long practice. Eventually, she'd learn how to do that, but it was better left for another time and an empty trailer.

Climbing down from the cab, he was followed immediately by Johnny and June, who wasted no time, running directly to Willow to greet her. As she scratched their ears, Dale waved her forward. "Come on—let's get them unloaded and into their new home."

Nearly bouncing with excitement, she quickly pulled her phone from her pocket and snapped a selfie with the barn and truck behind her, grinning broadly and giving a thumbs up. Nathan had requested pictures of her big day. If he couldn't be here with her in person, she was going to do what she could to share this event with him, since he'd been so supportive of her new venture.

Smiling at her enthusiasm, Dale opened the barn doors and stood to the side, waiting for Jeremiah to join them. "I figured we'd unload the alpacas and goats first, then the horses."

Loud shuffling of feet and *baaing* of goats split the air. "Sounds like they're ready to get out of there," Willow said. "Tell me what to do. When it comes to this kind of thing, I bow to your superior knowledge."

"Stand to the side where you are, and I'll stay here, while Jeremiah opens the trailer. Our job is to make sure they don't panic and run off. Johnny and June will help herd them. In my experience, they follow the leader and go right in. Cattle are similar, right, Jeremiah?"

"Yeah, just meaner." Her friend stood beside the trailer door, his expression unreadable under his hat brim.

"You've never had an alpaca spit on you, have you?"

"Can't say that I have, Dale. But why don't we get this done? Still a lot to do and I have my own ranch to think of too," Jeremiah snapped in an uncharacteristic display of temper. Willow frowned at him, but he didn't look in her direction. "Ready?"

Dale nodded wordlessly, his mouth a grim line of displeasure. Clearly, Jeremiah's ire wasn't directed at her in any way. *I'm staying out of it for now,* she thought to herself. She had too much to do without playing referee or, heaven forbid, matchmaker.

Jeremiah swung the door to the trailer open and eighteen fluffy, giant, irritated alpacas barreled out, followed by two noisy goats. As Dale had predicted, just standing to the side while the dogs did their thing was enough to keep the herd directed into the barn. Once the trailer was empty, Dale said, "Come on. We need to get Alfie and put him into his own pasture."

"If you two have this, I'm going to get the horses settled," Jeremiah said, already walking backward away from them.

"Thanks Jeremiah." She'd never seen him like this. He'd been helping her a lot recently, but was she asking too much of him? She frowned at his back as he reached the horse trailer. He'd been doing so much for her, and she hadn't returned the favor, aside from sharing a few meals with him. Vowing to treat him to a new hat or something, she returned her attention to her foreman.

"Don't worry about it. It's me he's pissed at, not you," Dale said, handing her a lead rope and glancing over at Jeremiah unloading the horses. "He's right though—there is still a lot to be done. Let's get these guys taken care of."

Willow worked side-by-side with Dale and Jeremiah for hours, taking the second trip back and forth from Redworth with them. All the animals were finally settled in their respective barns and stalls, cozy, warm, and fed. The feed and

ATVs were stored, and all that was left to do was help Dale get his trailer in place.

Jeremiah stood next to her, as the wind, now biting and frigid, blew flurries into their faces. Willow was tired, and her temper was on a short fuse. The men had been sniping and bickering at each other for hours, and she'd had just about enough of their shit.

Raising her hand, she motioned to Dale, directing him as he backed his RV into the sheltered area between the barns. He would be close to the animals and have a measure of privacy from the house. Willow had hired a contractor to come to the ranch last week to run electrical, water, and sewer lines from the existing systems, so they could be connected to the fifth wheel. If all went well, she'd look into getting a prefab cottage for him in the spring that they could set further away from the house to give both of them more privacy.

"What is your problem today?" she demanded of her friend who stood several feet away, watching the other side of the RV as it was backed into place.

"I have no idea what you're talking about. I'm frozen solid and exhausted—maybe that's my problem?"

"Too fucking bad, princess. This isn't like you. You're my best friend—you've been here for me ever since I moved in—now let me be here for you." She met his eyes briefly, before waving Dale over to the right a bit.

Jeremiah sighed heavily, and chagrin flooded his face. "Willow-girl, I'm fine really. I'm just beat—it's been a long day, and he gets under my skin. Don't worry about it."

Not believing him for a second, she decided to let it go. He was a grown man, and if he said he was fine, well, there wasn't much she could do about it now.

Willow and Jeremiah both signaled for Dale to stop, and he cut the engine before getting out of the truck and striding back to them. "Honestly, I'm cold as fuck. I'll unhook it tomorrow. Thanks for your help today, Jeremiah." Dale extended his hand to the other man.

It took him a long moment, before he accepted the gesture, shaking the man's hand firmly but not meeting his eyes and letting go as if the touch had burned him. He was clearly giving off the vibe that he couldn't wait to get away from Dale.

"I'll be by in a few days, Willow. Give me a call if you need anything." He hugged her quickly before rushing off to his own truck that he'd left parked next to hers. His hurry to leave apparent to them both.

"No need to be rude, you know!" Dale shouted at his retreating back. Jeremiah froze, his shoulders stiffening, before he turned and glared.

"Listen here, I don't know what your fucking problem is, but get the fuck over yourself, Dale. I'm not doing this with you every time I see you. I'll be here sometimes, so you'd better get used to seeing me and learn how to keep your fucking fool mouth shut."

"Guys. Please. Can we not do this right now?" Willow's attempt to calm their flaring tempers failed as Dale's long legs ate up the distance between him and Jeremiah, irritation evident in his every step.

"Get over myself, huh? You first, fucker!" Dale shouted as he stopped in front of the other man, propping both hands on his hips.

Willow's head bounced back and forth like a ping-pong ball, as she tried to figure out what in the hell was going on with the two of them and stave off the headache they were giving her. She'd obviously missed something but hadn't a hint as to what it was. Whatever had happened between them at the rodeo was coming to a head like a festering wound.

"What? You're pissed that I won't fall to my knees for you? You act like you have some sort of clue what my life is like! Newsflash, dipshit, you don't! So, yeah, fuck off, fuck you, and fuck yourself while you're at it!" Jeremiah was right in Dale's face, jabbing his finger in the bigger man's chest. "My life, my call. You don't get to judge me."

Dale snarled, slapping Jeremiah's hand away from his chest. "Yeah, I do. The way you look at me is just *begging* for me to judge you."

Willow hesitated, not sure what to do. One man was her best friend and the other was now her employee. Deciding she'd let them continue unless it came to blows, she stayed well back and observed. Maybe they just had to blow off some steam after being at each other's throats all day.

"Begging? Begging! Not on your sorry fucking life will that ever happen!" Jeremiah's face was bright red with the combination of anger and the cold air. She'd never seen him so pissed off and didn't want to ever again.

"I don't recall asking you to, now did I? I said what I said at the rodeo, and I meant it. Until that day comes, not that I think it ever will, you need to keep your pissy fucking attitude around me in check. You have no one to blame but yourself."

"Again, asshole, you have *no clue* what my life is like." Throwing his hands in the air, he gave the foreman his back. "I'm not doing this. Not now. Not ever. What I do or do not tell people about myself is none of your fuckin' business." Opening the door to his truck, he glanced over at Willow. "I'll see ya, Willow-girl. Tell Nathan I said hey. Call me if you need me."

Crossing her arms over her chest, she watched her best friend drive away before turning toward her new foreman with a scowl. "Way to spend your first day at a new job, huh? Baiting my best friend who left his own ranch to help us? I don't know what's happening with you two, but if I see that sort of display again, I'll be finding a new foreman." She kept her tone cold and firm. "This sort of macho dick-measuring contest bullshit is a waste of everyone's time. You don't have to like him, but you'll be civil toward him when you're on my property."

Looking at his boots, Dale had the grace to look ashamed. "Yes, ma'am."

"And for crying out loud, don't call me ma'am." She allowed herself to smile, just a little, trying to soften the blow of her words. She needed his respect, but she didn't want him to dislike her. They would be working closely together every day and needed to maintain a good relationship.

The corners of his mouth ticked upward, but he was smart enough to keep the smirk or smile from fully forming. "Understood." Burying his hands in his coat pockets, he continued, "I'm going to get a few things set up in the RV and have some dinner. I'll do another check on the stock later before getting some shuteye. I'll see you in the morning. I'll be up at dawn, but you're the boss—I won't expect you until I see you."

Nodding once, he spun on his heel and walked to his trailer. The door slammed behind him as he went inside, and Willow questioned if she'd handled the situation correctly. She'd have to ask Nathan when they Skyped later tonight.

Stomach growling, she saw it was dinnertime—not only for her, but for the chickens and Ethel too. Once the hens were safe and secure for the night, Willow headed back into the house, cold and hungry. She threw some kibble in the cat's dish in the laundry room, then checked the pantry for something for herself. Soup sounded good—it was fast, easy, and hot, just what she needed to warm up and still be ready in time for Nathan's call. Grinning for the first time in hours, she hurried to fix her meal, anxious to talk to him.

RECLINING IN BED, Willow propped her laptop on her thighs and opened the Skype app. She tapped her fingers and watched the clock tick over, impatient to see Nathan. Every time they spoke, she struggled more and more not to confess her feelings and beg him to come live at the ranch with her when he was finally discharged from the army. She was desperate to tell him she loved him but knew it would be more meaningful coming from her in person, not over the internet. She would only get the chance to say those words for the first time once, and she didn't want to screw it up.

She tried not to think about Andrew, but the man had pissed her off to no end—again. He'd called twice while she'd been eating her dinner. As usual, when she saw the Philadelphia area code, she'd sent both calls to voice mail. Since she'd blocked his number, he'd started calling her from other phones---she didn't know or care who they belonged to. She listened to the messages for all of two seconds to confirm they were from her ex, and not someone else trying to get in touch with her for some reason, before deleting them. The man wasn't going to get a dime from her no matter how much he begged. Let him find someone else to bail him out of whatever trouble he'd found himself in.

The chime sounded on her computer, and when she connected the call, Nathan's face and upper body appeared on the screen. He was shirtless and coated in a fine sheen of sweat. She grinned into the camera. "Nathan, why are you all sweaty? You know that's mean right? Teasing me . . ."

Laughing, his eyes dancing, he swept a hand down his shiny face. "My workout with Ramsey ran long, and I didn't get a chance to shower yet. I didn't want to keep you waiting."

"Well, I can't say I'm complaining about your appearance,

since seeing you all flushed and glistening with sweat does things to me." She gave him a sassy wink.

"Don't distract me, woman. All settled in there?" He grabbed a towel from somewhere off screen and wiped his face and chest off. *Lucky towel.*

"Yes!" she exclaimed, knowing he was talking about the animals. "They were no trouble at all. It was a long day, but so worth it. Dale said he was going to do another check this evening, but I'll go out too when we're done talking. I just want to see for myself that they're doing okay. I feel like a first-time mom or something. Well, a second-time mom since I already adopted Ethel, and Fred sort of adopted me."

"I'm so happy for you, and I can't wait to see them. You'll have to take a video of them tomorrow and send it to me. I loved all the pictures you sent throughout the day. Especially the one with Lucy mugging for the camera. Or was that Desi?"

She giggled. "It was Desi. Apparently, he loves getting his photo taken."

Reaching out, he ran a finger down the computer screen, no doubt tracing the image of her face. She could almost feel his touch along her jaw. His expression softened into something akin to longing. "I wish I was celebrating with you." They stared at each other in silence for a few moments before Nathan suddenly sat up straighter. "Which brings me to my other news. I'm only working a half day on Friday. I can fly up to you that afternoon and stay until Sunday afternoon."

"Really! You're sure? You can really come?" Her exhaustion faded and pure elation flooded through her.

"Yes, Wannabe, I'm sure. I was just about to look at flights. As soon as I get it booked, I'll text you the details. Will you be able to get away to come pick me up?"

"Are you kidding? Nothing could keep me away. I can't

wait to see you! I miss you." She figuratively bit her tongue, stopping herself just in time from telling him how much she loved him, how much she wanted him in her home and bed. He belonged here with her—she knew it in her heart. She just hoped he knew it too.

"I miss you too, Wannabe, more than I can say. I'll see you Friday, baby. Clear your calendar and tell Jeremiah to occupy himself elsewhere. This trip, I want you all to myself. Understand?" His tone dropped low, causing shivers to break out along her skin. Her nipples tightened and her panties grew damp, and all because he spoke to her in that commanding tone of his that made her knees weaken. *Damn the man.*

"Y-yes." She couldn't wait to experience everything his wicked grin and desire-filled gaze promised. *Twice.*

CHAPTER THIRTY

Willow barely had the front door shut behind them before she was pinned up against it. Nathan's mouth was on hers in a heart beat, and all thoughts of what to make for dinner fled from her mind. She kissed him back with fervor, giving as much as she took. His tongue swept into her mouth as he pushed her coat off her shoulders.

Moans, gasps, and sucking noises filled the air as they quickly divested each other of their clothes. Boots *thunked* against the floor, and she stumbled as she kicked her jeans off. Willow hoped like hell Dale didn't need anything or Jeremiah stopped by. Both men always knocked before opening the backdoor to her kitchen, but there wouldn't be enough time for her and Nathan to duck out of view if either of them entered. Being caught standing there in her underwear by her employee or her best friend, while being ravished by her boyfriend, wasn't how she wanted to start her weekend.

Today hadn't come fast enough for Willow. Since she'd found out Nathan was coming up to see her again, she'd been counting the hours and then the minutes until she'd met him at the airport.

"Bed-bedroom," she managed to tear her mouth free of his and blurt out in between gulps of air.

Grabbing her hips, Nathan lifted her. "Wrap your legs around me, baby," he demanded before resuming his assault on her mouth. They were both in just their underwear, and she hissed in pleasure as his bare skin pressed against hers. His chest hair rubbed against her stomach and breasts, sending tingles all through her and raising goosebumps on her exposed arms and back.

His hands cupped her ass as he carried her down the hall to her bedroom. After he deposited her onto the mattress in a heap of wanting flesh, he knelt between her legs and flicked the front clasp of her bra, letting her breasts fall free. He crawled onto the bed, his body covering hers, surrounding her in his warm scent, as his mouth latched onto one of her nipples. His tongue flicked her piercing causing her to gasp and moan in pleasure. Willow writhed beneath him running her hands through his short hair, over his strong shoulders, and down his back. His skin was hot under her palms, fueling her desire. She couldn't get enough of him. She wanted to touch and taste him everywhere, all at once. "Mmm, hurry, please."

Apparently, that'd been the wrong thing to say because he slowed down immediately. Sitting up, he straddled her thighs and reached for her right wrist, bringing it to his lips. He'd done this before, and it drove her crazy—in a good way. His tongue snaked out and licked where her tattoo sleeve began, before tracing the interconnecting designs upward to her elbow and then further to her shoulder. Occasionally, he'd stop and suck on her skin for a few moments before moving on. Whenever they were naked in bed, he loved to study the ink, finding new things to comment about each time.

While he teased her, she moaned and twisted her hips, desperate for friction where she needed it most. By the time his tongue worked its way across her upper chest, her clit was throbbing in time to her pounding heart. "Nathan, please," she begged again. "I missed you. Need you so bad. Tease me later, please . . ." She was so wet and nearly incoherent with need.

He slid just a bit down the bed, and she spread her legs, so he could nestle his hips between them. His hardness rubbed against her mound, and she lifted her pelvis to try to increase the pressure. Rubbing against him, she cried out as the head of his cock bumped her clit directly, shooting an arc of pleasure through her.

Nathan kissed his way down her torso, licking, sucking, and tasting as much of her exposed flesh as he could. He tongued her nipple rings, pulling on them gently with his teeth, knowing it drove her crazy, before nuzzling the undersides of her breasts, kissing the soft skin there. She touched him everywhere she could reach, scratching her nails along his shoulders and arching her back to get closer to him.

When he reached her hot-pink lace panties that matched her bra, he knelt by her feet, lowering the material down her legs and off. His gaze roamed her naked body, almost reverently. "God, you're so damn beautiful, Wannabe. What did I do in my life to deserve you?" He didn't give her a chance to answer before he dipped his head, parted her folds with his thumbs, and buried his face between her legs, forcing a gasp from her throat. "Damn, you taste amazing." He groaned against her flesh, alternating between sucking on her clit and licking inside her until she grabbed his hair, pulling him up and off her. His face was glistening, and he grinned before wiping his face on the sheet.

Smiling, she reached between them and palmed the bulge

in his boxer briefs, making him groan and shift his hips closer to her touch. "You just had to be you, Nathan . . . nothing more, nothing less." She paused for a moment before meeting his blue eyes, blazing with desire, and letting the words she'd been holding back spill from her lips. "I love you." Her voice was soft and hesitant, as her heart hammered against her ribs with both desire and fear.

His eyes widened, then he leaned forward, pressing his chest to hers and propping his hands on either side of her head. He lowered his mouth to hers, giving her the sweetest, most heart-felt kiss she'd ever experienced. "I love you too, Wannabe. I think I fell in love with you the moment I read your first letter." He whispered the words against her lips, his breath puffing against her mouth. "And I'll love you to my dying day."

Before she could respond, his lips were on hers again, taking possession of her mouth. In that moment, she knew . . . he owned her. For the rest of her life, her heart would belong to him and no one else.

He quickly removed his underwear and ran two fingers across her pussy lips, dipping them inside her, making sure she was ready for him. She could've told him he didn't have to bother though—she was soaked. When he lined his cock up and entered her, her body yielded and stretched to accommodate him as if the final piece of its complex puzzle was sliding into place. With a few short strokes, he was soon buried to the hilt. This wasn't sex between them . . . not anymore. It was the melding of two hearts and two souls.

As they climbed a precipice of pure pleasure, Willow's senses were aware of nothing but Nathan. The way he touched her and murmured endearments and promises into her ear. The way his scent surrounded her, and how his skin tasted on her tongue. The way he moved within her with deep and sure strokes, touching every part of her heart and body. All of that didn't send her over the edge though, until he lifted his head just enough that she could see the love burning in his eyes. When he said, "Come for me, baby," she shattered and screamed his name as her orgasm crashed over her, sending her tumbling into a sea of bliss.

When Nathan followed her, Willow felt his heated release bathe her insides. It made her feel so close to him, without the barrier of latex in the way. She never wanted anything to keep them apart, not even something as simple as a condom. The possibility of children was a concern, but not a big one. A little girl or boy, with Nathan's dark hair and her eyes? Maybe one day.

Lying sated, with her head on his chest and Nathan's fingers in her hair, she now understood the impassioned love her father had felt for her mother. She also understood how Jason's heart had shattered at the loss of the woman who'd been his soul mate.

Willow caressed Nathan's taut abdomen, her fingers playing with the dark hair there. She could almost feel her father channeling the courage he hadn't been able to find until it was too late into her mind as she lifted her gaze to Nathan's. She refused to repeat Jason's mistakes and let fear and regret prevent her from seizing her happiness. "When your discharge is final, move in with me?"

His eyes filled with hope. "You mean it? This isn't just my superior love making skills messing with your head, right? You really want me here?"

Laughing, she shoved him. "Jerk," she teased, kissing his chest before nipping at his nipple. "I've thought about it almost constantly since you left. I love you. I love being *with* you. If it's not something you're ready for, I understand, but I really hope it is."

He continued to run his fingers through her hair, letting the strands fall against his bare arm. "Yes, Wannabe, I'd love to live here with you. And no, I don't need time. If you hadn't asked, I'd planned to just keep showing up and slowly bring more of my stuff with me each time."

"What?" Giggling, she moved to straddle him, folding her arms on his chest and resting her chin on her hands. "You didn't think I'd notice?"

"Oh, I know you would, but I thought you'd be so taken with me you wouldn't mind too much. And if you said anything about it, my plan was to distract you with sex."

She wiggled her hips, bringing his cock twitching back to attention. "There are definitely some perks of you living here, soldier-boy. Someone to do heavy lifting, your omelet skills, hmm . . . what else? Bed warmer?"

"Boy!? Woman, I'm your soldier-man, dammit. How many times do I have to tell you that? Do you need another demonstration to remind you of the difference?"

"Hell yes, will *always* be the answer to that question."

Laughing with delight, Nathan rolled them over, drew back, and flipped her onto her stomach. Hauling her up onto her knees, he drove inside her with one hard thrust. "Oh, hellll yessss."

FOUR HOURS after she'd picked him up at the airport, Nathan sat next to Willow at the kitchen island. He couldn't stop staring at her. From the moment he'd met her, maybe even before then, she'd taken his breath away, and now, she'd asked him to move in with her when he was discharged! She'd told him she loved him! There wasn't a bastard on this planet luckier than him.

He hadn't hesitated with his reply—he wanted to be wherever she was. He loved her, more than he could express with words, although he'd done his best to tell and show her that in bed a little while ago. He'd meant what he said—if she hadn't asked, he'd planned to slowly creep into every facet of her life, until one day, she turned around and realized he was living there.

They were seated side-by-side, eating sandwiches and recovering from their bout of mind-blowing love making. Reaching across to her plate, he snagged one of her Doritos, popping it into his mouth and crunching down.

"Hey! That's mine. You have your own!" Willow stole some of his chips in retaliation, but he just grinned.

"What's yours is mine, right, since I'm going to be living here soon?" After leaning over and pecking a quick kiss on her lips, he finished the last of his food and gathered their empty plates, setting them in the sink to be washed later. He had other things he wanted to do right now. Namely being with his woman. To be near her was to want her.

He poured a glass of water, downing it in a few gulps. He'd need to keep hydrated.

"No, what's yours is mine, and what's mine is also mine. Duh."

Leaving the glass beside the sink, he looked over at her and grinned. "Cheeky wench." Swiftly rounding the island and grabbing her off the stool, he bent down and slung her up and over his shoulder. She squealed and slapped at his ass and thighs. Shifting her weight more evenly onto his shoulder, he made his way to the hallway that led to her, *their* bedroom.

"Put me down, dammit! Nathan!" She was laughing so hard and wiggling so much, he was afraid he was going to drop her.

He smacked her ass in return. "Keep it up woman, and you won't get your prize." Rubbing his hand over where he'd spanked her, he decided he kinda liked it, so he did it again, imagining her pretty ass bright pink with his handprints. His already hard cock thickened even further at the thought.

She immediately froze. "Prize?"

"Yeah, only good wenches get my prized stud services."

"Stud services! You've got quite the opinion of yourself, don't you!?" She dug her fingers into his sides, tickling him mercilessly.

"Stop it! Fuck, I—" A loud pounding on the front door interrupted them, just as they reached the entrance to the bedroom. Willow's hands stilled, and he set her gently onto her feet. Her face was flushed, and her eyes sparkled with laughter. Whoever was at the door better have a damn good reason for being there because, if not, they might just have to die—slowly. "Expecting someone?"

"Nope. I've no clue who that could be. Probably Jeremiah ignoring your mandate to stay away for the weekend, so you can have me all to yourself."

"If it is, I'll kill him."

The knocking came again—whoever it was, they weren't exactly being patient. Shrugging, she hurried past him into the foyer where she flipped on the porch light and opened the door.

"Willow, baby." A man's voice Nathan didn't recognize broke through the last of the lingering joy from their roughhousing. *Baby? No one gets to call her that but me,* he thought before following her to the door.

Willow's back straightened, and there was no mistaking the tension that suddenly appeared in her shoulders or the anger in her tone when she said, "What the fuck are you doing here? Did my shotgun not get my point across, asshole?"

Rushing forward the last few steps, Nathan stopped behind her and glared over her shoulder at a stranger standing on the porch. *Shotgun?* He remembered Willow telling him about confronting her ex, so this must be him—Andrew Phelps.

The asshole had some balls showing up here again. He wasn't dressed for the weather and seemed unwashed. Thick black circles lined his watery gray eyes. His brown hair hung limp and dirty over his sweat-dotted brow.

"Willow, who's this?" Nathan asked, even though he'd already figured it out. Placing his hand on her shoulder, he adopted the same expression he wore when dealing with idiot privates at work.

"Who am I? Who the fuck are you? Get your hands off my wife!" His face turned the color of a tomato, and his fists clenched at his sides as he glowered at Nathan.

Raising a brow, Nathan stared down at the smaller man, whose sweaty face and greasy hair shimmered under the yellow glow of the porch light. He knew the shotgun was beside the door but didn't think he'd need it. Hell, he probably wouldn't need more than one hand to deal with this arrogant nasty piece of garbage. What the hell had Willow seen in him?

"Wife? Try again, dipshit," he spat while gently pushing Willow to the side and confronting the asshole head on. "Actually, scratch that, no need. I know who you are—you're the sorry excuse of an ex-husband who was such a piece of shit that you thought sticking your tiny dick in Willow's best friend was a good idea." He stepped forward, forcing the smaller man to retreat to the top of the porch stairs. "*I'm* Staff Sergeant Nathan Casey, and I have the training, the ability, and trust me, the *desire* to kill you with my bare fucking hands. You're not welcome here, not now, not ever, and I suggest you get your ass gone before I take some frustration out on your face. Got me?" He punctuated his last words with a hard jab to Phelps's chest.

The other man blanched, going sickly pale as he stumbled

backward, tripping down the steps and falling flat on his ass in the snow.

"Willow?" The fight seemed to seep out of Phelps as he mewled pathetically. "Please. I just need help. Th-there's these guys—I owe them money."

She stepped out onto the porch next to Nathan, her arms crossed over her chest. She looked pissed and absolutely gorgeous in her anger. Fuck, he wanted nothing more than to get back to what they'd started before this asswipe had showed up. "None of that sounds like it's my problem. Nothing that has to do with you has been my problem for a very long time, and it's going to stay that way. I'm not giving you a cent, and nothing you say or do will ever change my mind. Leave. Now. I won't tell you again."

Nathan descended the steps and nudged the prone man's leg with the toe of his boot. "And don't come back. Lose her number too. Understand?"

Rage stole across Phelps's face again as if a switch had been flipped, and Nathan wondered if the guy was on something to promote such rapid changes in response. "Fuck you! You have her now, but I had her first." Scrambling to his feet, he glared at them both, his hate-filled gaze stopping on Willow. "You think you're so much better than me, you stupid bitch. You have no idea."

Nathan saw red, and his fist shot out before he realized he'd decided to act. His punch connected with Phelps's jaw with a *crack,* dropping him like a stone in a pond as his legs crumpled and he landed in an unconscious heap of tangled limbs.

A heavy sigh resounded from behind Nathan. "Well, guess I'm calling the sheriff, huh?"

He glanced over his shoulder at her. "Yeah, I'll stay here and keep an eye on him. Toss me my coat will ya, baby? It's cold as hell out here." He almost laughed about how nonchalant they both were considering what'd just happened. *Nothing to see here folks, just some jackass passed out in the snow.*

After throwing him the coat, she only left the door open a crack, probably to keep the heat and Ethel inside, and walked deeper into the house. Moments later, he could hear her muffled conversation with Sheriff Grady Minor. Glaring down at her ex, Nathan debated on hauling the asshole by his feet out of the snowbank and up onto the porch but decided against it. Let him freeze.

"This was *not* how I saw this night going, you fucker." He wanted to plant his boot into the bastard's side, but he had more honor than that.

Phelps was just coming to, groaning and rolling over, when Sheriff Minor arrived in his department-issued SUV. The lawman must not have been too far away, since he'd gotten there rather quickly.

"Sheriff Minor, evening." Nathan nodded, keeping his bare hands tucked into his coat pockets, since he'd left his gloves in Willow's truck when they'd gotten home. "Got some trash for you."

"I see that." Glaring at the man struggling to his feet, the sheriff grabbed Phelps's upper arm to help him stand, with obvious reluctance.

"I want to press charges! He punched me!" Phelps spit blood into the snow and tried to jerk his arm free from the sheriff's grip, like a five-year-old brat throwing a tantrum.

The only thing he succeeded in doing was pissing off Grady further if his thunderous expression was anything to go by. "Yeah, that's not gonna happen. You see, the thing is, you're trespassing. *Again.* I warned you not to come back here. Actually, I'm surprised you risked it after what happened last time. If you're not careful, boy, Willow will shoot your balls off. She's been practicing with that shotgun, and I doubt she'll miss the next time—intentionally or not. Now, hands behind your back." Pulling his cuffs free from his duty belt, he turned a loudly protesting Phelps around, before quickly and efficiently securing his wrists. "You're under arrest. I usually wait until I get a suspect back to the station before saying, 'you have the right to remain silent,' and all that jazz. But since I don't want to listen to your pathetic whining on the way there, you have the right to remain silent—please freaking use it—otherwise anything you say can and will be used against you in a court of law. You have a right . . ."

Nathan tuned out the rest as he glanced up at Willow who was standing on the porch with her winter coat on, scowling at her ex. He climbed the steps and wrapped her in his arms, wanting to reassure himself she was okay. He hated that Phelps had the power to upset her—he just hoped this was the last time.

When she slid her arms around his waist, he kissed the crown of her head. "Sorry, baby. I don't normally go around punching people."

"Nathan, honey, you didn't do anything I haven't wanted to do for years. Thank you." She tilted her chin up and brushed her lips across his. "You're like my knight in shining armor. Or rather, my soldier boy in body armor."

"Oh, really?" He liked the sound of that. Well, not the boy part, but he'd pay her back for that later—when they were both naked.

Grady finished loading the still complaining Phelps into the caged back seat of his SUV, shut the door, and walked over to them. "I'm going to assume this idiot was threatening you two, and that's why he got cold-cocked and is spitting blood."

"Yup." Trying and failing for a look of pure innocence, Willow tucked her free hand into Nathan's back pocket, as he swallowed a bark of laughter. Damn, he missed living in a small town.

"At least it wasn't the shotgun again this time. Less paperwork." Shaking hands with both, the sheriff bid them goodnight, got into his vehicle, and drove away.

Nathan pulled Willow back into his arms. "Tonight was eventful in a way I wasn't expecting. Next time you tell me you love me though, can we do it without the ex-husband and police?"

"No promises." Smirking, Willow rose on her toes, wrapped her arms around his neck, and kissed him. Groaning into her willing mouth, he grabbed her ass and hauled her up against his body, silently urging her to put her legs around his waist, which she did without hesitation. He wasn't sure how he managed to get them into the house and shut the door, without falling, but he did it. Not pausing, he carried her down the hall, into her room, and to her bed— soon to be their bed. Placing her on it, he followed her down, losing himself in the woman of his dreams.

"Now, where were we?" he asked against her throat, running his hand down her side and hiking her leg over his hip. "Ah, about right here, I think."

CHAPTER THIRTY-ONE

Four months later . . .

Nathan grabbed the last box from the horse trailer and carried it into the house. Ethan Rivers, one of Jeremiah's ranch hands, and his cousin, Shane, who was Willow's new hand, had driven to Kansas to help Nathan haul all his possessions and his family's stuff, that'd still been in storage, up to Wyoming. Over the past few days, he and Willow had slowly emptied the trailer and neatly piled anything they could unpack at a later date in one of the two spare bedrooms and the attic. His clothes and toiletries were already in the bedroom suite he was sharing with her from now on. He loved seeing his belongings next to hers—it gave him a sense of home that he hadn't experienced since he'd been a kid.

He was officially retired from the Army. A day after the farewell party his friends had insisted on throwing for him, he'd gotten into his truck and followed Ethan and Shane north to Wyoming. One of his buddies had taken over his share of the lease on his and Zach's apartment, moving in with the other man, so Nathan hadn't needed to worry about that. It'd been six weeks since he'd last been in Antelope Rock, and he hadn't been able to get back there fast enough to satisfy him. If he hadn't needed the trailer for all his stuff, he might've sold the damn truck and hopped on the first flight he could get with just the clothes on his back.

He hadn't taken leave for Thanksgiving or Christmas—he'd always volunteered to work those holidays, letting the guys with kids and big families have them off, so instead, he'd invited Willow to Kansas to celebrate with him. Jeremiah and Dale had promised her they could take care of everything while she was gone, including Ethel, Fred, and the chickens. She'd been nervous about leaving the two men to handle the ranch, worried there would be a bloodbath when she returned. But after both trips, she'd been relieved to find the two men still very much alive without any visible battle scars.

Nathan had loved introducing her to his buddies and their families. Several of the Army wives and girlfriends had taken her under their wings while she'd been visiting and helped make her feel like she was one of them. She had taken particular pleasure in seeing him come home from work in uniform every day. Not that he'd had it on long once he'd closed the door.

He grinned remembering how she'd greeted him Christmas Day in nothing but her cowboy hat and boots, and tattoos. As always, his eyes had immediately zoomed in on her nipple rings, but he'd gotten a laugh when noticing she'd changed the steel horseshoe shaped hoops for straight barbells with sparkling red Santa hats on either end. He'd murmured, "Merry Christmas to me," before pouncing on her.

For New Year's Eve, Nathan had surprised her by flying up and having Ethan pick him up at the airport. One of the

JP Ranch's barns had been cleared out, and it'd seemed like half the town had been there for the big party Jeremiah threw every year. Thousands of white Christmas lights had been hung from the rafters and around all the vertical supports. A potluck buffet table had been laden with finger foods, barbecue, and at least a dozen different kinds of dessert, while beer, shots, and champagne had flowed freely. A country band had been set up on a small stage in front of a dance floor. It'd looked like something out of the Hallmark movies that Willow wouldn't admit she liked to watch with Jeremiah occasionally. She'd been so bummed thinking she wouldn't see him for New Year's that he'd known he had to make it up there, even though it had to be a short trip.

Nathan's woman had squealed when she'd arrived at the party and found him waiting for her, with another potted succulent in his hands for his lover who didn't want flowers. He'd barely managed to keep it from being crushed between them before she'd thrown herself into his arms and squeezed the stuffing out of him. It'd taken everything in him not to haul her back over to her house and make passionate love to her long before the stroke of midnight.

Since they could walk home, they'd indulged in enough alcohol that neither had protested when a few people had coaxed them into participating in some line dancing. The guests had cracked up watching how Nathan and Willow would go right whenever everyone else had gone left, and vice versa. The couple had knocked into the other dancers, laughing hysterically, and ended up clinging to one another to keep from falling on their asses. But they'd been having far too much fun to be embarrassed about it. It'd been one of the best times Nathan had experienced in years.

Before he'd returned to Kansas for his last six weeks in the Army, Nathan had gotten Jeremiah alone for a talk. Willow's best friend was the closest thing she had to family now, so Nathan had told Jeremiah he was going to propose to Willow after he moved in with her and asked for his blessing. One would've thought Nathan had given the man a million dollars the way his face had lit up in excitement. Of course, before giving his consent, Jeremiah had gone through a long spiel that covered what would happen if Nathan ever hurt Willow—in a nutshell, they'd never find his body. Wyoming was a big place, and Jeremiah was in possession of a woodchipper, so Nathan didn't doubt the man would follow through with the threat if he ever screwed up, which he had no intention of doing.

The engagement ring he'd bought her was burning a hole in his pocket. He'd been stressing for weeks over how and when he should ask her to marry him. His friends had peppered him with suggestions from the sickly-sweet romantic to the corniest and most inane ideas they could come up with. However, nothing had sounded right to him.

After humbling himself, he'd had a long conversation with Jeremiah over a few beers the other night and had come up with a plan. Today, he would execute that plan. He'd been on countless missions during his career in the Army, but he didn't remember being this nervous before any of them.

Today, he'd woken up even earlier than normal, too nervous to sleep. He'd taken great pleasure in wearing Willow out last night, *twice*, hoping she'd sleep in. Not that making love to her was a hardship by any means. He swore every time was better than the last, and he was pretty sure his brain was going to short-circuit one of these days and he would just keel over from an overload of the ecstasy he found in her arms and body.

After finishing his preparations in the kitchen, he tip-toed to their bedroom to check on Willow. He breathed a sigh of relief when he saw she was still passed out, naked and sprawled on her stomach, taking up the middle of the bed now that he wasn't in it. Her beautiful, long hair, that was well past her shoulders now, was draped across her face, and she was snoring softly. Grinning, he left the letter he'd written on the bedside table, propped up on one of the first succulents he'd sent her and right beside the framed picture of his parents and sister.

Now, he just needed to wait.

Shit, I think I'm going to puke.

WILLOW AWOKE IN SMALL DEGREES, smacking her lips and groaning. Damn, she was sleeping like the dead lately. She knew the reason behind her exhaustion but was still trying to think of the best way to tell Nathan. Plus, he'd been the reason she'd gone to sleep very late last night—making love to her once in their shared shower and then again immediately afterward in bed. The man had mythical level stamina sometimes, not that she was complaining.

Going to sleep with wet, sex-mussed hair had been a terrible idea, she thought as she shoved the tangled mess off her face. Blinking open her bleary eyes, she noticed a folded piece of paper, with "Wannabe" scrawled in Nathan's handwriting on the front, propped against her plant. "Hmm, weird," she mumbled. *Maybe he had an early errand?*

Lifting herself up on one elbow, she grabbed the note and opened it.

Dear Wannabe,

A special something has been planned for you today. But first, breakfast is ready—drink your coffee and eat your bagel. (Don't cheat and skip that step!)

When you're done, Lucy's best friend will have the next instructions for you to follow.

Now, hurry and follow my clues, if you want to keep me from having the blues . . .

XOXO,
Nathan

Grinning, she dressed quickly, brushed her teeth, quickly ran a brush through her hair, wincing when it got caught on a few knots, and hurried to the kitchen. Sitting in her cat bed was Ethel, wearing a red bow tied around her pink collar with an attached scroll. "Oh my God! What is that crazy man up to, Ethel?"

After wolfing down her waiting bagel and coffee, she untied the bow from Ethel and unraveled the scroll.

Wannabe,

You've had your food and drink, so come and find us next before we fall into a ring of fire. We have a love like them . . .

XOXO,
Nathan

"Holy shit balls, Ethel! It's Johnny and June!" Willow exclaimed, but the feline just blinked at her and then went back to cleaning her paws. Clearly her cat wasn't excited as she was. "For a man who claims to hate country music, he can sure quote it, huh?"

Pulling on her muck boots, coat, and hat, Willow raced to the barn. The dogs began barking like mad as soon as they spotted her. Dale was nowhere to be seen, which was unusual, but a quick look around confirmed the morning chores had been done. The alpacas were out in their pasture, eating their hay.

Willow felt like a kid on Christmas morning as she entered the barn.

"Johnny, June, c'mere guys," she coaxed, noticing another scroll, this time around June's neck. When the dogs rushed over to her, she patted their heads, earning her some licks and nuzzling, before untying the scroll.

Wannabe,

Retrace your steps.

Go back to the beginning, to the place where your lips first touched mine. There you'll find another couple lines . . .

XOXO,
Nathan

She had just enough sense to make sure the barn door latched behind her as she sprinted for the driveway and her truck. Her grin wouldn't quit, and her heart was racing. She couldn't keep a thought in her head beyond where she needed to go next. Coming to an abrupt stop beside her truck, she jerked open the driver's door and found another scroll, this one resting on the driver's seat. Sliding the red ribbon off, she unrolled it.

Wannabe,

With your words, I fell. With your kisses, I burned. With

*your touch, I shattered. Now, turn around, baby, so I can
ask you . . .*

Whirling around, Willow gasped when saw Nathan
behind her, down on one knee in the snow, holding a small
black box open.

A squeal escaped her before she found her voice. "Holy
shit! Oh my God! Holy shit, Nathan! What are you . . . Oh my
God!" She jumped up and down, happiness exploding within
her, making her hands shake so hard she could hardly hold
onto the stack of notes. Tears of joy blurred her vision, and
she swiped them away with her hand.

He looked more nervous than she'd ever seen him. Sweat
dotted his handsome face and brow, despite the frigid
February temperatures, and his hands trembled almost as
badly as hers. "Willow, the day I received that letter from you
was the day my world brightened for the first time in years.
You gave me something to live for, something to fight to get
back to. I want to spend the rest of our lives fighting for each
other, building a life together. I want to make love to you,
argue with you just so we can make up, and adopt more
animals with clever names. And when you're ready, I want to
start a family with you. Will you marry me?"

Dropping to her knees in front of him, she clasped his
hands, ring box and all. Her watery gaze met his. "Yes! Yes, I
want to spend the rest of my life with you. I want to be your
wife and wake up next to you every day. But there's
something else you need to know before you put that ring on
me." She wiped new tears from her cheeks, smiling through
them.

"Willow, what . . . I'm . . ." Seeming to not be able to help
himself, he took her mouth in a deep kiss. "Baby, you're
killing me here."

"We should probably hold off on adopting any more

animals because I'm ready to start that family. In fact, it's already on its way."

He blinked at her owlishly, in surprise and shock, and then an indescribable expression of jubilation broke over his features. "You're pregnant? We—we're having a baby?"

Grinning, she nodded. "The shot failed. My doctor says it happens sometimes."

"I'm going to be a dad?" Not waiting for another confirmation, he threw his arms around her and pulled her close, burying his face in her neck. "God . . . Willow, I love you."

He lifted his head and stared at her, clearly overcome with the emotions coursing through him. Tears fell from both their eyes. The moment was so perfect and precious, she thought her heart would give out from the sheer joy of it. "I love you too. Based on how far along the doctor said I am, it happened when you were here for New Year's." She brushed the tears from his cheeks and kissed him softly, pouring all her love for him into her actions.

"Woman, next time I try to surprise you, can you maybe not steal my thunder?" Nathan said, helping her stand, but not releasing his hold on her. His sappy grin told her he was just teasing her. "Dale and I already did the chores, so you and I have the rest of the day with nothing to do but spend it together." Bending down, he picked up the ring box that'd gotten dropped at some point during their celebration. "Take your glove off, baby."

Doing as he asked, she tugged her left glove free and stuffed it into her coat pocket. Holding her hand out for him, she watched as he slipped the ring onto her finger. The diamond was set flush into a white gold band, a practical setting that wouldn't catch on anything while she did chores around the ranch. "I know you can't wear this all the time, so I was thinking after the wedding, we could get our wedding bands tattooed on, but I wanted you to have this too." Kissing the ring where it rested on her finger, he met her eyes. "I love you more every day I spend with you. And now, we'll have a child to love too. You've made me the happiest man in the world, and I hope I can make you even half as happy as you've made me."

"You already have, Nathan, you already have." Cupping his face in her hands, she brought his mouth to hers for another deep kiss. After a few delicious moments, she pulled away and smiled. "Now take me to bed—I'm cold and I need my fiancé to warm me up."

"My pleasure." With a broad grin, he swept her up into his arms and carried her into their home, into a future that was looking bright indeed.

CHAPTER THIRTY-TWO

Dear Willow,

If you're reading this, it means I've passed and you're at Skyview. You have the letters now and, with them, our history. With all my heart, I wish I'd had the guts to come and meet you. I bet you're beautiful, just like your mother. Time and distance did nothing to temper the love I held for her. She was all that was good and bright in this world, and when I received word of her death, I gave up. I'm ashamed to admit that, but in the back of my head, I'd always hoped that, maybe one day, fate would be kind to us and allow us to have a life together. Once I learned it was no longer possible, I had my will changed, leaving you this ranch. It isn't much, but I hope you'll have the means to create the legacy you want for your own children, whatever it might be.

Two months ago, I was diagnosed with advanced pancreatic cancer. The doctors tell me I only have a few weeks left in this world. I've taken care of as many details as I can think of, so you won't have to. My lawyer, Howard Smith, is a fair man that you can trust with helping you navigate the transfer of the estate. If you need anything else, your new neighbor, Jeremiah Urban, is also a good man, but don't tell him I told you that. He embarrasses too easily. He doesn't give himself enough credit, but I hope he might be a friend to you.

Many see my diagnosis as a death sentence, but I see it as something more. I will finally be able to be with my beloved Cherry again. Treatment would just prolong the agony, and I don't want to die like that. I want to go quickly. I'm in a hurry, you see. I've spent a lifetime without half my heart and soul, and I'm eager to be reunited with her.

Having never known me in life, I don't want to subject you to watching me take my final breaths. You might think of me as selfish for leaving this world without meeting you, but as I told your mother in one of my letters, I don't deserve you. I didn't want your only memories of me to be of a broken, miserable bastard on his deathbed. My letters to your mother show a different man than the rest of this town knew—the man I wish I could've been for you. Someone you could've looked up to. Don't be surprised if no one has a kind word to say about me, because I wasn't worthy of any.

I hope this ranch and this land bring you the peace and happiness that always eluded me. Fate and circumstances weren't kind to me, but I pray they are to you. My advice, Willow, be happy. If you see the chance for it, don't let it go. Hold onto it with both hands and fight for it with every ounce of courage I didn't have. You deserve it. All I've ever wanted, other than your mother, is for you to have the life I never had. I allowed shame, anger, and regret to make me a bitter, cruel man. Be better than I was.

I love you—I always have. Be true to yourself and don't let others dictate who you should love. And tell whoever wins your heart to be good to you, or I'll come back and haunt them.

With all the love I was never able to show you,
Your Father

WILLOW WIPED HER WATERY EYES, then folded the letter and slid it back into its envelope, which she placed on top of the others in the ornate cherry box she still kept them in. She'd finally gotten the courage that morning to look at the letter Jason had addressed to her, and this was the second time she'd read it in as many hours—third, actually, if she included when she'd recited it out loud to Nathan over breakfast.

She softly closed the lid until she heard the little *snick*. Setting it on a little, round table next to her, she used her foot to start the double-seat swing moving. They had two of them now—one on the side porch and one on the back deck where she was now. Nathan was in the kitchen behind her, cleaning up from the breakfast he'd insisted on cooking for her before kicking her out the backdoor to rest. He'd been the stereotypical first-time father-to-be, not letting her do things he deemed too strenuous or too exhausting for her. On one hand, it drove her crazy, while on the other, it made her feel cherished.

Ethel jumped up on the swing and rubbed her face against Willow's swollen belly, purring loudly. She had five weeks left before her due date, and it couldn't come fast enough for her. She was ready to walk without waddling and being out of breath, not to mention see her feet again. As her pregnancy had progressed, she'd had to stop doing a few things she'd grown to love, including helping Dale and Shane with barn chores and riding her horse, Poppy, a Palomino with a white blaze down her nose. The gentle mare had become Willow's favorite since arriving at the ranch with most of the other animals, but she hadn't been able to climb up into the saddle for the past two months. She was certain Poppy missed their riding time as much as she did.

Who would've thought a pink-haired, tattooed chick, with a nose stud and nipple rings, from Philadelphia would turn into an alpaca rancher in a small town in Wyoming with less than a thousand people living there? Certainly not Willow. But there was no denying this was where she belonged—this had been her destiny, even if it'd taken her thirty-three years to find it.

She touched the simple silver and black band that encircled her left ring finger. With all the work they did around the ranch, they'd decided to get their wedding bands tattooed on, not wanting to catch any actual rings on the various equipment. But Willow's OB/GYN had advised her to wait until after the baby was born and no longer breastfeeding. Nathan had insisted on getting his right away though and had purchased the band for Willow to wear to ensure everyone—meaning every *guy*—knew she was taken. As if her round belly wasn't already a sign. For now, she'd gotten into the habit of putting the ring on a chain around her neck whenever she was doing something that it might get caught on.

The small alpaca herd was thriving and had welcomed five newborns about three months ago. The babies would eventually be sold, since they couldn't be bred with Alfie, their father, and Willow had no doubt she would cry when the time came. While she knew the animals weren't pets, she'd grown attached to each of them as their personalities had emerged.

Nathan and Willow had been discussing with Dale the possibility of adding another male and several females to the herd next year. Willow was also looking forward to the first shearing at Skyview Ranch next month, but Nathan had warned her she would have to watch from the sidelines—that is if she didn't go into labor before that. Dale had already arranged for a professional shearer to come help him and Nathan remove the fleece from the animals, so it could be sold.

The alpaca ranching community had embraced their new members at a recent event Willow and Nathan had attended in Cheyenne with the Brodericks and Dale. No one had cared that the two were greenhorns, and they'd become friends with quite a few people that weekend.

Their garden was flourishing, and Willow was even researching canning. Nathan kept sneaking the cherry tomatoes off the vine and eating them. He refused to admit he was the culprit and complained they almost never had any for their salads, but he only had himself to blame. Willow would just stare at him and not say a word, both of them knowing he was the thief and not the rabbits or prairie dogs.

They'd had a going away party for Cody Moore last week. As his high school graduation had approached, he'd been struggling with what he wanted to do afterward. At first, he'd been planning to go to college but hadn't known what he wanted to major in. After spending a lot of time talking to Nathan about the Army though, the young man had decided to enlist. He'd left for bootcamp a few days ago with the promise he'd email or write to everyone when he got the chance.

It seemed as if Andrew was finally out of her life for good.

He hadn't called or made an appearance since the sheriff had arrested him. He'd been released on his own recognizance with a fine the next day, and Grady had advised him to get his ass out of Wyoming and never come back. She had no idea where her ex was or what he was up to, and honestly, she didn't care. Okay, maybe she cared just a little because, while she wanted nothing to do with him, she did hope he hadn't been hurt or killed by whoever he owed money to. After all, she had been married to him, and she wasn't so callous that she wished him harm.

The screen door opened, and Nathan strode out, carrying a mug and a small gift bag. He handed her the coffee—decaf no doubt—and kissed the top of her head as he ran his hand through her long pink hair. The coloring was temporary, and safe for the baby, and had been her idea for the gender reveal. She'd known they were having a girl since she'd been four months along, but Nathan had waffled back and forth about whether he wanted to be told or not. When he realized he couldn't paint the nursery in the colors Willow wanted without figuring out if they were having a boy or girl, he'd finally agreed she could tell him. The alternative had been to allow her to paint the walls herself, but that had been a no-go for him.

Instead of just blurting out their child's sex to him, she'd asked Ginger Moore to come over and dye her hair pink. After drying Willow's hair, her friend had helped her tuck it all up under her cowboy hat before leaving. Willow had then called Nathan into the house and told him to sit on the couch. She'd come out of their bedroom wearing nothing but the hat, her tattoos, and her nipple rings, which she'd just removed yesterday in anticipation of nursing, and straddled his lap the best she could with the baby bump between them. When Nathan had lifted the hat from her head, the long pink strands had tumbled down past her shoulders. It was the third time she'd ever seen her husband cry—the first time had been when she'd told him she was pregnant after his proposal, and the second time, at their wedding when he'd recited his vows to her. To say he was thrilled they were having a girl was an understatement. He was already planning to teach her how to shoot and defend herself. Willow had a feeling the poor girl wouldn't be allowed on a date until she was at least twenty-five, maybe not even then. Shannon Cherry Casey, named for Nathan's sister and her mother's nickname, was going to be the most well-protected girl in the county, with her veteran Daddy and a ranch full of honorary uncles between all the men at both the JP and Skyview ranches.

Moving Ethel out of the way, Nathan sat next to Willow and handed her the pink and purple gift bag. She took it, finding it heavier than she'd thought it would be for such a small bag, and set her coffee down on the side table. "What's this?"

More presents? Their kitchen windowsills were full of succulents now, and it seemed every time the man went to town, he came home with something for her, even if it was just one of the chocolate bars she'd been craving.

"Open it."

After she removed several layers of tissue paper, the rich smell of wood and lacquer wafted out. She reached in and lifted a rectangular object out of the bag. She gasped when she saw it was a box, identical to the one her father's letters were in, right down to the cherry blossoms and puzzle to open it. "How? Where?"

Nathan chuckled and reached across her to grab the older box from the table beside her. "You never noticed the initials on the back of your father's box, did you?"

He turned it over and pointed to three small letters carved into the bottom right corner. *JPU*. They could only stand for one person she knew. *Jeremiah Peter Urban.* Stunned, she ran her fingers over the letters, and then checked the bottom of the box Nathan had given her. The same initials had been carved into the same exact spot. "Jeremiah made these?"

"Uh-huh. I noticed the initials a few months ago and asked him if he'd made the box. He said your father had him design it after his divorce. Jeremiah was around twenty at the time. I guess Jason wanted a safe place for the letters after Chasity almost burned them."

She reverently fingered the cherry blossoms on the new box. "I know he likes to do woodwork, but I never realized he was this talented. He never lets anyone else in his little workshop, not even me."

"He calls it his sanctuary. I think it's because he can just be himself in there. No one is watching him, judging him, or criticizing him. I get the feeling his parents never encouraged him to be anything but a cattle rancher who would take over the family business after they died. Even after they moved away, he still can't find the courage to show the rest of the world his talent. If the box had been for anyone else but you, I don't think he would've made it. Apparently, it had taken quite a bit of convincing and some money, at a time when Jeremiah really needed it, for him to give in and make the box for your father. Jeremiah said when he'd finally delivered the box to your father, it'd been one of the few times he'd seen something other than misery and anger in Jason's eyes. He said the best he could describe it was a combination of longing and regret."

Leaning over, she kissed Nathan on the lips. "Thank you for this."

His eyes sparkled. "Open the box, Wannabe."

She gave him a quizzical look but did as he'd requested. Her eyes filled with tears when she lifted the lid and saw a stack of letters inside, wrapped up with baling twine. The top envelope had her scrawled penmanship on it and was addressed to "Any Soldier".

"Both my letters and yours are in there, and I put them all in order. When our daughter is old enough, I figure she'll want to know all about how we met and fell in love. She'll also want to know about her grandparents—all of them—and also my sister. I have plenty of pictures and stuff from my family, but your father's letters tell so much more about him, your mom, and you than any photograph ever could."

Willow kissed him again. "I love you so much. Thank you doesn't feel like a big enough thing to say."

"You're welcome, baby." He took both boxes and put them on the table. "Ready to go?"

She nodded. "Yeah, if you can help me up."

Chuckling, he said, "My pleasure," and stood before taking both her hands and helping her to her feet.

Today would've been her father's fifty-eighth birthday, and they were taking flowers to the cemetery to leave on his grave. The headstone Willow had ordered a few months ago was finally in place. She'd selected a rose-colored granite slab and had requested that cherry blossoms be carved into it along with the names of both her parents, with their years of births and deaths. She'd arranged for her mother's ashes to be removed from a mausoleum in Philadelphia and sent to her, so she could bury them with her father. Fate may have only given them a short time together in life, just long enough that Willow came into existence, but now they could be joined forever in the afterlife.

As Nathan gathered the boxes and her coffee mug, movement out of the corner of Willow's eye caught her attention. "Well, look who finally decided to show up. Fred, why're you running late today and who do you have with you?"

The prairie dog sniffed the air as Ethel rushed over to greet him and his much smaller companion, nosing and circling them both. "Looks like he brought one of his offspring with him—maybe showing his kid the ropes," Nathan suggested.

Willow concurred with him. Without fail, Fred made his daily mecca to the dish of seeds she left out for him on the back porch. To keep the birds, who had their own feeders on the property, from eating it all, she'd put a dome cover on it and turned the opening, so it was facing the wall. She left just enough room for Fred to climb in and stuff his cheeks with the goodies. He would then take them back to his family. "I guess we should name him Little Ricky then, even though that was Lucy and Desi's son."

"That works for me, but how can you tell if it's a boy?"

"I can't. But then again, I have no idea if Fred is a boy either." She shrugged. "I mean, it's not like I ever got close enough to take a peek to see what sort of parts he's packing."

He stared at her in shock for a moment then burst out laughing. "And all this time I've felt like a clueless idiot, trying to figure out how you knew it was a male!"

THE DRIVE to the cemetery was quiet but comfortable. It was one of the things she loved about Nathan—he didn't always have to fill the silence and it never felt strained. When they arrived, Nathan helped her from the truck. Her center of balance was so wonky lately, he refused to let her get in or out of the vehicle alone, terrified she'd fall. Most of the time, she let him mother her, knowing it came from a place of love, not control.

Standing at her parents' grave, Willow cradled her stomach with both hands, rubbing circles around the bulge as Shannon kicked away happily. The headstone was gorgeous. The cherry blossoms were carved so intricately that she was sure the flowers would burst from the stone at any moment.

"Do you want a minute alone, baby?" Nathan asked from where he stood by her side, his large warm palm resting on the small of her back. If he was near her, he had to be touching her. It was a habit she didn't mind a bit.

"No. To be honest, I'm not really sure what to say. I know I'm glad they're resting beside each other. I know I'm grateful that he taught me all he did through those letters. I'll probably always be sad when I think about what they lost out on—the life they could have had. I'm not overly religious, you know that, but I really hope they're together somewhere. If anyone on this earth ever deserved to be with the love of their life, it's those two."

"Well said, Willow. He'd be proud of you—they both would."

Tipping her head back, she stared at the endless blue Wyoming sky. The breeze ruffled her hair, blowing a pink strand across her face where it caught on her lips. Brushing it aside, something moved on her left, catching her eye. Turning her head, she swore there was a man standing with a woman in the shadows near the base of a large oak tree, waving. She blinked, and the image disappeared, but a perception of rightness remained in her heart. Maybe it'd been a shadow, a trick of the light, or maybe it'd been something more. Either way, a feeling of peace settled on her, a sense of calm and completion. She knew, unequivocally, that she was exactly where she was supposed to be, with Nathan by her side and their child growing under her heart.

Smiling, she met his gaze. His eyes were so blue, so bright and clear, they rivaled the cloudless sky above. In her womb, their daughter kicked out, once again making her presence known. Willow reached for Nathan's hand. "C'mon—take me for ice cream. Your baby girl is craving some mint chocolate chip again."

Laughing, he tucked her against his side, and his familiar warm scent flooded her senses with a comfort that she didn't have words to describe. With a kiss to her temple, he said, "Sure thing, Wannabe. Let's go."

EPILOGUE

JEREMIAH STRODE down the path that ran along the fence lines of both his and Willow and Nathan's ranch. Over the past year, the dirt had gotten well packed from everyone using it to either walk or ride the horses or ATVs on. He tucked his hands into the pockets of his jacket. Autumn had arrived along with colder temperatures. He didn't know why he'd decided to walk over to Skyview Ranch, home to the woman who'd become his best friend and her husband. Being neighbors in Wyoming didn't necessarily mean you could even see your neighbor's house.

He was tired to the depths of his soul, but the fresh air on his face and the endless sky and wide-open vistas of this land made him feel a little less alone for some reason. After the rodeo and argument with Dale last fall, then watching Willow and Nathan fall in love and start a family, he was out of sorts. Staying in the closet was just something he did. He'd never considered coming out, not ever. He'd heard too many homophobic comments and seen the damage even rumors could do to other gay men in the ranching community, that he'd resigned himself to making do with one-night stands in

Cheyenne. He was forty-two years old, and he'd spent thirty of those years hiding who he really was. He didn't know any way to live other than behind closed doors.

Drawing closer to the house, he saw the couple curled together on the side porch swing, a blanket covering them, their heads touching. They leaned against each other, speaking quietly, the hushed words broken only by the occasional giggle from Willow. Jeremiah's chest clenched in envy, and he spun on his heel. He might be a lonely asshole, but he wasn't going to break up such an intimate moment because he was feeling maudlin.

The sound of a door opening drew his attention. Glancing to his left, he saw a strip of light appear between Skyview's two barns. From where he'd stopped in his tracks, he had a perfect view of Dale's trailer. The gruff man had stepped out onto a small slab of concrete that served as his patio. A flame flared, briefly illuminating the man's handsome face, and then went out, leaving behind a red glow at the end of a cigarette.

Jeremiah's feet moved of their own accord. Was it the thought of his empty house behind him that had him closing the distance between himself and the man he couldn't stop dreaming about? Hell if he knew. It'd been months since Dale had confronted him at the rodeo, and Jeremiah had thought of little else ever since. In the past, he would've headed into Cheyenne to blow off some steam and put whatever was bothering him behind him, leaving it at the feet of some random hook-up. But since meeting Dale, Cheyenne no longer held an allure for Jeremiah. He knew something had to give before he went insane, but he didn't know if he was ready for it. He'd avoided the man as much as possible over the past several months, but it'd done nothing to quell the desire he felt whenever he caught a mere glimpse of Dale or even when someone mentioned his name.

"Come on, cowboy, I can hear your footsteps," Dale said in a low, husky voice as Jeremiah drew closer. It sent delicious shivers down Jeremiah's spine. "Don't worry though—the lovebirds just went inside and never saw you."

Ignoring the evident dig about him being in the closet, Jeremiah murmured, "Evening." *Seriously? That's all you got? Who says blah shit like that?* Him, apparently.

Chuckling, Dale finished his cigarette, stabbing the butt out in a small, metal bucket filled with sand. "Want a beer?"

"I'm not a man that ever says no to a beer." One step . . . two . . . three . . . he kept moving. His palms became sweaty, and a thick lump formed in his throat. He was close enough now to see Dale's face. Wreathed in shadows from his hat, he was even more handsome. He looked mysterious and dangerous, a deadly combination that woke Jeremiah's libido up with a jolt of electricity, shooting straight to his cock, making him half-hard. Willing the response away, he walked even closer.

Dale smiled wryly. "This one you might. It's my new batch of home brew. Might be good. Might taste like an old man's nut sack—no way to know until you try it."

"You've tasted an old man's nut sack?" Jeremiah laughed, feeling lighter than he had in months.

Reaching behind him, Dale pushed the trailer door open and waved him forward. "Come in, I'll tell you all about it."

Doffing his hat, Jeremiah walked up the steps and through the door, feeling as if he'd just entered a wolf's den and he was the prey. Heaven help him.

AFTERWORD

Want to send your support to a US Soldier, Marine, Sailor, Airman, or Coastguardsman?

Visit the Any Soldier, Inc. website.

OTHER BOOKS BY J.B. HAVENS

ABOUT J.B. HAVENS

J.B. Havens lives in rural Pennsylvania, and is a wife and mother of three, a boy and twin girls. She has a love for a good cheesesteak and anything that involves coffee or chocolate. When she's not caring for her family, she is busy researching and writing her next novel.

Find JB on her website where you can find character bios and even a short story or two. She loves to hear from readers, so reach out and tell her what you think!

Connect with J.B.

Facebook
Steel Corps Stalkers Group
Twitter

OTHER BOOKS BY SAMANTHA A. COLE

SPECIAL PROJECTS

First Chapters: Foreplay Volume One

First Chapters: Foreplay Volume Two

First Chapters: Foreplay Volume Three

Word Search For Warriors: Authors For a Cause

Word Search For Warriors: Volume II

Trident Security Coloring Book

Shaded with Love Volume 5: Coloring Book for a Cause

Cooking with Love: Shaded with Love Volume 6

USA Today Bestselling Author and Award-Winning Author Samantha A. Cole is a retired policewoman and former paramedic. Using her life experiences and training, she strives to find the perfect mix of suspense and romance for her readers to enjoy.

Her standalone collection of short stories, *Scattered Moments in Time*, won the gold medal in the 2020 Readers' Favorite Awards in the Fiction Anthology genre. Her standalone novel, *The Road to Solace* (formerly *The Friar*), won the silver medal in the 2017 Readers' Favorite Awards in the Contemporary Romance genre.

Samantha has over thirty books published throughout several different series as well has a few standalone novels. A full list can be found on her website listed below.

Sexy Six-Pack's Sirens Group on Facebook
www.samanthacoleauthor.com
Subscribe to my newsletter: eepurl.com/b2hNQj
www.samanthacole.allauthor.com

facebook.com/SamanthaColeAuthor
twitter.com/SamanthaCole222
instagram.com/samanthacoleauthor
pinterest.com/samanthacoleaut